Christopher Hood was born in 1943 in Lancashire. He lived for some years as an unskilled labourer before starting to write his first novel. In 1970, this novel found its way to Chatto & Windus, and was published in 1971 as *The Mullenthorpe Thing*. His next book to be published was *The Other Side of the Mountain* (1979) which was shortlisted for the 1980 National Book Award for Fiction. He has also published some stories for children, including *Contact With Madonna*, which was written with his son Jasper.

Christopher Hood lives in Swansea where he writes articles and reviews, and where for two years he was director of the Swansea Fringe.

for Josie Caryll, Iris Murdoch and Frank

*This dizzy, ditchwater town at the end*
*of the railway lines.*

Dylan Thomas

*Poachers of pirates*
*Crowd in the creaking wynds of daybreak,*
*Prising a gintrap welcome in the spyglass dawn.*

not Dylan Thomas

Christopher Hood

# BANANA CAT

First published in Great Britain by
The Alison Press/Martin Secker & Warburg Ltd 1985
Published in Abacus by
Sphere Books Ltd 1987
27 Wrights Lane, London W8 5TZ
Copyright © 1985 Christopher Hood

I am grateful to the Dylan Thomas Estate for permission to
quote extracts from the following works by Dylan Thomas
published by J. M. Dent:

The Followers
How Shall My Animal
Under Milk Wood
The Hand That Signed The Paper Felled A City

Set in Garamond

Printed and bound in Great Britain by
Cox & Wyman Ltd, Reading

# Part One

# 1

The Magistrates' Court in Port Morris is down a side street, in a converted swimming baths; the façade of the building has no pretensions to legal grandeur. There is a surprising and rather pleasing depth inside, and several modern courtrooms with a sense of austere plush, geometric lines to the dark wood fixtures and the HMG logo stuck up above the bench like the trademark of the old firm. I got there with two minutes in hand.

Inside the entrance there was a pretty good crowd awaiting Her Majesty's vicarious displeasure, punctuated by lawyers and policemen and social workers and people who were here to make a living, including a woman selling plastic cups of tea and coffee out of a little room like a cupboard. On a notice board to one side was a much studied charge sheet, pinned up for perusal like a list of today's runners.

The weird and rather crazed air of prevailing expectancy reflected this. At the start of business in court the punters seem indistinguishable from the punters in a bookie's, and I suppose that in either case the motivation is similar; the lucky ones are going to get off with only a mild clobbering. If you ask me, masochism is vastly underrated by the social sciences. As I lunged towards Court Number Two, Fat Boy Jones came over and touched my arm.

'Mr Waddin'ton?' Sweat beaded dewily on the still pubescent skin of his face, which otherwise did not betray emotion. 'I bin thinkin',' he said. 'Didn't I ought to 'ave a lawyer?'

'Probably,' I said. 'About four weeks ago. As I seem to

3

remember telling you about six weeks ago.'

'We-ell. I thought I'd juss gerrup in court, like, and ask 'em.'

'By this stage that is a bit irregular.'

'Oh.'

'But you may as well give it a try. There's always a good chance the bench won't know the right procedure either. Now excuse me, I'm going in.'

The bench had not emerged yet, so the courtroom still had that sense of summery relaxation which courts wear when the top table is empty, a strangely healing balm which descends on everything like soft light. Paid habitués salute one another with real pleasure, or sit together whispering languidly like lovers. The usher treats officials, observers and accused with the same quietly deferential charm they might receive from the nicer type of restaurateur.

The only possible explanation for all this is that the court is actually a church, the house of our true national religion, our real gods. You might expect this to confer a priestly status on the bench but it doesn't.

The first case that day was a double act by two borstal graduates, up for joyriding other people's motorbikes and trying to con the arresting officer with false identities. As the charges were read out they stood side by side in the dock in an attitude of laconic brotherly indifference, while the leader of the bench reeled at the mental effort of adding up the maximum penalties in his head before listening to the evidence. One of the accused had counsel, some dithering junior who only made things worse, and who in the end was reduced to grovelling for time to pay oncoming fines, in view of the HP agreements his client had with regard to previous ones, all coming out of his pension from the Social Securicor.

The proper penalty would have been about ten quid apiece and a Probation Order. What they actually drew was a couple of stiff benders and a string of fines which would mop up their Social Securicor allowance till about the end of the century.

Then Fat Boy Jones was paged, and I was jerked awake from a daydream about machinegunning the bench to assume my role as his Probation Officer. He lumbered into the dock like a lost cow, mumbled a sentence which included the word lawyer and was granted an adjournment just like that. That concluded my business here for the day and I followed him out. In the entrance hall I grabbed his sleeve.

'Don't forget to pick up a legal aid form,' I said.

'Uh,' he replied, and shambled off into the wastes of Port Morris. I supposed it had sunk in. I was there to prosecute him for defaulting on a Community Service Order, one of those schemes of basically decent and liberal intent which had caught on with the judiciary because it was cheaper than prison. His original offence had been going equipped for burglary after dark, perhaps in search of a window large enough to accommodate him. He was a very typical punter; he seemed to lead a life of blandly tedious attrition whose high points were prosecution. He lacked the least clue about life, just struck at it ineptly and got clobbered.

I drove off thinking that crime was the biggest growth industry in Wales except suicide and I was jolly shrewd to be on the payroll, which was a pathetic attempt to compensate for my sense of futility. The truth was that like nearly anyone I drew my pay and railed inwardly. At bottom I was no better than Fat Boy Jones. Merely a lot more intelligent, which meant I had less excuse.

Port Morris is a lump of suburban scab tissue at the far end of Swansea Bay, a dying steel town whose Welsh stone terraces are planted thick with new brick town houses, small clean monuments to postwar delusions about universal affluence. All this makes it a solidly depressed place which is trying to remember solidarity, bound against the sea by an arc of low dirty mountains, its best feature the chimneys and cooling towers and mad, skyward scrambling clusters of pipe which proliferate like spires beside the dual carriageway. After dark, from the other end of the bay the place is lit up like Hell or a gigantic fairground with a galaxy of lights. Sometimes a ball of flame will yawn out into the night and send a red reflection bouncing on the water. One day the whole lot will sink back into the dirty ground like Maya.

Halfway to Swansea I pulled off down the lane to the Old Barge, a lighterman's pub stood in the shadow of a motorway bridge, in a landscape of rotting dinghies, bits of scrub and

5

rusty metal, mud and flat water, with abandoned sheds and derelict bits of factory about the background. The air down there seems always to be toned by mist, and a flaccid trade still goes on up the immobile water of the inlet when the tide is in, and filthy boats unload valuable cargoes watched by men with suits and Mercedes cars, who later call in to the bar and pay for large rounds of drinks with large banknotes. There is a long, verandah-like room off the bar where you can get lunch looking at the river. I can never look out of those windows without a creep in the solar plexus somewhere between desire and despair, a voluptuously melancholic near surrender to a feeling I don't understand.

'Ah. George. Hello.'

I jumped. 'Oh – hallo Dugdale.' I made a hesitantly expansive gesture at the seat opposite. It is an occupational hazard of mine to know all kinds of people with whom social intercourse is not desirable, which means I creep around in public with the rather tense discretion of a doctor from a VD clinic. However quite a lot of my punters are likeable, and Dugdale was likeable enough to make me cross over the line. Eloquent, charming, in spite of a tramplike appearance even rather beguilingly urbane, he was the kind of man you'd take home to mother without hesitation provided the spoons were locked up.

He settled into his chair nursing a near empty beer glass and his confidence while he gazed through the window and tried to think up some conversation. I started mentally counting my money.

'Fascinating, isn't it?' he said eventually, meaning the view.

'Yes,' I said.

'Ever been for a walk out there?'

'No. Funny you should mention it, though. I keep meaning to.'

'You really must, some time.'

'Yes.'

'I could show you round if you like.'

'How kind. We really must do that.'

'Yes.'

He lapsed into a painful silence, broodily tilting the beer which was now little more than a stain on the bottom of his glass, the tension in his body affecting mine by sympathetic vibration. Sweat broke out on his forehead as he looked up at me and said: 'George...'

'What about three quid?' I asked, fishing it out. 'I don't seem to have all that much cash.'

'Good *heavens*.' He did the surprise so well I almost added a quid by way of applause. 'You must be psychic,' he said. 'Well look...' He drained his glass and stood up in the same motion. 'I'll just...'

'Right.'

'Can I get you...?'

'No.'

'Fine. I'll pay this back as soon...'

'Please,' I said. I hate to hear a man perjure himself. 'Pay me when you've got it.'

In common with a lot of people I didn't the least mind buying his company with a few pints from time to time. It was inconceivable that he should not be aware of this; he talked about paying one back merely out of respect for the mutually face saving rituals of scrounging. Two pints later he was relaxed, convivial, bending my ear with his theories about painting.

'The so called modern stuff belongs in a museum, of course,' he said. 'Futurist, expressionist, abstract. Where is it? And we won't even mention pop art. But since then what? Retreats towards Constable on one hand, gimmicks on the other. Hyper realism. You know?'

'Yes,' I said, meaning no, not really. 'Didn't know you were interested in painting,' I said. 'I mean you're more the literary type.'

'Of *course* I'm interested,' he said grandiloquently. 'Art is One. The point is it's all in dire need of a *rapprochement* with reality. That's all. It was given us as a means of facing the human condition and finding it bearable. Right?'

'Erm...'

'Of course it was. But,' he said, holding up an elegant if rather grimy finger, 'what do we find? People can't face the truth of their condition so they fantasise. You know,' he said, 'the way the English all think they're descended from Walter Raleigh. The Scots think they're Robbie Burns, the Welsh

7

think they're Owen Glendower. Now George – I'd like you to ask yourself something. What's the truth of our condition? Where do we actually live?'

'Er...'

'In an industrial graveyard.' He raised one finger like a semaphore signal to point sideways through the window, not following it with his gaze. 'It's *out there*,' he whispered.

So flabbergasted that I at last had a clue what he was going on about, I started nodding dementedly.

'Doesn't that view give you the *strangest* feeling?' he asked me.

'Yes, actually. I...'

'Have you ever asked yourself why?'

'Frequently.'

'With, I assume, no very conclusive result?'

'No.'

He leaned back in his chair and beamed at me with deep satisfaction; evidently I was a star pupil. 'That's because you're not an artist,' he explained kindly. 'If you were, you'd *know*. Permit me to show you something.'

He took from beside his chair a large flat cardboard bundle done up with string, which he began to undo. It surprised me to think that the bundle must contain something; it had looked simply like a badge of residence at the local doss house, where he was currently staying. 'How are you getting on down there?' I asked him.

'Oh fine,' he said. 'The place is run by a lot of dedicated Marxist nuns who do insist on certain standards. Two square meals a day, you know, and no pissing on the staircase after ten o'clock. I'm really quite comfortable. Ah.'

He now produced an A3 sheet of paper with a scene depicted on it which was very like the view we were looking at. I gazed at it for a while without speaking, while Dugdale's eyes flipped shrewdly from the picture to my face and back to the picture.

Rough grass, chimneys, a few sheds, thin lines of houses and hills behind, in the foreground a still pool of water reflecting the dirty sky. It *was* good; I found myself nodding.

'Doesn't that *say* it?' he demanded.

'Yes. That disturbing pleasure you get from the reflected sky – he's got that.'

'That's what an artist does,' he said. 'Illuminates your feeling about the world by depicting his. Because contrary to popular belief, feeling is objective.'

'Mmngh,' I said, not really listening. 'Who did this in any case?' I was trying to read the signature. 'Not you, I gather?'

'Good Lord no. That's Sky Hendersen.'

'Sky?'

'So he says.'

'And he's where – Swansea?'

'Yes. Why?'

'I've never heard of him.'

'Nor has anyone,' Dugdale said. 'Bloody man won't try to sell anything. Alright, so he's a bit crude in some ways, but that's not important compared with the rest, is it?'

'No...'

'That's why I bought it,' Dugdale said. 'To encourage him. But I think I've made a pretty good investment too.'

'Mm.'

'I must get it framed, of course.'

'Yes. Where in the doss house could you possibly hang it?' I wondered.

'That's a point,' he said gloomily. 'Not only that, but how the hell am I going to frame it?'

'Well that's no problem,' I said impulsively. 'I'll do it for you.'

'*Would* you?'

'Yes of course.'

'Oh – but I could never afford to pay you.'

'Dugdale, listen,' I said. 'I've got the wood, the tools, the skill. As it happens I've even got the glass. So what's it going to cost me? A piece of mounting board and two hooks. I'll be happy to do it.'

'George, that's terribly good of you, but ...' He was chewing his lip and looking uncomfortable. 'Well I tell you what,' he said. 'By way of return, you've got to hang it in your house on unlimited loan.'

'Oh...'

'I insist. Please George, I'd feel better. And I've nowhere

9

to put it at the moment, as you say. So you look after it till I get a place of my own.'

'And when will that be?'

'Possibly never.'

'Exactly.'

'Well alright,' he said. 'Keep the thing. Take it. It's yours.'

'Oh I *couldn't*.'

'You must. The only important thing is that it has a good home.'

'I can't just *take* it.'

'Well okay,' he said. 'If it makes you feel any better I'll sell it to you dirt cheap.'

'Fine. That's a good idea.' I reached for my wallet.

'Mind,' he said. 'I mean dirt cheap. I won't take a penny more than twenty five pounds.'

I said: 'Ah', having been thinking more in terms of a fiver. But a painting is a painting. It was a good painting and I didn't want to be chintzy. 'Alright, twenty five,' I said.

'Less the three I just borrowed.'

'Of course. Would you like me to deduct the two I lent you last week as well?'

'Naturally,' he said, not batting an eyelid. 'You took the words out of my mouth.'

'In a few years,' he said, taking the twenty before I could remember any more debts, and putting it away, 'it will be worth several hundred, you realise that?'

'No doubt it will,' I said, joining in the face saving exercise with my usual complicity. I finished my beer and picked up my investment. 'May I keep the cardboard?'

'Please do.'

'Right.' I stood up. 'I'll see you on Wednesday for your usual.'

'Of course,' he said. 'Bye bye.'

I took another look at the picture before placing it in the car. Having just parted with a cow, I wanted to make damn sure the beans still looked magic when Dugdale wasn't there, because if not I was going to have a hard time living with the Jack's mother side of myself. But yes – it was good. It was quite worthy to hang beside my Monet and Modigliani reproductions. I set off for Swansea and the office, the back of my mind already wondering how long it would take to lose twenty five quid through my not particularly generous expense allowance.

Dugdale was one of those people who made my job worthwhile, not because his character made progress but simply because his company was a welcome relief from that of my conventionally recidivist punters, a fact which of itself should have made me far more wary of him than I was. He would sit and regale me with stories of his crimes, secure in the knowledge that my willingness to be amused by them sprang from a tacit approval.

As a con man he was virtually an artist, who worked more for devilment than profit, with a grasp of his victim's prejudice which was positively satirical. He generally went from house to house collecting for some worthy cause which was shamefully ignored by the authorities and in need of funds. For example there was the delegation to the European Parliament to stop the French eating horsemeat, or failing that to stop them importing it from Britain. 'Do you want the Derby winner to end up in a French restaurant?' was, he said, the phrase which really got people. Then when Christianity and anticommunism came back briefly into vogue, he collected quite a tidy sum for Displaced Albanian Priests.

He didn't come badly unstuck until the Falklands war, when he was sponsoring a delegation to the United Nations to dissuade General Galtieri from putting Welsh speaking Patagonians in concentration camps, and then only because he had the misfortune to call on a house in Sketty whose relatives lived in Patagonia, from where they phoned regularly twice a week. He was prosecuted with quite ferocious animosity and was lucky to get probation, but then his manner in court was as plausible as out of it.

I had realised at our first meeting that applied psychology and avuncular guidance would get neither of us anywhere, and as time went by had simply given myself over to being entertained. When not remembering his exploits, we generally passed the time discussing Dylan Thomas.

# 2

The world seems to be divided by telephone neurosis; there are people who daren't answer it and people who can't let it ring. The dividing line runs right down the middle of my personality. As I came up the path and heard it belling through the front door, it became evident that I had just flipped over from behaviour type one to type two.

It was the beer, briefcase, meat, new painting, milk and bread under my arm which were the problem. I left them on the step in the end, broke through into the hall and took the phone up in a flying lunge.

'George. Ah.'

'Oh. Hi.' I sat on the stairs with an old familiar creep of feelings crabbing through my stomach. It was, and I might have known it, my rather tenacious partly ex wife Alice, She Who Must be Appeased.

'What can you do for me?' She actually said that. It was an old private joke.

'Yes,' I said. 'What?'

'Rodin,' she said.

'Really?'

'And his contemporaries. They're coming to Swansea.'

What an utterly beguiling thought that was. Renoir caressingly portraying barmaids, Degas peering in through bathroom windows, Modigliani stretched out pissed in Castle Gardens with a nude on either arm, while Rodin himself knocked up a grandiloquent three times lifesize statue of Dylan Thomas, possibly a rubber one which swayed in the breeze.

'I suppose,' I said, 'you mean their work?'

'Of course I do,' she said briskly. 'Their sculpture. The private view's tomorrow at the Oscar Lewis. I've got two invites.'

'How nice,' I said. 'Who are you taking?'

'Oh har bloody har. George it's ages since you took me anywhere. You can't possibly not want to go.'

The trouble was she was dead right.

'Where shall I pick you up?' I asked.

'At the gallery, darling. Half seven. Then you can take me for a meal.'

'Oh good.'

'We've lots to talk about.'

'Have we?'

'Of course we have,' she said. 'You haven't spoken to me for yonks.'

'I spoke to you last week.'

'*God*. You and your mulish pedantry. I mean talked to me properly. You know perfectly well what I mean.'

I did too. Getting a talking to was her private euphemism for claiming her conjugal rights wholesale.

'Alright we'll eat,' I said. 'But I'm not going to the Death Wish again.' I was referring to Swansea's most venerable restaurant, of which it is said that they will on request bring you a mortgage application form or a loaded revolver with the bill.

'No of course we can't go there again,' she said, in a dismissive tone which rather implied that I'd said we should. 'It's stuffy and poisonous and quite impossibly expensive. Anyway someone actually died there last week.'

'Who?'

'How should I know? Some venerable old bugger who'd subsisted for years on Windsor soup and gin. The funny thing was they didn't discover it for about three hours,' she said. 'Then of course when they did they got into a frightful tiswas in case he scared all the customers away. So some silly geriatric cow of a waitress stuck a tablecloth over him. Can you *imagine* it?' She was snorting with laughter now. 'Of course, within about two minutes everyone was screaming. Then when he fell sideways off the chair there was pandemonium. Oh dear ...' I could picture her wiping away tears of laughter with her knuckle. Alice was positively wicked in the real archaic meaning of the term. It was the side of her I still found hard to resist. 'They just left him there in the end,' she said, 'lying on the floor like a poleaxed Shakespearian ghost till the ambulance came.'

'You can't put a corpse in an ambulance,' I said. 'It's illegal.'

'George, I wish I was there with you.'

13

'Why?'

'So I could stuff the phone down your throat, you pompous bastard. Till the hearse arrived, the knacker's van, the Lord Mayor's Rolls. Who cares? The point is it's *funny*.'

'Yes,' I conceded. 'It is rather. How do you know all this?'

'Oh, that poor old cow got the sack,' she said, changing gear downwards to a more mundane voice. 'The waitress. We're handling her case. Anyway no, I can't possibly have you spending your money in the Death Wish. I tell you what – you can feed me at your house.'

'Oh thanks.'

'I'm only trying to save you money,' she said. 'You can give me one of your nice surprises.'

'Okay,' I said, fighting to keep the sigh out of my voice. 'See you tomorrow. Bye.'

I stared at the phone for a while after replacing it, continuing my dialogue with Alice in an *esprit d'escalier*. She knew damn well that I knew that she knew that eating *chez moi* meant there was no chance of leaving her with a kiss on the doorstep. She would always perpetrate her outrages by reasonable stages, leaving me three courses of action. Shooting her, pissing off to South America, giving in. I was indecisive so I gave in. She knew this of course. On average I gave her about three days a month. Still, three days a month Community Service was an improvement on a life sentence, so I was making progress.

Strains of dying summer came in through the open front door, on a soft aromatic breeze from across the town and sea below, shot through with bouncing sunlight and the sound of birds careening in the warm air. I picked up my things from the step, pausing to persuade the next door dog that sniffing my meat and pissing on documents nominally owned by Her Majesty came under the heading of unacceptable behaviour, then went in to slump across the sofa with a can of beer, painting propped up at the far side of the room while I decided how to frame it.

Alice kept getting in the way. We had been separated for six months and I could see no reason why she should still want me, other than the fact that she hadn't got me. Now she had schemed herself into an invasion of my sanctum, purely

14

because it was mine. She just wanted to piss on my briefcase, like the next door dog.

It took four cans of strong lager to bring my brain round to the question of the picture, and by that time I couldn't trust myself with a saw. I made a few notes about moulding and mounting, then promptly mislaid them before settling back onto the sofa for an unexpected snooze.

# 3

'You can see Renoir never did the washing, can't you?'

'Why d'you say that?'

'Because I mean *look* at her. The way he's got her holding it.'

'Yes,' I said consideringly. 'I see what you mean now.'

We were studying a small Renoir statue of a woman doing the washing – me and this rather personable girl I'd never met – and I was strongly impressed by her capacity to look straight through the shroud of reputation to what had actually been done. Now she had pointed it out, I saw the way the woman was holding up a garment rather soppily for inspection, a bit like Marie Antoinette merely playing at kneeling and pounding clothes in a stream.

'He's better than bloody Rodin anyway,' this man said, joining us. 'He was nothing but a ham.'

'I do rather agree there,' I said.

'Well I wish you wouldn't do it so loudly,' the girl said. 'The French attaché might not like it.'

'The French attaché can stuff himself.' The man panned the crowded gallery with a jut of his red beard, spoiling for an international incident. He was a good deal taller than the girl, who I assumed to be his wife. She had a soft classic profile and a distinctly Jane Austen type dress arranged fetchingly about rather small round tits which made me think of fruit.

15

'Usual bloody gang,' the man observed laconically. 'Plus a few respectable corpses since the occasion is so auspicious. I haven't seen you here before.'

'No, I...'

'Listen I'm just going to get a drink. Can I fetch you one?'

'No.'

'Charlotte?'

The girl shook her head and he lurched off. I wondered if he were slightly drunk or just one of nature's lurchers. Perhaps both. I was on the lookout for Alice but she was only about twenty five minutes late. It was one of her little tactics. I'd start off not wanting to meet her at all, then disprove this by getting frantic as I waited for her to show up.

'*Santé*,' the man said, lurching back with two glasses of red wine. He made as if to put one on Renoir's pedestal and then thought better of it.

'Who's the other one for?' his wife asked.

'Me,' he said. 'They were running out. Let me introduce ourselves. Sky and Charlotte Hendersen.'

'George Waddington.' I shook her hand. Since he still had a drink in both his we nodded at each other ceremoniously. 'I'm terribly pleased to meet you,' I said, smiling, 'I've just bought one of your paintings.'

'Impossible,' he said. 'I've never sold any.'

'But I tell you I have. A kind of industrial scene in some kind of poster colour, with a big dirty pond in the foreground.'

'That *does* sound like mine,' he said. 'How odd. Oh wait a minute – you don't know a man called Dugdale, do you?'

'Yes I do,' I said, for some reason adding: 'I'm a Probation Officer.'

'That figures.'

'Why d'you say that?'

'Because Dugdale's a klepto,' he said simply.

'Oh. That isn't why he's with me at all. He...'

'No don't tell me,' he said. 'I'd rather not know.' He made a dismissive gesture with his drink bearing hand and gave Renoir's washer girl a faceful of Chianti. 'I mean I absolutely love Dugdale but he's a pain in the arse.'

'I know what you mean. So he stole it from you?'

16

'Looks like it.'

'How awful.'

'Oh, I dunno,' he said philosophically. 'How much did you pay for it?'

'Twenty five quid.'

He threw back his head and laughed, loudly enough to distract a claque of local aldermen, Arts Council officials and freemasons from their intent determination to kiss the French attaché's bum in two and a half languages. I spotted Bill Haydock Williams, a short eager councillor like a grizzled hamster who spent most of his life running after gravy trains which had just left; he looked round at us with a school-marmish frown, then recognised me and gave an ingratiating wave. His name had been coming up in Alice's conversation recently, which must mean she was softening him up for one of her little schemes.

'Twenty five quid, dear Jesus,' Hendersen said. 'I must sign Dugdale up as my agent.'

'I think it's a very fair price,' I said stoutly. 'And I must say I can't understand why you haven't sold any before.'

'Because he's a prawn,' his wife said. 'How do you exhibit paintings from the back of a cupboard?'

'I suppose she's right,' he said. '"Hide not thy light".'

'Exactly.'

'Well it's your fault,' he said, rounding on her. 'You never encourage me. She's never once told me I'm a genius,' he informed me. 'She never poses in the nude for longer than five minutes. Fidgets. Complains of the cold. I ask you. What's the point of the woman? Look – would you like to come to dinner?'

'Er, yes.'

'Oh great,' he said. 'I love having people to dinner. Especially when they're richer than me and bring lots of drink.'

'How d'you know I'm richer than you?'

'Everyone is,' he said simply. I was to discover that he based his entire philosophy on this assumption. 'Maybe I can flog you another painting. You can look at them anyway.'

'Not quite sure when I'm free.'

'I'll phone you up,' he said, so I gave him my number.

'Ah *there* you are,' said Alice, taking my arm. She gave the Hendersens a rendition of her Brides of Dracula social leer and said: 'Excuse me, but you've got my husband. And I want him,' and whisked me away to look at a rather nice mask like head by Modigliani, and a pair of giant hands by Rodin which were reaching up yearningly, writhing in agony or ecstasy or perhaps simply groping blindly for a bar of flying soap. Her main reason in wanting me alone was to dig her fingers in my arm.

'Oh *nice*,' she said with carnivorous relish. She never stopped till she saw the pain flash in my eyes. 'Now you do me.'

'Not *here*,' I said through gritted teeth.

'Yes,' she said. 'Here.'

'Alice *please*.'

'I'll do something really embarrassing otherwise,' she said, more in anticipated sorrow than insistent threat. I knew she meant it.

'Oh alright.' I glanced round furtively, took hold of her upper arm as though drawing her aside, then employed my not inconsiderable strength in digging in my nails. 'That do?'

'No. More,' she insisted. 'I want marks.'

So I did it again, until her knees sagged slightly and her eyes rolled; I suppose it was cheaper than heroin.

'Mmmn. Goody.' She swept up the loose cream sleeve of her blouse and rubbed her wounds appreciatively. 'Now we go eat.'

'You've only just arrived,' I protested. 'I want to finish looking at the exhibition.'

'No you don't,' she said.

'I do. I had a bit of bother getting in, since you've got the invites. I had to pull rank in the end.'

'*Hah*!' Alice treated the room at large to a fortissimo example of her Cruel Empress laugh. 'You pulling rank is something I really wish I'd seen,' she said. 'What did you do? Flash your corporal's stripes?'

'Alice don't be bitchy.'

'Why not?' she asked reasonably. 'I'm a bitch. Anyway do come along.' She took my arm and pulled me away, leaving her glass in the care of Rodin's giant hands, then kept me waiting for ages in the entrance hall while she fetched her jacket from the cloakroom.

I was standing looking at some posters when Sky Hendersen appeared beside me and coughed.

'Listen,' he said. 'You can't lend me a quid?'

There's nothing like the direct approach of course; I might have expected this from a friend of Dugdale.

'Alright,' I said, giving it to him.

'Thanks.' It seemed to afford him immense relief. 'Of course, if you should buy another painting this would be a down payment, wouldn't it?'

'I suppose so.'

'I'll see you,' he said, taking to his heels at the sight of Alice as she came clacking out of the cloakroom, shaking her blonde hair loose from her collar to fall around her broad, straight shoulders. She went in generally for severe grey suits with tight, discreetly split skirts, black heels, spray-on stockings and frilly blouses. With her wide birdlike face and beaky red lipstick she looked like a depraved civil servant with ambition, which was just what she was. We'd hardly gone five yards up the street when she stopped a taxi.

'Why?' I asked.

'You chintzy bastard.' She skewered my foot without conspicuous malice with her left heel as we sat down.

'It's not far,' I said reasonably. 'That's all.'

'It's uphill isn't it? And if you can afford to lend money to smelly painters,' she said, 'you can certainly afford to take me around in the proper style on an evening out.'

'Didn't know you saw that.'

'I didn't,' she said. 'I guessed by his manner. I can spot scroungers a mile off. It's a pity you can't.'

'It was only a *pound*,' I protested. 'I don't *mind*. He is an artist after all.'

'Oh *Jesus*. George, when *will* you learn that you're not some largesse besotted Whig patrician from the eighteenth century? Hmm? I mean when will you look in the mirror and see an underpaid civil servant from the wrong end of the middle class with not enough ambition, and respond accordingly? Do you lend money to your recidivists as well?'

'*No*. Of course not. Well – only to one of them,' I said.

'Very occasionally.'

'And I suppose he's an artist too?'

'You could say that,' I said, bristling rather. 'In a way.'

We were pulling up. We'd only been doing about three miles an hour in any case; the dividing glass had been open all this time and you could tell by the driver's ears that he'd been enjoying the conversation so much that he was reluctant to drop us off.

'So here we are,' said Alice, getting out and stretching happily as she left me to pay the tab. 'You know I've never seen the inside of your secret new abode.'

# 4

'So you've finally made it.'

'Yes,' she said. 'Unless you push me down the steps.' She began ascending them, looking around her. 'You know, this view is far too good for you, George.'

Behind the town centre Swansea rises abruptly like an amphitheatre, and Matabele Road got full advantage of the rake. Beyond the Toytown grid of streets below stretched a lot of dazzling grey sea, out to Mumbles Head and right across the channel to the blue hills of Exmoor, a view which was pretty stunning at the worst of times. With her born-again Tory conviction that greed was a virtue and the primary dynamic of civilisation, I could see that Alice was narked by this. She could contrive no means of owning it, and a lot of people were enjoying it for next to nothing. I laughed.

'It isn't funny,' she said. 'Why am I stuck down there in Dresden Street looking at back windows and washing lines?'

'Because you thought Dresden Street was going up.'

'You bought the house,' she countered.

'At your insistence. Anyway it is going up. And you threw me out.' I unlocked the door and held it open.

Don't be absurd, George. We had a perfectly rational

discussion and decided it was the best thing to do.' She stepped over my threshold. 'You need a new front door,' she said.

'I'm perfectly happy with that one.'

'That's what I can't stand about you,' she said, quite without malice. 'You're perfectly happy with a lot of things.' She prowled into the living room.

'Well?' I asked.

'Not bad,' she admitted. 'Apart from the carpet.' She scuffed at it with her toe. 'I mean where did you get it? Somebody's office?'

'It is a perfectly agreeable carpet,' I said. It was – a rough, durable burnt sienna colour. 'You dislike it merely because it doesn't reek of money.'

She flopped back onto the sofa, twinkling at me. 'I like it when you get pompous and indignant,' she said. 'You should do it more often.'

'Why?' On my way to pour a drink, I paused. 'I get indignant at things I find objectionable, which it follows as a point of logic that I don't want to live with.'

'Oh – points of logic up your bum.' In the act of taking off her shoes she threw one at my head. It narrowly missed Sky Hendersen's newly framed masterpiece and fell back onto the drinks table, smashing a tumbler. 'Your idea of the good life is to hide from everything which isn't bland and agreeable.'

'No it isn't.'

'Yes it is. You'd fall asleep if no one tortured you.'

'No. It's just that you understand nothing but the imposing of one will on another. What did D.H. Lawrence call it? The Great American No.'

'The Gnome of Nottingham. Did he? And why America, for Christ's sake?'

'That's what he happened to be discussing at the time. The thing is you know about nothing but competition. The best things always happen in a state of peaceful rapport.'

'Oh yeah?' she said in her gutter voice. 'Like what?'

'You wouldn't know, would you? You've always driven them away.'

'Oh shit,' she said, visibly rattled. 'Why don't you stop preaching and pour me a drink?'

I poured some vermouth, pondering on how furious it made her to think of another type of being enjoying life more than she did. In fact this was the clue to her continued interest in me; she was convinced that I had a secret garden, which she wanted to possess and destroy.

'Ah, warm bianco,' she remarked, sipping it. 'This is your current notion of a smart drink, is it?'

'Oh, do let me get you some ice. I forgot it.'

'No please don't bother.'

'But I insist,' I said, going out to the kitchen. 'I can't have you carping about it all night.'

I was trying to hack my way into the ice compartment with the bread knife when she came in and said: 'What an unim*peach*ably squalid kitchen,' making me jump. 'You don't mean to say you eat in here?' she added.

'Why not?' I went over to the sink, sucking my cut finger.

'What's the matter?'

'Oh nothing much.' I ran it under the tap. 'It isn't deep.'

'Look, skip the ice,' she said. 'Seriously. I think I'll just have the wine. I see we've got a nice fat bottle of Algerian brasso. What's the meal?'

'Curry,' I said. 'It's all ready.'

'Oh George.' She clapped her hands happily. 'What I always love about you is your casual capacity for getting things wrong. It's almost insouciant.'

I smiled. It was the nearest she ever got to friendly banter, standing there with her big shoulders and her tight uniform skirt like a wardress trying to be a tart. Maybe she was too stupid to enjoy life but she got a great deal of pleasure from attacking it.

I wrapped my finger in my handkerchief, put a low light under the curry and a kettle on to scald up the rice, and showed her round the workshop I'd built by roofing in the back yard with transparent sheets. I showed her my lathe, half made chair, pepper mills and bowls, my slabs of apple and cherry wood, oak, elm, mahogany, lime, olive, black-thorn, yew. The whole thing was an ambiguous and highly formal dance. I was saying this is what I can do when I'm alone; it's my secret garden and you haven't got the key. Alice made glinting hieratic steps about it all, impressed

22

enough to hold back but licking her lips the while. I told her my plans for the house, showed her my indoor plants and some new books, Modigliani, Sky Hendersen and Monet. It was all my weakness and my strength: we were terribly nice to each other through the entire performance. I came close to showing her a very promising bit of ash, on which I intended testing a long dormant ambition to sculpt, but something told me to hold back.

Then we went into the kitchen and had our dinner. I lit a candle because Alice insisted on it, and she regaled me with the devious career schemes which were what she had in place of an inner life. Not so much a secret garden as an assassination bureau. She began by saying that so-and-so had her hand in the till but there was nothing to be got out of screwing her at the moment. Let her get some way up the ladder and give her enough rope, was how Alice felt. Her immediate boss at the obscure den of industrial relations speciality where she worked was a weakling and a sentimental phoney, and she was moving in to cut his throat and take over his job. She was co-opted with him on a project which she was sabotaging in such a way that the blame would fall on him. I wondered if this might include the poor old cow who got the sack from the Death Wish over the dead customer incident and she said yes definitely. She was going to build up an unshakable case and then blow it on a technicality which would quite unmistakably be down to him.

I wondered if she didn't realise the way people at her boss's level hung together self protectingly to make cooperative defensive attacks when any one of them was threatened and she said yes of course. But it depended on the style of the attack. If one hit hard enough and in the right way then an opposite syndrome came into play, as with bent coppers. Nearly all of them were, but when one got properly nobbled the others would all stone him to death in furtherance of the myth that he was just one rotten apple among many good ones. Her boss would quite certainly get demoted and she would take his job, and in a few months she'd find an opportunity to clobber him again, so he would always be too squashed to get back at her.

Then she told me a few more titbits about who she had

snubbed, who deflated, and whose progress she had blocked over something or other, but the main course was over. Her manner through all this was neither contrite nor exactly boastful nor even adolescently exhibitionist and take-it-or-leave-it. She told it all in a low uninflected monotone which was strangely intimate. She had always had this tendency to treat me as a kind of priest whose vows included a strange injunction to fornication on demand after confession, not so much a sex object as a Dad object with orgastic attachments. We were sitting back with coffee and two of her small cigars when Beau walked in.

Beau lived in my upstairs front room on a diet of jogging magazines and meditation, a hell of a nice boy but nervy as a racehorse, and in his own opinion just as delicate. He shied over to the sink and leaned back on it, then peered forward through the greasy yellow gloaming of the candlelight.

'This is Alice,' I said.

'Hello.'

'And that's Beau. Do have a glass of wine.'

'Thanks.' He leaned forward to accept one, and leaned back again.

'How are things?' I wondered.

'Oh ...' he explained, elaborating the word with a look of anxious disgust and jerky backward flicks of the hand near the side of his head, which might have been International Sign Language for bugger it, the bats are nesting in my ear again.

'Otherwise not too bad,' he said. 'I've got plenty of energy but I can't get things to relate. They won't mesh together, you know?' he said, putting down his glass to make failed meshing motions with his fingers.

I grunted. Of course what people study afflicts them throughout life like malaria. Qualified in sociology, Beau could understand nothing until it was transcribed into the Abstract, by which time nobody else had a clue.

'I'm dealing with too many wankers,' he concluded. 'The trouble is I can't seem to get any of them to understand what I'm talking about.'

This might have been a reference to his purgatorial job. He had been given an insecure temporary salary and the task of making flesh from an inspired piece of municipal plagiarism called the Swansea Fringe, assisted by a board of amateur directors with whom he coexisted on terms of permanent blind rage. Seeking a change of subject I said: 'How's your knee these days?'

'Terrible.' He leaned down wincingly to rub it. 'Went for a run earlier,' he said. 'Shouldn't have done it of course. It's my tendon, you know?'

Beau's second subject was biology.

I fed him a cue. 'What – your left tendon?'

'No. The right one. But it is because of the left one. You're right there. You see . . .' He put down his glass again, the better to address both of us. I could positively feel Alice eating him up with her gaze. He was strikingly good looking though not very much aware of it or the effect he had on women; where'er he walked they tended to spring out of the long grass like predatory grouse and frighten the life out of him. 'The weakness of my left leg caused an excessive use of the right one,' he said. 'To compensate. And this in turn meant that my right leg grew very slightly longer . . .'

'But nobody's legs are precisely the same length are they?' Alice said.

'No they *aren't*,' Beau said, leaning forward animatedly and holding up one finger. 'But. What happens is that people *adjust* to that because it's a stable situation. And this extra bit of length to my right leg is *additional* to that. Or separate rather. Irrespective of whether my left leg was originally a bit longer than the right one or not, say for example that it was. That doesn't matter. Or wouldn't matter. D'you see what I mean?'

'Not entirely.'

'Look, it's really very simple . . .'

'I think I know what you mean,' I said impatiently. Simply watching his gestures had brought out beads of sweat like pearls along my forehead. 'Say someone was born with their right leg half the length of their left, and learned to hobble around. Then if in the middle of the night their right leg suddenly assumed its full length, the next day all the rest of their body would be thrown out of kilter when they tried to walk. Their back and everything.'

'*Exactly*,' Beau said, describing in his gratitude a kind of

25

swimming motion of the arms in the near darkness. 'And it's my back it affects. You see, this problem doesn't really arise unless you do advanced running, but now, *because* my left leg's better, my *right* one is giving what amounts to too much thrust. So there's a slight inswing of my right knee. Especially when I'm turning corners to the left.'

'Why don't you just run in straight lines?' Alice wondered.

'That's a pretty good idea,' Beau said, quite seriously. 'Except that crosswinds have the same affect usually, and you nearly always get one down on the beach, which is the best place for running in straight lines. I've just been overdoing it.'

'You haven't thought of giving up running?' I said.

'Of course not.' He threw back his wine. 'I shouldn't really drink with these pills,' he observed, going over to open the fridge. 'I think I'll go to bed.'

'What pills?'

'Some kind of painkillers. Make me feel bombed out of my mind all the time. I have to take these other ones to bring me down.'

'And they make it okay?'

'Not entirely. They give me headaches. Oh, *shit*.'

'What's the matter?'

'Some fucking idiot's stuck a knife through one of my ice packs. It's leaking all over the butter.'

'Oh dear. I believe that was me,' I said. 'Look, I'll...'

'No, it's okay. I've got another one.' He plugged in the electric kettle and shortly filled up his hot water bottle, which had been lying where he always kept it in the vegetable rack. 'So I'll bid you goodnight.'

'Yes. I hope you sleep well.'

'Thankyou,' he said, with a lack of conviction which was positively aggressive. 'I'll probably stare at the ceiling for about six hours thinking about my income tax.'

'An ice pack and a hot water bottle?' Alice whispered as Beau's unequal legs tramped wearily upstairs. 'What does he *do* with them?'

'Uses them on differently afflicted bits of his anatomy,' I said. 'According to need. I mean I don't know, he does all sorts of things. Sometimes he ties a heavy weight to his foot and swings from the banisters. Frightened the life out of the gas man last week.'

'Oh dear. Perhaps he ought to have more sex. Hasn't anyone got him?'

'Females do leap on him occasionally,' I said. 'But generally not if he sees them coming.'

'Hmm.' She was chewing her lip. 'I wonder...'

'Alice. Don't you dare.'

'Why?' she said. 'Jealous?'

'Not a bit. But I mean I'm a horrible old sinner and you're bad enough for me. He's nice, considerate, sensitive, full of promise. And one thing you emphatically don't represent is healthy sex. In fact you're the only woman I've ever met who gives me hangovers.'

'And why is that?'

'Because you're foul.'

She exhaled a low pleasurable sound somewhere between a moan and a hum. 'That's right,' she said. 'I'm filthy.'

I nodded. 'You're a disgusting bitch,' I said flatly.

'Good – come on.' She snatched up the candle. 'Let's go to bed.'

'Oh alright.'

She took my hand and dragged me upstairs to my room, where she placed the candle on the bedside table and closed the door. 'Now,' she said, eyes shining. 'I'm a disgusting bitch.'

'Okay.' I took her by the scruff of the neck. 'You foul, disgusting bitch...'

'George *please*. Can't we have a bit more conviction?'

I cleared my throat, seized her harder and gave it a more savage growl. Her knees sagged and her eyes grew glutinous with compliant lust. 'You foul, disgusting bitch. You filthy little cow, take off...'

'Oh *no*,' she said, springing awake again. 'Take *down*.'

I sighed deeply and had another go, with an anger increasingly less difficult to simulate. 'You foul, disgusting bitch. You filthy little cow. Take down...'

Of course participation would have been impossible without my coming to enjoy it in some way, and participation was compulsory. I could only hope that Beau had somehow managed to fall asleep.

27

# 5

The day did not begin well. It took me longer even than usual to leave the house without my glasses, go back for them and leave my briefcase, look for my mac, write a note for the milkman and lose my pen. Once I had taken everything down to the car, it only required that I come back and get my car keys, go back to the car, get in it and start the engine.

I leaned on the steering wheel and let go a big sigh, and pointed the nose towards the steppes of outer Swansea and the valley towns beyond, homeland of so many of my punters, the numb Siberian exile of a post industrial working class.

The middle of Swansea town addresses itself to the sea and feels compact and metropolitan. There's an urban expectancy in the air, a rapport. Streets cluster beside the happy miles of beach, ships slide with ponderous grace into the docks from Hamburg, New Jersey and Bombay, and London is less than three hours journey up the railway line. But less than a mile out, the world becomes a long drag into nowhere, pile after pile of dwellings smeared across the landscape like some great big convalescent camp for a disease whose name has been forgotten.

My first call was in Pleasant Avenue, a wide street of uniform dirty pebbledash houses the approximate length of the Salisbury Plain. Soapy Protheroe did not respond when I knocked at his front door but I didn't let this bother me.

I went down the side path and encountered a small boy in the back garden, driving a big plastic tip-up lorry loaded with earth back and forth across the vegetable patch. 'Is your dad in?' I said.

He interrupted his engine noise for long enough to say: 'Who's askin'?' and then the back door opened.

'Alright, you don't 'ave to involve the kids, do you?'

'I'm sorry, Soapy. I did knock at the front first. Anyway, you must have been expecting me.'

'Well – kind of.' He stuffed a greasy shirt tail into the taut waistband of his trousers and held out a hand for my HMG envelope. 'Wha's this then?'

'A summons.'

'Oh ah?' He ripped it open.

'You really must have been expecting that too.'

'Well,' he said, perusing it casually. 'It don't really surprise me, purr it like that.' He reached into the kitchen to put the summons on the draining board. 'So what d'you reckon then, Mr Waddin'ton?' He rubbed his hands. 'What'll they give me?'

'Your initial sentence. Which as I seem to remember was twelve months for warehouse breaking.'

'I know about that,' he said. 'But wharrabout the Community Service I've put in already? Don't that count for nothin'?'

'They gave you two hundred hours,' I said. 'Of which you appear to have done twelve. I'm afraid not.'

'Good God A'mighty, I'da bin better off goin' down the big 'ouse right away,' he said bitterly. 'Saved all this aggravation. I'da done 'alf my sentence by this time.'

'I thought Community Service was a better option,' I said. 'So did you at the time.'

'Ah,' he said. 'I was bloody conned, tha's why. Finished up doin' that and goin' in nick and all, haven't I?'

'You could still...'

'What?'

'Well, you could still plead to try and fulfil it if you wanted. I could soft pedal my testimony. If you could produce reasons why you weren't able to make it.'

'Ah, reasons,' he said. 'You don't know nuthin' about bloody reasons. Nuthin'. I mean no offence Mr Waddin'ton, you do try. Not like some – we know that. But you live in another fackin' world, you people. Another world.

'I mean you take it,' Soapy went on, lowering his voice. 'I got the wife upstairs cryin' her eyes out now. Always bad, she is. 'Aven't been right for *years*. All this business is just another screw in the coffin, like. Plus I got the kids on my 'ands. One of 'em always in bother in school, mitchin' off all the time. The other one isn't right with his ears. I got the garden, this bloody 'ouse the Council never do fuck all to keep up to scratch. *I* can't go poncin' off up the valleys, doin' up old people's community centre like a boy scout, mun.'

'Why not?'

'I juss *can't*,' he said. 'There's people up there don't like me anyhow. I'll be better off in the nick out the way. Jus' do my time an' that's it. Eight months good behaviour, finished.'

'But what's going to happen to your family while you're away?'

'I *dunno*, do I? There's nothin' very brilliant goin' on with 'em now.'

'Yes I see what you mean,' I said. 'I'm sorry.'

'Why?'

'I just am. I wish I had it in my power to hand you a clean slate.'

'And what will I do with it?' he said. 'I'll only go thievin' again. I bloody *will*, I'm tellin' you. I don't care if you knows it or who bloody knows it. Wharr else have I *got*? Look – if I'da known when I was young wharr I know now, I'da done myself in when I was twenty. Full wages, no worries, one Saturday night – boomph. Oblivion. I'm serious.'

'Really?'

'Yeah. Oh, don't look like that – I'm not gunna do away with myself now. It's too bloody late *now* – I may's well ride it through. When He wants me He'll send for me.' He jabbed a finger skywards. 'Meantime, I done four stretches an' I can weather another one. Easy. I 'spect there'll be a war before long anyhow.'

'You don't.'

'Aye. I do. Why not? Sort *everybody* out, that will.'

'Fry everyone up, you mean.'

'Exactly. There'll be nobody left,' he said, 'except Margaret Thatcher, down a deep 'ole in the ground, makin' rules and regulations for the bugs under the bloody carpet. I'll see you.'

'Yes,' I said. 'See you in court.'

'Don't put money on it,' he said wearily. 'P'raps I'll juss take off for the mountains with a bloody shotgun. Tara.'

I drove off half hoping he would take off with a shotgun; the story rolled through my mind like a film until I realised with a jolt that the hero was a dreamlike hybrid of Soapy and myself. He was up in the Brecon Beacons by this time, starved and dangerous: the local Tories were after him with foxhounds but it was the SAS who got him, dropping silently by parachute to cut his throat while he was stalking a sheep for his breakfast.

My next call was even further out into the hinterland, across the old grey ribbon of Carmarthen Road, on an estate where weeds fought through the asphalt and the sagging contours of an empty factory took up the visible horizon. I was looking for Charles Edward Andrew Phillips, a skinny teenager with persistent backache, a penchant for other people's cars and an Oedipus complex. His mother answered the door.

'Duw, Mr Waddin'ton, I phoned your office yesterday,' she said. 'I dunno *what* they think they're doin'. I left very clear instructions.'

'Yes, I got the message, Mrs Phillips, that isn't...'

'Well if you got the message that's it,' she said. 'What are you doing here? Yiw are not gunna go draggin' 'im out carryin' heavy objects round a buildin' site, not in his condition, surely to God?'

'No, but that's not...'

'I mean he is up there now,' she said, pointing up the spick and span staircase behind her, 'in 'is bed, on a board we 'ad specially from the 'osspital, sufferin' terrible. Under the doctor,' she added. 'I got notes and everythin'. Here.' She delved into a pocket of her pastel orange nylon overall to thrust a medical note in my hand, telling me for one thing that my visit was far from unexpected. 'See?' she said triumphantly.

'Yes,' I said. 'But I mean he was supposed to start Community Service six months ago and he hasn't been once. This only says he's had backache for a fortnight.'

'All 'is *life* 'e've 'ad it,' she said. ''E've *never* been right. It's 'is bones. All 'is father's family got weak bones ...' There came an interrogatory groan from upstairs and she said: 'It's Mr Waddin'ton, darlin'. Don't worry, I'll deal with it.'

'Oh Mam – I better talk to 'im.'

'You juss get back in that bed *now*,' she said, actually starting up the staircase as though about to storm the Bastille. 'You are not in no condition to talk to nobody. Now then.' She came back down again. 'He is not fit to talk to you, Mr Waddin'ton,' she said, folding her arms, 'and that's it.'

'I don't want to talk to him, Mrs Phillips.' I passed her the billet-doux from HMG.

'What's this?'

'A summons.'

'How is it a summons?' she said on a rising note. 'What've he *done*?'

'Nothing,' I said. 'This is the point. Look Mrs Phillips, I forget the sequence exactly, but since his original court appearance he's had the most extraordinary number of afflictions, hasn't he? I mean apart from backache there's been earache, flu, palpitations, sore throat, diarrhoea, piles, gumboils, skin rash, chest pains, head pains, agoraphobia, warts, bladder trouble...'

'That's *right*,' she said. 'I keep tellin' you people – he is not a well boy.'

'Not *well*? Your phone messages read like the Seven Plagues of Egypt. Then there were two occasions when he had no shoes and one when he had no trousers.'

''E 'ad swollen feet,' she said. 'The poor love. His shoes was pinchin' something terrible. The other time, 'is trousers was in the wash.'

'What – all at the same time?'

'Only the one pair we 'ad,' she said. 'Plus one other pair what 'e'd bought 'imself, what were totally unsuitable so I'd chucked 'em out. Now then.' She waved the summons at me. 'Are you *still* going to give this thing to me this mornin'?'

There is simply no limit to the delusions an inflated maternal ego can inflict on itself. 'Yes,' I said, not without a certain satisfaction. 'Mrs Phillips I am. As a matter of fact I've no choice, but I'd give it to you even if I had.'

'So – they are just gunna drag 'im down that court and say the same things to 'im all over again, is that it?'

'Not exactly. They'll probably lock him up.'

'*What*? Yiw are kiddin'.'

'I'm not.'

'Bloody *wasters*,' she said, advancing on me. 'You wanna try catchin' some *real* villains. I could tell you – right in this street where we're standin' now. 'E've never been a bad boy, not underneath. 'E've been brought up tidy. If 'is father 'ad listened to me years ago we'd've 'ad a nice 'ouse by now.

32

Proper education, private medicine, the lot. It's a phase,' she said. 'Bad comp'ny. *You will take that boy to prison over my dead body.*'

Driven right down the path to the gate, I managed to rally by jabbing one finger at her like a pistol.

'Usually,' I said, 'sending people to prison gives me the creeps. But if you ask me it'll make a nice change for your Charles. It does represent his best chance of getting away from you. Now do please make sure you wipe his nose and get him off to court on the appointed day, complete with trousers. The police really do get rather shirty when they have to come out and fetch people, and it tends to result in longer sentences. Get him a lawyer, get legal aid and for Christ's sake resist the temptation to say too much in court. Or they might lock you up as well. Good morning.'

I took off with a screech of tyres. This was one occasion when I caught myself rather enjoying the nastier side of my work. However it wasn't long before I started feeling guilty about it. The feeling grew into a morbid remorse of near Raskolnikov proportions and I found myself tempted to pull up at some traffic lights and leap out to tear my shirt and declare myself a sinner to the passing traffic. I reached Ritchie Pritchard's place in a state of emotional collapse.

Ritchie lived nearly all the way back into town, at the top of a tower block near a major road junction, in a world of panoramic views, no streets and permanently defunct lifts which the Social Securicor used as a dumping ground for people with not enough clout to complain about it. He came to the door in his underpants and a torn shirt, leaning on the jamb all skinny knees, aquiline hooter and Charles the Second black locks while his eyes tackled the tricky problem of perspective.

'Hah!' he exclaimed, having focused on me. 'Who loves ya, baby? 'Sarright,' he called over his shoulder. 'It's George. Come *in*, mun.'

I followed him into the living room, which apart from the permanently closed curtains was furnished with a horsehair mattress, a hi-fi and about three dozen bottles. Two of his accomplices were stretched out on the mattress, and he now kicked the off switch on the hi-fi and reached down to pour me a drink of some greenish fluid from one of the bottles in the fireplace. On the wall behind him a large graffito said: LEGALISE IT NOW, without any further details. Ritchie was one of those people for whom history stopped with *Easy Rider*, which must have come out not long after he was born.

In response to my drink I said: 'Thanks' rather doubtfully. 'Look Ritchie...'

''Assles, is it?' he asked cheerfully.

'Yes it is rather.' I opened my briefcase.

'Ah – save it, mun. No rush is there? I mean 'ave a drink first, straighten your bloody 'ead out. You can arrest me after.'

'Well, I'm not necessarily...'

'I told you,' he said, laughing. 'Can it for a while. I can't 'andle that stuff this early. Siddown or somethin'. You look knackered.'

'Yes alright. Thanks,' I said, looking round for some means of doing this. I didn't really want to sit on his friends, both of whom were comatose. One of them had distinctly green tinted skin; I looked on my drink with renewed alarm.

Ritchie had meanwhile fetched me a chair. 'Wanna sandwich?' he asked expansively. 'Or a birra meat and salad or somethin'?'

'Er – no thanks. I...'

'Ah go on,' he said. 'We got plenty.'

'Alright, yes. Thanks. Maybe I will. It is nearly lunchtime isn't it?'

'Is it?' he asked, seized by another fit of laughter. 'I dunno. We've banished time yere, see.' He lurched off towards the kitchen. 'Sally,' he called. ''E will 'ave some. Give 'im summa that pork.' He came back, clutching his head in mock embarrassment. 'Duw George – I forgot to ask,' he said. 'Yiw are not Jewish or nothin', are you?'

'No.'

'Oh tha's good.' The laughter had got him again, a spluttering and high pitched seismic hooting, and he leaned back into a corner of the room for support. 'Otherwise,' he said, with difficulty, 'otherwise we coulda done you – oh *Christ* – done you a kosher – fa-ckin 'ell – kosher bacon bloody *sandwich*,' he finished, sliding all the way down to the floor where he lay clutching his stomach in some apparent agony, going: 'Kosher bacon sandwich. Ah Duw – I'm dyin' I am.'

A large, amiable girl came in with a huge cold meat meal on an oval plate, and gave it to me. I presumed this to be Sally, whom I had not previously met. Built on distinctly potato-lifting dimensions, she was not at all unattractive and seemed already to understand Ritchie quite well.

'Der – looka the state of 'im,' she remarked. '*Gerrup*, you daft bugger, will you?' She prodded him with her toe. 'An' put some bloody trousers on or somethin'.'

'Hello Sally.' He waved.

'Ner' mind 'allo,' she said. 'Get bloody dressed.' She turned to me, shaking her head, and clocked the motif on the flap of my briefcase. 'Oh, I geddit,' she said. 'Wunna them, are you?'

'I beg your pardon?'

'An official. Come to run 'im in I 'spect. Wharr is it this time?'

'Sellin' kosher bacon sandwiches,' Ritchie said. On his way out of the door he was struck by another bolt of laughter, as if he had been shot. 'Without a bloody *licence*. Ah dear . . .'

'Get *on*, will you?' Sally gave him a boot up the arse. 'I'll not tell you again. An' you two can bloody shift an' all,' she said, applying her foot to the nearest figure on the mattress. 'There's got to be alteration round yere – I've 'ad a gutsful.' She took hold of the curtain – which was tacked to the window frame – and ripped it off, at which five thousand kilowatts of daylight zapped into the room, affecting Ritchie's friends in very much the way it might affect Dracula. After blinking around them in terror for the merest couple of seconds they slunk away like dogs. I heard the flat door slam.

Ritchie came back in wearing trousers, gazing at Sally in astonishment. He said: 'Where's Gareth and Terry then?'

'Out.' Sally finished folding up the curtain. 'Permanently.' She picked up a jacket, a shoulder bag and a shoe from around the mattress, opened the window and dropped them out.

'Tha's Gareth's things tharr is,' Ritchie said, pointing indignantly.

'Well 'e can bloody pick 'em up then, can' 'e?'

Ritchie shook his head slowly, and turned to me. 'Duw, I got to laugh,' he said. 'I 'ave honest. Be back in a sec. I'll juss get my shoes.'

In my head, I was already composing my report for the bench: 'Though a persistent petty offender, Mr Pritchard has never shown a truly vicious character, and it now seems as if his easy charm, which has landed him in trouble on many previous occasions, may at last be working to his proper advantage. His common law wife, who is standing by him, shows a stalwart and determined character. If, as I suggest, we give him a second chance to fulfil his Community Service Order, we can I think be assured that her steadying influence will be a help to him . . .'

'Sally,' I said.

'Yeah?' She had hold of a broom now, sweeping bottles, dust and cigarette packets into a pile in one corner.

'Look, Ritchie keeps not turning up for his Community Service . . .'

''Is wha'?'

'He'll explain it to you. The point is they're probably going to give him one last chance. If he's lucky. Otherwise they'll stick him in the nick.'

'Bes' bloody place for 'im if you ask me.'

'Well hardly. And I mean he really is quite useful when he does turn up.'

'Tha's right,' Ritchie said, coming back in. 'I bin a few times, 'aven' I, George? Painted a complete ceilin' down that welfare 'all, I did. On my own. Can't seem to gerrit together to make it as a reg'lar scene like, tha's the trouble. All this bloody times and dates and places. That's alien to my nature, see? I'm too laid back, like.'

'Too bloody dull, you mean,' Sally said, bustling off towards the kitchen in search of a dustpan. 'You never even tol' me you was supposed to be anywhere.'

'The las' time,' Ritchie said to me confidingly, 'I did remember. I got myself up in time and everything. But George, I got to confess it – the magic mushrooms got the better of me.'

'Oh?'

He nodded. 'Shouldn't 'ave 'em for breakfast, see? Duw I

36

was sat in yere for hours, mun. *Hours*. Stock still, talkin' to a giant cockroach. *Yuge* thing it was, the sizea you. Wearin' jackboots, I remember that. Three pairs. We was discussin' Chinese philosophy.'

'How nice.'

'Aye,' he said. 'It was, believe it or not. She went spare,' he whispered, pointing at the doorway and grinning in recollection. 'Absolutely *spare*. Nearly 'ad 'eart attack over it. Course, she could only year one sidea the conversation naturally. Thought my fackin' brains was on fire, she did. Nearly phoned amb'lance to 'ave 'em lock me away. She've never done nothin' like dope or mushrooms or nothin', see?'

'No?'

'Uh uh. *Very* straight upbringin',' he said. 'Strong ale, work and sex. Mind you – not bad, I got to give it to 'er. An' I does,' he said, nudging me gleefully as he spotted the *double entendre*. 'Anyway 'ow's the drink, George?'

I had in fact been sipping it quite often, probably because I was eating. It had an interesting taste, not unlike sour hock laced with gorgonzola. I said: 'Well . . .'

'Good stuff, innit?' he said, refilling my glass. He swigged from the bottle. ''Ome made, see?'

'Really?' I said. 'It's certainly alcoholic.'

'Alcohol, oh aye. Among other things. Anyhow George – we're off now, are we?'

'Off where?'

'Down the nick or the bloody court or somethin'. Soon as you've finished your food. Are we?'

'*No*.' I took a deep breath and prepared to explain. Not that Ritchie was by any means stupid; the problem was caused by the fact that we were talking across an existential chasm. 'Look,' I said, 'there was your original offence . . .'

'Jointa meat from Tesco,' he said, nodding. 'I remember.'

'Right. Then there was your sentence, which in view of your record was a bit stiff. Three months or one hundred hours Community Service.'

'Was it?' he said, squinting back into the past. 'Oh ah. I remember.' He seemed to bear no grudge against a world which was determined to persecute him for leading a normal

37

life, but by the same token he couldn't be bothered trying to understand it. In all this he evinced his own version of that masochistic resignation which the voiceless and powerless have thrust on them by circumstance. ''Undred hours,' he was musing. 'Tha's only two and a half weeks' work when you think about it.'

'Mm.'

'Pity I couldn't do it all at once and get shot of it.'

'Yes. They gave you the weekend slot. That's because you pretended to have a job,' I reminded him.

'Well – thought I'd make myself look respectable,' Ritchie said. 'Little white lie, like.'

'White lie? It nearly got me sacked. Anyway. Look ...' Sally came in. 'Sally,' I said.

'Wha'?'

'Buy an alarm clock. Buy a calendar.' I gave her the summons. 'Get him into court on whatever date you'll find here. I'll be there pleading for another chance. If they give it him, mark off his attendance days on the calendar and make sure you get the bastard out of bed. Even if you have to use a pitchfork. Alright?'

She nodded. The word pitchfork had brought it all home to her – she was probably going to take that literally.

'Thanks very much for lunch.' I stood up and drained my glass.

'So – I'm not goin' in nick after all?' Ritchie asked, puzzled. 'Or wha'?'

'Probably not,' I said, making for the door. 'And in the meantime for Christ's sake stop pinching things. Or if you can't do that, stop getting caught.'

'Yes, I get you,' he said, nodding judiciously. 'Sensible. Burr I mean don't worry about me, George. I'm gettin' better alla time. Aren' I, Sal? I mean f'rinstance that birra pork you 'ad just now was pinched, and that was *gigantic*. Wasn' it, Sal? Off the cooked meat counter. Stuck it in my 'oldall, see, and then ...'

'Ritchie *shut up*. I didn't hear that. You never said it. I'm going now. See you next week. Goodbye.'

I slammed the flat door behind me and ran down the stairs. The laughter got me as I was pulling out into the main road.

# 6

Someone had been doing something funny to my front steps. Otherwise how come they were three times as steep as usual? And why wouldn't they keep still? In the end I resorted to hands and knees.

This was all rather odd because my brain felt perfectly clear and driving home had presented no problem beyond the faint though rather alarming delusion that I was travelling sideways.

I crawled up the path and the last few steps to the door. Finding my key and using it were out of the question so I sat down.

My state of mind was beginning to alter now, and it was clear that I was going mad, or dying, or more probably suffering the effects of the magic ingredient in Ritchie's green hock. If he was bombed on this stuff all the time it was a wonder he got out of bed at all.

I found myself gazing in wrapt adulation at the view. Swansea is all nuances of grey shot through by thin gold light, especially the seaward aspect; this heart-wrenching kick in the brain of a view from my house had never been the same twice over. Today it invaded me with a dreadful and delightful sense of loss and slow elation.

Perhaps I would die here. In this house, or this town, under this high grey bowl of sky, this year or next, or sometime. It struck me that until that very second, my image of death had always been a child's one, of something fixed firmly in another time and place like a foreign war in a history book.

But now it was out there somewhere to the far side of the smudgy Devon shore horizon, waiting with demonic patience to close in and find me.

This thought was all bound up with a very odd sensation like an electric shock in slow motion which went on and on. I felt that if it speeded up it might be fatal. The solid objects around me were now dissolving in a rainbow shimmer.

It was more exciting than fearful, though it was so exciting that I was rather scared. Death had revealed itself to me.

Therefore it had made me a present of the rest of my life. I was alone and the rest of my life belonged to me in a way it never had done.

If I tried too hard to understand the feeling it tended to vanish, so I just sat back on the sunny doorstep stunned with rapture, watching as from a distance while my faculties of sight, feeling and imagination became entwined. The light struck the sea and the grass and a vital force ran out of my fingers like a spectral dust storm through the haze. It ran down the path and into the plants and houses, up into the vaulted reaches of the sky and down again to bless the ships and tugboats in the shipping roads.

I started humming to myself. It gave me no particular surprise to observe that my pieces of wood were now parading in solemn dumb procession before my eyes, a palpable illusion; I could have reached out and sculpted each one just how I wanted it, with my thumb, as though it had been wet clay. It was some time before I heard the phone.

I found my feet – they were on the other end of my legs – got up on them and opened the front door quite easily.

'Yes?' I said, passingly convinced that it was Death on the line.

'George?'

'Yes?'

'Sky.'

'Sky?'

'Hendersen.'

'Oh. Hallo.'

'Hallo,' he said. 'How about tonight?'

'Tonight?'

'For dinner.'

'Oh that sounds nice.'

'Great. Do bring your charming wife.'

'No.' I was half glad and half sorry to observe that things were returning quite rapidly to normal. 'I won't. She's only my part time wife.'

'And this is one of her days off, is it?'

'No. One of mine.'

'I see.' He laughed. 'Well come about seven,' he said. 'Let me give you the address...'

40

# 7

The Hendersens lived in Poland Street, overlooking Kilvey Hill and the docks and the eastern sweep of the bay to the furnace fires and chimneys of Port Morris, at the top of a series of steep and shabby backstairs lanes which clambered up behind the Oscar Lewis Gallery. The street felt like a frontier. One end reared high into the air above the skybound world of Swansea, while the other ran into a dark hillside with rubbish tips among the twitching bushes, quite definitely in Wales. The Hendersen house was halfway along, a plebeian terraced shoebox with a mock baronial front door.

'Horrible, isn't it?' Sky remarked, opening it to me. 'Beware of the dogs.'

By this point one of them was backing me up against a bicycle, two cardboard boxes and a bag of cement which took up most of the tiny narrow hallway; the rest of it was full of a pushchair, a plastic sack of something or other and about six abandoned overcoats. Afraid I might drop it, I gave Sky the carrier bag containing a litre of cheap red and three bottles of my elderberry wine which was not bad and quite popular among the omnibibulous, which I assumed him to be. He examined them appreciatively and said: 'Great. I've got some polish removing champagne in the fridge too. It should mix well.' The dog was still barking and he kicked it, expertly and without malice, and it yelped and ran off to another part of the house. 'Don't let it worry you,' he said. 'They almost never bite people.'

He showed me through to the dining room where I encountered the other dog, some kind of long-haired miniature which was bouncing up and down on four feet yelping dementedly. All it lacked was a giant key sticking up out of its back. Sky shouted at it and it jumped up onto the table, licked my hand and barked even louder, then he pushed it off and it crawled under a chair and lay there, growling and fawning at me by turns. I sat down, feeling already somewhat overwhelmed.

That whole evening is still rather a blur. I do remember that I developed a powerful predilection for staying put in my chair since any kind of movement was fraught with peril. During one journey to the lavatory I was twice attacked by a tricycle, chased by one of the dogs, nearly stepped into a plate of bones which had been left in the middle of the bathroom floor where several cats were foregathered growling at one another absentmindedly, then on the way back I was pounced on by a tin plate which hurled itself off a shelf when I shut the kitchen door.

'Don't worry about it,' Charlotte said reassuringly. She was standing at the other end of the tiny kitchen, almost entirely obscured by clouds of steam pouring from about six saucepans at once. 'That often happens. The wall vibrates, you see. It's wooden.' She carefully removed a large comb from the butter dish, dropped the comb into the sink and added a slab of butter to something in one of the pans, probably potatoes. 'Look sit down for a minute. Dinner won't be long,' she said. 'These boring children don't eat curry so I'm having to feed them first.'

I sat down for less than a minute since one of the boring children she was alluding to – presumably the youngest – had pissed on the chair, possibly one different from that on which I'd been sitting earlier. It was made of fibreglass and had a concave seat which held about half a pint, imperial measure.

'Sorry about that,' Charlotte said. She placed a steaming pan on the dining room table, tipped the contents of the chair onto the floor and dropped a newspaper on it. The paper was part of a pile stuck up on top of a chest of drawers like a frozen avalanche. Several pens, a paperback book, a plastic dog and an apple core cascaded down as she removed it, and she kicked them into a corner, leaned her head round the bottom of the narrow cottage stairs and screamed: '*Din-ner*', presumably at the boring children who were in some upper part of this crazy and vociferous rabbit warren watching television. I had to admire the gracefully distraught way she accomplished everything. A number of alarmingly boisterous children began falling down the stairs prior to gathering around the table and arguing either with or about the dinner, followed by a much smaller one who was griping about something. Charlotte came in, placed it on her hip and dumped a pile of wet forks in the middle of the table. Then

42

she picked up a large spoon and began distributing peas, potatoes and some sort of stew in the general direction of several plates, and the larger children took one each and bore them off upstairs to continue their argument in front of the television. A door slammed, a solitary pea bounced slowly down the stairs and there was an instant or two of silence, broken by a loud and terrifying bang behind my ear.

A champagne cork hit the stew, having bounced off the ceiling, and Sky apologised for the froth down the back of my neck and poured me a drink. He had spent a solid quarter of an hour washing and polishing some tumblers which had been covered in a film of kitchen grease, like everything else in this dark and clamorous little dining room where there was just about room to swing a cat and always a couple of cats handy should you wish to test this amenity. Sky pushed one of them off the table, where it had been creeping up on the stew, sat down in a chair and said: 'Cheers.'

I grunted assent, feeling that I was beginning to understand some of the reasons behind his apparently vast intake of booze. Since both of them were perfectly intelligent I had to conclude that they'd planned things this way; I was terribly mystified as to the source of Charlotte's exemplary good humoured sanity. She was back in the kitchen at the moment, doing something to some rice while the small child swung like Tarzan from the back of her skirt.

Sky lurched off to the kitchen with the saucepans of juvenile dinner, had a brief and not acrimonious argument with Charlotte and returned with a sponge with which he pushed most of the spilled food off the table onto the floor, where the dogs and cats fell on it. Clearly this was their main function. Charlotte had now started blowing a fuse and was screaming at the small child to let go of her while she took the lid off the pressure cooker, and Sky went in and grabbed it and brought it in to try and interest it in some dinner, but it lay squirming and straining on his lap and he had a lot of trouble just holding it down. He – it was a boy – then stood up on Sky's lap and started pissing on the table, so Sky placed him in front of a pot in the corner, and after that he climbed up onto a chair and started eating his dinner quite happily. Sky wiped the piss off the table with a rather grimy looking towel which had been hanging on the back of his chair, and then dinner was served.

'Why are there four plates?' I asked, then there was a knock at the front door, Sky went to answer it and Dugdale walked in. He looked at me and said: 'Oh.'

'This is my new agent, Mr Dugdale,' Sky said mischievously. He slammed the door leading to the hall. 'Though I believe you've met.'

'Yes,' said Dugdale faintly. He was sweating. His face muscles wrestled with his dismay in the attempt to produce a smile and he sat down in a chair as though somebody had pushed him. One or two flies bounced off his forehead as he struggled with something in a deep inner pocket of his mackintosh. All of us were now watching him intently; the youngest child had a forkful of stew arrested in mid air as he gazed in rapt expectation, probably of a joke. Finally something in his mackintosh ripped and Dugdale put a bottle of brandy on the table with a clownish placatory gesture, looked at me wide-eyed and said: 'We can't go on meeting like this.' Whereupon we laughed. It was a display of quite extraordinary spur of the moment virtuosity.

'You see?' Sky said, as though this demonstrated something he'd been trying to explain earlier. 'Dugdale does his best to be a criminal but he always ends by enlarging life. That's because he's a great soul. Mahatma Dugdale. I mean take his theft of my painting,' he said, emphasising the word theft and pouring Dugdale a drink. 'On the face of it one could hardly think of anything more loathsome than to steal an artist's work for gain, but what happens? You get a perfectly good painting for a reasonable price, I at last acquire the confidence to regard my work as saleable and Dugdale gets a nice commission and is good enough to plough some of it back into this bottle of –' He examined the label '– disgustingly cheap brandy. I'm sorry about this rather awful glass,' he concluded, 'but you seem to have stolen all our good ones.'

'Have I really?' Dugdale said. 'Oh dear.' He took a sip of champagne. 'You know, I'd absolutely no idea you two knew each other.'

'I should hope not,' Sky said. 'How much money have you got?'

44

'Erm . . .' Dugdale placed a wallet on the table.

Sky pounced on it. 'Six quid,' he said, removing it. 'That'll do.'

Then Charlotte, who had been watching all this with what was either amused resignation or weary tolerance, removed a pound note on the basis that Sky owed it to one of the children, I claimed another pound myself and we all had dinner. I was amazed at this atmosphere of seething vitality in which money changed hands without touching the ground. It was exhilarating too; there were no holds barred but some sort of rules were in operation somewhere. The curry was very good and we ate a great deal of it, then all of us except Charlotte got absolutely steaming drunk and by about eleven o'clock Sky and Dugdale were locked deep in an argument about Dylan Thomas.

I think it had something to do with what precisely was meant by originality; due to a few echoes of my earlier feeling compounded by the drink I'd just swallowed the world kept switching itself on and off in waves and I wasn't terribly clear about a lot of things. At any rate it was one of those arguments where people suddenly realise to their embarrassment that they've been saying the same thing and casting one another as Devil's Advocate, then they take a little bit of time discovering a way of owning up to this without appearing to back down, and finally they dig in at opposite sides of the table going: 'Precisely!', 'Exactly!' and '*Yes*, you've *got* it' at the tops of their voices until they flatter one another into a state of crooning and gooey eyed harmoniousness. The upshot of this edifying discourse was as follows. I know this because Sky wrote it all down:

1) Originality really was originality, not merely a new combination of extant phenomena.
2) Dylan Thomas really had it.
3) Even though much of his character and work could be explained in simple psychological terms. These really didn't count because thousands of people with a similar psychological makeup had not become great writers, since they lacked the quality of originality (see 1)
4) However. Once something original had been made, it

was possible to reproduce it since by existing it had ceased to be original and become an extant phenomenon like any other.

5) Therefore. It must be possible for someone of reasonable talent to produce a new Dylan Thomas poem which looked at least passably genuine.

After that we all sat around actually writing one. Dugdale contributed most, followed by Sky, though I'm happy to feel that there are one or two words and phrases of my own knocking around in there somewhere.

Since it was to have so many profound repercussions, amounting practically to a life of its own which was to be quite original and not to be explained away in terms of extant phenomena, I here append the poem itself in all its reeking pulchitrude.

# 8

*How should my wellspring cat*

How should my wellspring cat,
Electric lard within a mottled tomb of cancer
And the shouts of praise,
Forsake the succour of oblivion's womb
And copper bindweed on the husks of time, to ride
Out on a shriek of stars
Athwart the foghorn bark of bailiffs
And the iron tit pip whistle of the priested air,
Streak on the streaming tiles
And, pistil hammered in the heart of night,
Conjour the treacle dark into a nest of spells,
The giddy winds of heaven and the kiss
Of polyp rotten daisies in the darling
Reek of creation's plundered well?

How should he hypnotise
The squalling female in her frozen rage,
Unpetrify the channels of the blood
In speaking capsules of his bony gaze,
Rant of his mummer's tale in delving throngs
Of wailing, and the reach of want
To spin, on ashtip summits of the skullwise loins
A clawtooth minuet of hair raise mawk,
Neckbreak and headlong southsea making
Cant of the slanted tongue,
Kick, trigger and conjoin the maw
And muscles in a wrack of rain
And warm spreadeagle down in spurts of ooze;
Split of his sprung banana to her inward glades?

Poachers of pirates
Crowd in the creaking wynds of daybreak,
Prising a gintrap welcome in the spyglass dawn.
I mind my keys and mumbled
In the rustle of my paging room
Rehearse my lies,
A pour of words beneath the clockshed skin,
Surging in milksop clouds to soak the hearthstone
Heated watchdog of my windowed brain.
The clattering tiger's ghost I forge in milk
Sketches a welcome in the dustrime book
Of hours in the fathered library
Where I await a strangled fever
Below the cuckoo silent sunrise of the summer town.

O cat, my fast and silent shiner of the flight
Hold hard, lie flat. Steel habits honed on nerve
Leaping the spavinned yards towards you
In an ambulance of shrouds:
My felled, fell name is ringing
Strident as spinsters at your shaggy pelt;
Hold hard. The minutes die,
Blood turns to black behind my ravaged nails;
The cat, king of his vanquished youth and stark
Ancestral rager of the waxing moon

Is loping home. The window an aureole of amazing shards
Is flat like cardboard and as sharp as fear:
The cat flops, spent as money at the lockjaw fender's rim,
His own dead, bright banana in his hangdog mouth.

Laurence Dugdale
Sky Hendersen
George Waddington
with insufficient apology
to Dylan Thomas.

# 9

Dugdale said authoritatively that it was of course an early
work, and Sky attempted to make some coffee but had to give
it up when he scalded his fingers and knocked the sugar on
the kitchen floor. So we had another glass of brandy instead
and staggered out into the blackness of the night to Sky's
studio, which was located somewhere in the garden at the
bottom of what I remember as a particularly uncomfortable
flight of concrete steps. Then in spite of the fact that we
couldn't see anything much we started looking at Sky's
paintings. In fact the effort of this did induce focus of a kind,
and Dugdale and I were both extravagant in our praise, if a bit
repetitive.

'That's marvellous. Isn't it?'

'It's great. I mean it's really – really great.'

'You think so?' Sky was holding onto the wall and
simpering myopically. 'Seriously? You think so?'

'Oh yes. It's great. Isn't it?'

'Oh definitely,' Dugdale said. 'It's marvellous.'

'I agree. I think it's great,' I said. 'You're a real idiot
sticking them all away down here where no one can see them.
They ought to be framed, for a start.'

'*Hah*,' Sky said. 'How the hell am I going to afford *that*?'

'I'll do them for you,' I said expansively.

'Really?'

'Cost price. On one condition. You then display them.'

'Where?' he said. 'How? How does one do these things?'

'You hire one of these little galleries and hang them,' I said. 'It's perfectly simple. I intend doing it myself next year,' I added unwisely. 'Maybe during the Fringe.'

'Why next year?' he asked. 'And what do you want a gallery for anyway?'

'My sculpture,' I said defensively.

'Really?'

'I haven't actually started yet,' I admitted. 'But I've got the wood. And the tools. I've had the wood for years. I know,' I said, making descriptive passes in the air, 'the forms that I want.'

'You start.'

'Mmn?'

'Now,' Sky said. 'Tomorrow. Otherwise you're just going to go on talking about it for the rest of your life. And there can't be a hell of a lot of it left.'

'I'll have you know,' I said, 'that I'm only forty seven.'

'Exactly. Now it's my turn to make a deal with you,' he said. 'I'll hire a gallery during *this* year's Fringe, and we'll both use it. My paintings and your sculpture. Get busy.'

'Alright,' I said. 'Sounds like an excellent idea.'

'Good. Now I think I'll put these fucking pictures away,' he said, 'before we all tread on them.'

It was probably a good thing he did. Dugdale had been perusing the actual paints, which were ready mixed poster colours in plastic containers like washing up liquid, and he now took the top off one, squirted the front of Sky's shirt and said: '*Hah*! My green period.'

Then Sky retaliated with a yellow period and Dugdale began warming up for a red and blue period, and I decided this was all getting very silly and it was time I returned to the house. So once I'd found it I gravitated to the dining room where Charlotte eventually came in and found me talking to a tank full of fish on the window sill that I hadn't noticed before. She wore a black silk dressing gown and an air of charming dishabille which suggested that she'd been lying in bed. I apologised for talking to the fish and she said with quite natural composure that that was perfectly alright only I wasn't to give them anything to drink. She added that she had only just begun to forgive Dugdale, who a few weeks previously had given them a glass of retsina, whereupon one of them had swum upside down for three days and eventually died.

She went back to bed then, and much affected by the tale of the fish I began weeping silently into the tank with my face slipping closer and closer to the water. More and more enchanted by the strange globular universe I started singing them a lullaby, though in retrospect I really must own that the effect of this, what with my voice echoing round the upper part of the tank and reverberating through the water, was not particularly pacifying for the fish, who began darting madly in all directions and even leaping into the air in an apparent attempt to bite my nose. Luckily Sky came in at about that point and pulled my head back under the serious misapprehension that I was trying to drown myself. Most of his face was a virulent riot of primary colour and I emitted a small shriek before I remembered the innocuous cause of it.

Evidently Dugdale had now passed out on the studio floor and for a while we debated the moral desirability of throwing a coat over him, as against the truly appalling logistic difficulty of actually getting hold of one and making our way down there with it, further exacerbated by the fact that Sky left strange coloured footprints wherever he went, some of which would have to be cleaned up for example the ones up the kitchen wall which had resulted from his demonstration to me of a rock climbing technique known as chimneying.

So we forgot about Dugdale and got busy with a mop and bucket, the bucket being that good old fashioned galvanised type which inflicts quite substantial minor wounds to the shins and forehead when they come in contact with it, and shortly after that Sky ran himself a bath and I passed out under the dining room table where I slept until about five o'clock, kept reasonably warm by a few newspapers, a cat or two and the larger dog.

Calling at the lavatory I noticed that Sky had left the bath by this time, possibly aroused by the temperature of the water which was an intriguing coffee colour from all the mingled paint. I let myself out and walked home with the light of cold grey dawn tearing into my brain like nitric acid, and collapsed into an armchair where I was woken up at eight by Beau shoving a cup of coffee under my nose. I crawled up to the bathroom for a shave and a change and then dragged myself off to court, where luckily I had absolutely nothing to do but sit holding the two halves of my head together waiting for one of my cases to be remanded till a later date. From time to time I amused myself by trying to compute the rate at which all us paid lackeys of the Penal Racket were clobbering HMG for little more than the honour of our presence.

When it came to making a living I really had it cracked, the ritual of court being totally immune to cuts.

# Part Two

# 10

I suppose that if it hadn't been for Dylan Thomas and the fact that this was something like the thirtieth anniversary of his trip to Manhattan to have his brain massively insulted, life might have been different, which is to say it might have gone on being just the same.

I had a sense of change anyway, or rather a feeling that change was possible, I might be anything I wanted, as though I'd been thrown suddenly into an autumnal adolescence. The relative absence of Alice from my life had made me light headed, so had dinner at Sky's; there really were so many ways to approach life when you thought about it.

Suffice it to say that in my forty eighth year, being of sound mind and a servant of Her Majesty's Home Office, I found myself disturbed and elated by all kinds of vague notions about opening my front door wide to the dark and Dionysian, wrestling with it, giving it form.

I actually had my front door open, my bit of ash was on a plinth in the middle of the living room with a flood of evening sun playing over it. I'd even brought myself to take a few bits off with a chisel. In a strung out and hungover way I was feeling very happy.

My mind had been making momentary feints towards hallucination all day, and I was not insensible of the possibility that my blood might have been permanently altered by Ritchie's evil green hock, but this did not seriously lower my mood. I seemed to remember Beau telling me that whereas about one person in a thousand was allergic to marijuana, a somewhat higher proportion was liable to long-term effects from hallucinogenics. As a veteran of the drug culture and a professional hypochondriac he'd be able to advise me if the flashes continued too long or got worse. He was out somewhere at the moment pursuing his lifelong mission to repair his health, pounding twenty five lengths of the beach, buying homeopathic painkillers or having his inside leg measured by a physiotherapist. The phone rang and I went out whistling to answer it.

'Ah good,' Alice said. 'You're available.'

'Available for what?'

'Don't be so mulishly defensive,' she said. 'It's a sign of failure.'

'Alice what do you want?'

'Nothing, if you put it like that.'

'Fine . . .'

'No *don't hang up.*'

'Well?'

'Ooogh!' she said. 'I just wanted to ask you if you'd be terribly sweet and come along to a little gathering this evening. I mean it would be just lovely to have you there. But please don't bother if you've something more important to do.'

'Well,' I said. 'I was thinking of having a bath.'

'Gosh, a previous engagement. Well in that case . . .'

'No hold on,' I said. I'd been wondering about my sculpture, but now that I'd actually begun it, it gave me a sense of infinite leisure which made me feel generous. 'It's alright, I'll come. Where is it?'

'You are sweet, George. I knew you would. It's at Tom Delderfield's house.'

'Who?'

'Are you kidding?'

'The name sounds familiar but I can't place it just at the moment.'

'George no wonder you never get on. He's only one of your chief POs, for Christ's sake.'

'Oh *that* Delderfield,' I said. 'But good God, the man's absolutely revolting.'

'I'm not asking you to go to bed with him.'

'But I mean Alice really. The *company* you keep. You

know he's widely rumoured to have raped his secretary about three years ago?'

'Of course I do,' she said. 'And it was only attempted. He couldn't go through with it because he's impotent. Anyway it never got as far as court so it doesn't count. And there'll be lots of other people there. JPs,' she said. 'Local businessmen, a councillor or two, Lady Gowerton...'

'*Le tout* Swansea.'

'Quite.'

'What is it, in any case?'

'The Dylan Thomas Memorial Affiliation.'

'Oh my *Gawd*.'

'I thought you liked the man.'

'I do,' I said. 'What's that got to do with it?'

'Oh George,' she said. 'I do so desperately need someone presentable who can chat poetry to people. You see they asked me to find a speaker...'

'Alice...'

'No don't worry,' she said. 'I've already got one. But he's disastrous. Some pompous little leftist twerp – I can't *think* what possessed me. Maybe I thought he must be intelligent because he's ugly.'

'That doesn't follow,' I said. 'Life really is quite delightfully unfair.'

'Yes I know. That's the annoying thing. I knew already. Anyway there's nothing I can do to stop the bugger now. I'll cut him as short as possible but everyone's going to *hate* it and I just want to have you there to wheel round afterwards.'

'And take away the taste of the nasty medicine?'

'Quite. Anyway George, I'm so glad you're coming. It's at eight.'

She gave me the address, somewhere in the Uplands. Beau came in at that point, absolutely dripping wet.

'I didn't know it was raining,' I said, replacing the receiver.

'It isn't,' he said truculently, squelching past me up the stairs. 'I fell in the sea.'

I thought he was being sarcastic but when I looked outside the sky was still perfectly clear. I went upstairs to change into poetry association clobber, then since I still had more than an hour I opened a bottle of elderberry wine, gazed at my piece of ash for a while, caressing it and thinking about the form I wanted to get from it, then went through to the kitchen.

Beau was there by this time, wearing a dry tracksuit and a towel round his head, drinking a mug of that wholefood marmite which is called something like Vetzyme and making dire predictions of pneumonia. He declined a glass of elderberry wine on the basis that it was made with white sugar which made the DNA cells revolve in the wrong direction and led to convulsions. I had been wondering whether to ask his advice about my wee flashes of hallucination, but decided after not much thought that this was best left until some other time.

# 11

'So if we can have your attention?' Haydock Williams said. 'Thankyou. If we could just all gather at this end of the room? Yes, over there please, if you could possibly drag yourselves away and forgather down here . . .?'

He was doing bookie signals and trying to speak directly, and first, to the knots of people furthest away from him in Tom Delderfield's seedily sumptuous living room. In common with so many of his efforts to do anything this had a compound negative effect: the people close to him instinctively ignored him since he seemed so clearly to be speaking to somebody else, while the people he was trying to reach reacted with the instinct of kids at the back of a class being harangued by a teacher who is trying weakly to be sarcastic. The noise in the room became less general but louder, while a few people actually backed away from him when his arm gestures became positively threatening to their drinks and sandwiches and sausage rolls.

This at any rate created a little stagelike space around Sion Slugge, who stood with an ingratiating scowl waiting to

58

speak, holding some sheets of lined paper and moving his lips. He had chosen to be next to a gilt standard lamp with a pink shade which anyone but Delderfield would have owned for its wonderful bad taste. The stand ballooned in and out from the base upwards until, standing on one leg and bearing the lamp itself, it became a plump and severe but nevertheless extremely suggestive near nude figure which must originally have been intended to represent something – not inconceivably the Unacceptable Face of Industry. It seemed to me that the gilt of some of the more erogenous parts of her body was looking rather worn.

I could have forewarned Alice about Sion Slugge had she asked me, but she hadn't. His given name was John and had first mutated to Sean, until he moved to Wales where he felt Sion to have more radical clout. A few people had now begun looking at him expectantly although the general hubbub was still too great for him to begin, all of which put him in the excruciating position of being exposed but helpless, which I must own to finding rather a treat to observe; I began to be quite glad that Alice had talked me into coming.

Alice herself now took things in hand and transformed us all into an expectant flock by moving about the room making a few barely perceptible gestures. She had of course the natural instincts of the sheepdog – a desire to savage sublimated to a facility for manipulation, which in her case was simply a means to savaging more effectively. A few people dutifully coughed and it was time for Slugge to begin.

'You might wonder, ladies and gentlemen. Persons,' he said. 'You might wonder why we are all here, graveward with our furies, yet another committee seeking to disturb the winding sheet of a dead poet with the crooked worm of our ignoble curiosity.' He paused to allow time for his abstruse quotations and self deprecatingly sophisticated jokes to sink in, or perhaps to allow some celestial examiner time to tot up his marks. In fact everyone looked blank except Lady Gowerton, who stood on my right discussing onions with a man in a brown tweed sports coat and thick glasses. 'Well,' Slugge resumed, 'this is the halfway house – I shall be returning to that theme – and we can only trust that we are pointed towards the altar, upon which, in the capacity of the owl –' he gave that genial psychopathic leer which he fondly thought of as a sunny smile ' – I shall attempt to shed as much light as I can. Now we must begin our journey with the discipline of forgetting. And first we must forget that larger than Hollywood myth of the great and dissipated orator, that awful transatlantic grandiloquence by which people think he was made but by which he was in fact ruined . . .'

The audience gave its first stir of sympathy at this. It is axiomatic in South Wales to regard Thomas as a good boy really who was lured to perdition by dollar-flaunting Bad Company, by which token everybody one speaks to is his mother.

'But secondly.' He held up a finger. 'Secondly, and this may be harder, we must forget the safe and sound loller at the corners of Wales – the *brassy* orator. For if we are to disentangle the intricate image of Dylan Thomas, we must also disentangle his fond, sly, dithyrambic web of words if we are ever to discover the bones within the meat. We owe it both to him and ourselves to do this. After all, our aim is to *descend*, from *overview*, to the nub of his writing, whereas Thomas's particular device was always to proceed from *underview* towards some measure of light. Naturally there's a conflict of interests, though in the end, if we do our job right, these interests will coincide. Now I shall shortly be coming to analyse the structure of Thomas's poems – the symbols and patterns if you like – wherein I hope to demonstrate by numerological metaphor, that whereas the early poems can be presented as *bottom* heavy fractions, which give us an *upward*-driving fertility –' here he actually raised a fist through the air like a coarse phallic gesture ' – in the later poems we find a *top* heavy fraction – which in Thomas's case meant panic – or even a *perfectly balanced* fraction, which in anyone's case means nullity and for him, probably, indicated a desire for death. But first I think we had better look at this intricate image of his which strode on two cultural levels. In short, we must examine the always rather fraught question of his Welshness, or lack of it . . .'

He had now lost his audience totally but seemed blithely, almost maliciously not aware of it, which was quite consistent with his behaviour at any time. He had a deep egotistic need of other people to play bit parts or simply be talked at, and tended to recruit them with the small and well nurtured side of him which was attractive, like a salesman gaining entry to the hall; the world positively seethed with people who were once quite friendly with him for ten minutes.

'. . . the Halfway House,' he was now declaiming. 'The cultural marches. Oh, the agony of being poised between slatternly, proud old Cymru and the vast, cold, imperialist machine of the English language . . .'

'*What* did he say?' Lady Gowerton abruptly broke off a rhapsodic description of her compost heap; her voice was now almost louder than Slugge's. '*Machine* language?'

'Somethin' like that,' the man beside her said. His eyes looked absolutely terrified but I think that was their permanent expression. 'Ah.'

'Machines will *never* write poetry,' she declared. 'Dylan Thomas certainly didn't use one. There is no substitute for human genius.'

'. . . on balance his solution was not a sell out,' Slugge was saying. He threw Lady Gowerton a weak smile. 'Rather, he took the English language and subverted it with an essentially Welsh meaning. Of course we must regret that he didn't tackle the Welsh language itself but he can, I think, be absolved from the charge of having crossed over the tracks.'

He had now reached the end of a page and begun fumbling for the next one. Alice acted. The last sentence had sounded just conclusive enough, the pause was just long enough and she began to clap ostentatiously. The rest followed suit, most of them loudly in compensation for the fact that they hadn't been listening, a process in which I joined with cheerful vigour. Slugge's face fell open with wide, outraged surprise, but he soon recognised his position as hopeless and simpered sullenly in acknowledgement.

'Machines,' Lady Gowerton was still saying.

'I *think* they're called word processors,' the man beside her suggested.

'And they produce processed language,' she said vehemently, glittering with the triumph of her own wit. 'Can a machine feel dread? Or joy? Is it affected by the phases of the moon? Of course not.' She treated Slugge to a glare of barely controlled malevolence which was intended to let him know that he should be horsewhipped but she forbore to descend to his level by doing it, but he was deep in a conversation with Delderfield and didn't see it.

'Thankyou Mr, er Mr Slugge,' Delderfield said. 'Int'resting. Most.' He stuffed a small pastry into his face from a heaped plateful he was carrying, nodding at a piece of the floor. 'Valuable introduction to our ...' He made a casually room embracing gesture with his arm, which ended as he sent another pastry down his throat to follow the first one.

'Yes. Well actually,' Slugge said, 'my talk wasn't finished. In fact I wasn't even halfway through.' He looked accusingly at Alice, who stood at Delderfield's elbow and beamed at him radiantly. 'Still, maybe I can give the rest of it next time.'

'Nghmmh,' Delderfield said, eating yet another pastry. 'I understand you write, ah, write poetry yourself.'

'Yes I do,' Slugge said with a defensive pride which in fact sounded merely truculent and shifty, as though he were owning to some contentious view about the benefits of masturbation.

'Mmmh. Of course a poet has his own particular mission to fulfil.' Delderfield dropped a creased but expensively tailored arm onto Slugge's shoulder, smearing it with pastry crumbs, and began leading him away down the room. 'Criticism is of course a lesser art,' he said indistinctly through his full mouth. 'Best leave it to the critics I think.'

'Oh,' Slugge said. 'I understood I was to be the resident...'

I heard no more, merely saw Delderfield's fat, pink neck folds wink as his head rolled a ponderous, regretful negative. He offered Slugge a pastry which was disdainfully rejected, so he ate it himself.

Alice dug me in the ribs and winked. 'Well that's seen *him* off,' she observed. 'Could have been a lot worse. Come and meet people.'

She took my elbow between finger and thumb, wheeled me about and presented me first to Lady Gowerton, who was nearest.

'Waddington,' she said. 'Waddington – haven't we met?'

'I believe so,' I said, dimly remembering some weekend

parole board conference.

'Hah!' She sniffed. 'What a frightful man,' she added. 'What did you think of him?'

'Well . . .'

'Machines indeed. He looks dank to me. Definitely dank. Is he a homosexualist?'

'I couldn't . . .'

'I mean consenting adults is one thing,' she said. 'Letting them take over society quite another. It may be alright for MPs, but things like the police force and the judiciary are right out. Which they know quite well, of course. They'll never get in. All this computer nonsense is just their way of getting back at us.'

'You mean – computers are some sort of homosexual plot?'

'Of *course*,' she said, clearly having heard it from a burning bush, or perhaps her compost heap. 'They know we won't let them take over so they're trying to destroy the culture.' She tapped two fingers, heavily beringed with honest toil, into her opposite palm. 'Computers,' she said, fixing me with a glittering eye. 'The Enemy Within. Language Machines.'

'Of course,' Alice said encouragingly, 'Dylan Thomas hated them.'

Lady Gowerton looked at her, dottily benign. 'They weren't invented in his day, dear,' she said. 'He was lucky.'

'No no,' Alice said, smiling. 'I mean homosexuals.'

'Oh, I'll say,' Lady Gowerton averred. 'Loathed them. "Pansies", he called them. Filthy pansies.' She glowered over at Slugge and said: 'Pansies' again in a loud voice, but he stood alone morosely swallowing a tumbler of burgundy, and merely looked up vaguely as if unsure whether someone had called his name or not.

'Father knew him,' Lady Gowerton informed us.

'Really?'

'Lent him twenty five pounds.' She smiled indulgently. 'Never saw it again of course. Couldn't have cared less. Fascinating man, he always said. Of course I was just a gel. Pinched my bottom once but I think he thought I was one of the maids. Perfect manners really. Only rude to people who thoroughly deserved it. Loathed pansies of course. Of course he did. Computers indeed. Anyway nice to talk to you Mr

Er. Quite a good thing this, I suppose.' She gave the room a sweeping, predatorily assessing squint down her nose. 'Get ourselves some halfway decent speakers and we can get cracking. Computers! At least Fatty Delderfield always puts up a good thrash. I'll have whisky,' she announced, handing me a tall empty tumbler. 'Four fingers. Splash of soda. No ice.'

'Well done,' Alice whispered to me at the drinks table.

'But I didn't say anything.'

'You listened in the right way,' she said. 'Lady Gowerton's the really sticky one. If she'd left, half the room would have followed her. Go on, take her whisky over. I want you to meet the next one.'

The next one was some grubby councillor called Helmsdale or Winscale who was quite high up in planning, or it could have been drains. He had backed Haydock Williams up against the mantelpiece in the course of discussion, and was emphasising his points with downward jabs of the forefinger.

'... you *can't* tell me he had no sense of tradition,' he said. 'Look: "The *hand* that signed the *paper* felled a *city*; Five *sov*ereign fingers taxed the *breath* ..." And so on. That pattern goes right back to the sixth century AD, boy. I've done my bloody homework.'

'Alright,' Haydock Williams said. 'I'll *allow* that.' He was holding up both hands in a don't shoot gesture while his feet performed a clumsy reel about the fender, trying not to trip over it. 'But, all I'm saying is he was very modern in the way he *handled* his forms.'

'Oh, granted,' Helmsdale/Winscale said, backing off a bit. '*And* in his meanings. Dylan talks directly to the man in the street. He is *not* for ivory tower intellectuals. This association has got to become the basis of a mass movement, or it's worth bugger all. And that's what *I'm* saying. That bloody clown was just exactly what we don't need. Welsh language,' he said disparagingly. 'The bugger isn't even Welsh. Bet he's never joined a trade union in his life.'

'That was the impression I had,' I said. I was getting better at this. The glow of two brandies chased the elderberry wine along my blood; it was lighting up time in the tired streets of my brain.

'Right,' Helmsdale/Winscale said, allowing me a nod. 'See my whole point is – we got to *wrest* culture out of the intellectual closet. It can't *breathe* in there. That's why the left is floundering. Got to be. Anger is just the wine of socialism. Theory's the bloody Valium. Culture is the bread,' he concluded, proffering a fist as though it were a loaf.

'That's rather well put,' I said, with that odd lurch which occurs when you set out to dissemble and find yourself speaking the truth instead, but to the same end. 'Why don't you give a talk yourself some time?'

'Why should I?' he demanded. 'My knowledge is too scrappy. A discussion though – I'll join in that. We want some speaker who'll stimulate discussion. How about you?'

'Oh . . .'

'You're reluctant for the same reasons as me?'

'I suppose so.'

'There we are then.' He began turning his back, then swung towards Alice. 'You want to find a good speaker, my girl,' he said. 'Then maybe we can get this thing off the ground.'

'Oh we will,' Alice said placatingly. 'It is early days yet, after all.'

'Not a good beginning,' Helmsdale/Winscale said. 'But I will give it one more try.'

'George you're magic,' Alice muttered, wafting me off towards a knot of people in the corner. 'The other half of the room would have left with him. Except for a few people who don't matter anyway. All that remains now is a bit of mopping up.'

In the course of the next hour and a half I mopped up a brace of depressive, monosyllabic professors of literature, a small conspiracy of councillors, a lurching of barristers, a booming of businessmen, a gaggle of literary spinsters of both sexes, one lone lugubrious GP and about six brandies which Alice kept handing me with little pats of encouragement. I finished up sitting rather giddily in a tartan covered armchair listening with hazy, incredulous passivity while R.V. Mottram Davies, lay preacher, Tory councillor and purveyor of ladies' underwear, regaled me with his personal experiences of the presence of Christ. Unless I'd got it wrong, Christ first appeared to him in the lavatory about ten years ago at a time of deep spiritual crisis. I was to understand that it wasn't anything like an apparition as such, just a sense of joyful conviction which overwhelmed him when he pulled the chain, a feeling of Christ pouring down into Christ and filling the room with radiance. It had completely changed his life. If he was ever tempted to doubt Christ's love for him now, all he had to do was nip off to the lavatory. I agreed that the convenience of this resource which had been given him was clear evidence that Christ possessed both generosity and the common touch, then thankfully he put down his glass and left the house abruptly to go and get his beauty sleep. I noticed he had been drinking milk, confirming a long held suspicion of mine that after puberty the stuff is positively dangerous; Genghis Khan drank an awful lot of it.

I sat back with a sense of luxurious tedium and closed my eyes, and was rather nonplussed when I opened them to find a girl sitting on the arm of my chair and looking at me.

I'd noticed her before – I had kept on glimpsing her through the knots of thick, middle-aged, middle income culture punters – very incongruous and distracted, alone and palely loitering with a glass of gin and something. I had wondered what she was doing there since in the entire course of the evening I had seen her speak to no one except Slugge, presumably to tell him to piss off. He had been ogling her considerably and now appeared to have left. She was extremely pretty when you looked at her twice, slender with that olive golden, slightly oily looking skin, coarse blonde hair tied loosely back and startling grey eyes which matched her dress, a sort of voluptuous Quaker job which, like herself inside it, looked ordinary until you looked again. I had an immediate impulse to tell her things I didn't even know were on my mind.

'I'm supposed to be taking life seriously,' I announced.

'Oh really?'

'Yes. Well not seriously so much as urgently. I'm going to die, you see.'

'Uh huh? You mean soon?'

'Oh no, no. Not soon in that sense. Sooner than you, probably, but ... I just realised the other day – yesterday it was – that I was going to die. That's all I mean. In my opinion the vast majority of people don't. They muddle on, making all sorts of ridiculous plans which are based on unconscious delusions of immortality. D'you agree?'

She looked around the room, drawing on a cigarette. 'Yes,' she said.

'Oh.' I think I might have preferred it if she had said no. Now, my feelings about life and death had to be taken seriously, their validity having been endorsed. Clearly there was a side of me which felt nostalgic for immortality and muddle. 'Well,' I said, 'the thing is, here I am farting around at a gathering in which I've no real interest, telling all sorts of plausible lies to people just to please my partly ex wife whom I don't even like very much. Where's my sense of urgency, that's what I want to know? But then on the other hand,' I argued with myself, 'perhaps that's what living life fully is about. Sending things up. Playing with reality. I mean to hell with puritan notions of the good and the true – the really serious have a certain gaiety. Don't you agree? I think I read that somewhere.'

'Probably in Henry Miller,' she said, nodding.

'Yes that's it. You mean you agree?'

'Yes I suppose I do. But I also think you're kidding yourself,' she said. 'Is your partly ex wife that blonde female with the predatory features?'

'Yes probably.'

'Hmmm. Well anyway, if you want to send life up – what's your name anyway?'

'George.'

'If you want to send life up, George, you must learn that there's no point in doing it on someone else's terms.'

I said: '*Ah*', struck by a statement which seemed so simple it was brilliant.

'Why don't you take me home?' the girl asked.

'Er . . . home?'

'To your house.'

'Well . . . right,' I said. 'Okay.'

'I'm in need of a temporary refuge, you see.'

'I *see*,' I said ponderously, now entirely confused and feeling like a prize imbecile. 'Well – there is plenty of room.

You're welcome.'

'Don't get so het up.' She smiled and laid a hand on my arm. 'I am making a pass at you – you were right the first time. I also do rather need somewhere to stay.'

'Fine,' I said inanely, stirring my limbs. 'Excellent. Good.' This kind of thing hadn't happened to me for years. 'Well look.' I cleared my throat. Laced with brandy and libido my blood pumped hectically, like an old tune switched on suddenly at full volume. 'I'll just say goodnight to everyone, then we can...'

'Don't be a berk.'

'Mmn?'

'Just *go*.'

'Oh, but how can I do that?'

'You put one foot in front of the other,' she said. 'It's called walking.'

# 12

'That one looks promising,' Sky said.

'But I've hardly touched it.'

'Exactly,' he said, stalking around the plinth. He caressed the wood along the grain. 'Avoid the temptation to take too much off. Don't be too polished.'

'Alright,' I said unhappily.

'Sorry,' he said. 'The other rule is, don't let yourself be bullied by people like me. Look.' He placed a large folder of pictures against the wall. 'These are for framing. I'll talk about them some other time. Goodbye.'

'Bye,' I said, thoroughly bewildered by his abruptness; it was as if he were running out on himself.

The phone rang.

'*Hallo*, George,' Alice said with massive affability. 'And how are you after yesterday evening?'

'In the circumstances, fine.'

'Went well, wouldn't you say?'

'Yes.'

'And of course you were a godsend. Pity you had to walk off with Bill Haydock Williams's secretary. I don't think he was terribly pleased.'

'You don't mean to tell me he's been trying to have it off with her?'

'Of course not. He hasn't tried to have it off with anyone since his youngest child was born, about sixteen years ago. But that doesn't obviate sexual possessiveness, it merely changes its form. The best thing you can do is be casually brazen about it, if you can manage that. Then he'll simply have to give way before your superior masculinity. Though if you want my opinion she's a bit U for you.'

'A bit me for me?'

'*No*. U,' she said. 'Opposite of non-U. I mean your usual speed is silly little typists who haven't heard of women's rights and think you're distinguished just because you're greying and vaguely good looking and can spell Habeas Corpus without looking it up. I just don't want you to get in out of your depth.'

'Thankyou very much.'

'Not at all. Look George, everyone was terribly impressed with you, apart from your minor rudeness at the end, and most of them were too drunk to notice that.'

'I'm so pleased.'

'But George . . . the thing is I've simply got to have you.'

'Eh?'

'As a member. If not Mister University of Life Professor then at least the chief steward.'

'No.'

'Everyone *loves* you,' she protested. 'They think you're a real intellectual Mr Nice Guy. I should have realised your appeal a long time ago. It's the jacket and the eyebrows I think, and the air of wood shavings in the pocket. You could be some old school rustic Labour MP or something.'

'Oh *wow*,' I said. 'That is my secret ambition of course.'

'*God*. You're so adolescent and bloody *negative*. Don't you realise what a lot of doors this could open for you?'

'The Dylan Thomas Memorial Affiliation? You're kidding.'

'I am not,' she said. 'Never underestimate the value of neutral territory.'

'For what purpose?'

'For people who have to pretend to themselves and everybody else that they hate each other's guts, to forgather behind a smokescreen of harmlessness and get on with the real business of life.'

'Which is?'

'Making deals,' she said. 'Hatching schemes. Making money. Getting on, God – I'm offering you so much on a bloody *plate* and you won't take it. What d'you think it's going to cost you? Your precious integrity?'

'Alice *no*,' I said. 'That's my final word.' I slammed down the phone, then took it off the hook and let it swing. I went and threw myself on the sofa and lay down bucked and disordered by a leaping rage with Alice, which I supposed had to do with her trying to take advantage of me but seemed all out of proportion. Some door inside me had been jammed open to release a boxful of feelings which were dangerously unschooled in self expression. Another example of this was Sophie.

Her name was Sophie. She was out somewhere at the moment.

What had she picked me up *for*, that was the question I was carefully not asking myself. She was certainly rather vague and impulsive but I didn't get the impression that she took this sort of initiative very often.

The question was quite urgent because we hadn't passed quite the night of friendly lust I had anticipated. Not to put too fine a point on it, I seemed to be in love with her.

At least I assumed that was what it was; I was beginning to realise that nothing quite like this had ever happened to me.

# 13

'Gentleman to see you,' Joan said. In common with all her statements it sounded somehow admonitory. Joan's official position was tea lady and dogsbody to our little den of middle class iniquity, though I was prepared to swear she was also paid a fat retainer by the Home Office for saying what time we came in and left and how much stationery we pinched.

'I have no appointments until half past two,' I said blandly. 'Meanwhile I'm rather busy. Unless he wants to wait a long time, you'd better get him to leave his name and come back.'

'Too late for that, I'm afraid,' she said. 'I've said you'll see him. I'll show him in.'

I actually picked up the nearest file and sank my teeth in it, so that as this character walked in I was worrying it like a dog with a rabbit, growling fiercely. This was not a good beginning. I replaced the file on the desk and said: 'What can I do for you?'

'Some kind of office therapy, is it?' he asked with a familiar grin, sitting down without an invitation.

'Yes it is,' I said. 'Who are you?'

'Oh sorry.' He pulled from his back jeans pocket a little leather wallet which flipped open to show a plastic card with a mug shot and some official stamp on it. 'Pollock,' he said, putting it away. 'Social Security. Pleased to meet you.'

He leaned forward to proffer a hand across the desk and I stared at it until, with a shrug, he took it back again. 'I understand one of your, uh, clients is a Laurence Dugdale,' he said.

'Yes?' I said, pulse notching upward. 'What about him?'

'He's one of ours and all, see. I've bin goin' through 'is file.' He drew Dugdale's file from the briefcase on the floor by his chair, and tapped it. 'I'm a Special Investigator.'

'Oh I see,' I said. 'That's why you wear jeans and cowboy boots and slouch around the place like a greasy little yobbo. Undercover job. Or does all that come naturally to you anyway?'

'We can play this thing any way you like,' he said, gratifyingly nettled. 'The fact is we're considerin' a pros-

71

ecution for persistently failing to maintain himself. Whether we do or not could depend very much on this interview. It's up to me.'

'Bullshit,' I said. 'If it was up to you you'd have already done it. I know your type. What were you till they offered you commission and a car allowance for being witchfinder general? Some harassed little counter clerk?'

'I don't find your attitude very helpful.'

'And I find your whole demeanour thoroughly distasteful but presumably we do have something to talk about so let's get on with it. Now I infer that failing to maintain himself means not working?'

'That's right.'

'Well I can't believe that even this government could regard that as an offence by itself, so you mean he's actually turned down a job?'

'He has turned down several jobs,' the Special Investigator said. His voice was shifting from vernacular to prim as he got rattled, rather than the other way about. 'In the first place,' he said, not consulting his file, 'lollypop man.'

'Oh yes – I can just see Dugdale as a lollypop man,' I said. 'He'd either fall asleep and let the kids wander all over the road, or get really enthusiastic and lead them over the hills and far away like the Pied Piper. What else?'

'Part time lavatory attendant. And that . . .'

'That isn't even worth considering.' I waved dismissively. 'Any more?'

'Yes,' he said. 'There was potato picking. New potatoes. Down in Pembroke.'

'That would be temporary?'

'Yes. The season comes round, see, and the old farmers put the word out. Get a good crowd down there. Good few people off our books this time of year.'

'I presume it's piece work.'

'Earn a good few bob, some people. Glad of it too.'

'You're seriously suggesting,' I said, 'that a man of fifty two or whatever he is, with obvious intellectual ability and no experience as an agricultural labourer, is wilfully failing to maintain himself by not picking potatoes?'

'The work was offered him.'

'I assume it was also offered to someone else, who took it?'

'Yes of course,' he said. 'And grateful. This is the point.'

'The point is the job went to someone it suited. I imagine the other two did as well. Good God, boy, you could stand out there now and hawk them on the street corner. You'd be killed in the rush.'

'I am not responsible,' he said, 'for the economic re-seshunn.'

'No, you just make a good screw out of it. *I'm* responsible for Dugdale's rehabilitation, and I...'

'Well rehabilitation might be the word,' he said, gathering his things together fussily and getting up on his spring heeled piggy legs. 'One of our resident retraining centres I mean. And that's from my chief – it's not me. You can phone him up and ask him if you like, on the telephone. Since you're this Dugdale's Probation Officer you might care to tell him that since all these jobs are so unsuited to his marvellous talents, perhaps he'd better find something suitable on his own. Otherwise we might start getting nasty. Okay? I'll see myself out.'

'Please do,' I said. 'The door's over there.'

He had no sooner left the room than my desk buzzer squawked.

'Someone on the phone for you,' Joan said.

'Who?'

'A lady,' she said, and switched Alice through.

'Alice, I've told you not to phone me at the *office*.'

'George how *sweet*. It sounds as though I'm your mistress. Anyway what am I supposed to do when you won't answer your other phone?'

'Take the bloody hint and leave me alone.'

'You know,' she said. 'You've become so volatile as to be positively hysterical.' She sighed. 'I suppose it's the sex,' she said. 'It's bound to do more harm than good at your age. Anyway listen...'

I put the phone down. About ninety seconds later Joan was through to me again.

'Seem to have cut yourself off there, Mr Waddin'ton,' she said, prepared to overlook the lapse just this once. 'I'll put her through again.'

'Now look, Alice...'

'No you look. I'm quite happy to play this game all day. I just want to put a simple proposition to you, then at the end of it you can say yes or no. Or do you so doubt your capacity for decision that you're scared to listen to it?'

'Alright,' I said. '*Alright*. Just get on with it.'

'Right, point one,' she said. 'We had a committee meeting. Our little affiliation's really getting into shape. Haydock Williams is pretty certain he can get some Arts Council funding...'

'What – to cover Delderfield's booze bills?'

'No. Well possibly, but that would be incidental. The really crucial necessity for a funded existence, would be some demonstrable proof that we were doing original work. In other words, that we had a real down home slant on the Beast of the Boat House which was not already covered either by American universities or all these smelly little amateur groups who sit around swilling real ale and arguing about his word patterns. So in short we need two things: a thesis and a project. Which means we need a presentable authority.'

'So why are you phoning me?' I said. 'You're thick with professors of literature already.'

'Thick is the word,' she said. 'They're all *hopeless*, George. Half of them bitch all the time about rival theories of criticism, and the other half can't even construct a sentence. And they're all about as charming as a dead badger.'

'Well I don't know anyone.'

'Yes you do,' she said. 'I mean how about you doing it?'

'Alice *no*.'

'Oooh! There's *money* in this, you stupid berk,' she said. 'I'm not just asking you a favour. I though you wanted to pay off your mortgage, retire early, I dunno. I told Tom Delderfield you'd do it, too. He isn't going to be too pleased.'

'Are you trying to threaten me?'

'No. Well yes, I was I suppose, but... *Honestly*, George, I just don't understand you. You already know a good bit about the subject, you can wield a pen, you've got the gift of the gab. You'd need to write a few thousand words, give a couple of talks, maybe swan off on a little paid lecture tour, conning middle aged females with your charm and erudition. It'd be such a *doddle*.'

It was the word con which did it. I had a very palpable sensation of a light bulb reading: 'IDEA' lighting up in the centre of my brain.

'Alice – okay,' I said. 'Thanks for putting it to me. I really don't want to do it though. But now I come to think of it, I do know someone. I can put you on to him if you like. He'd be ideal.'

'Are you *sure*, George? As good as you?'

'Oh, he's *much* better at this kind of thing than I am,' I said. 'Infinitely.'

# 14

I didn't normally buy bottles of vodka but several things had conspired to make this a special occasion.

To begin with, Sophie had gone out for a walk and hadn't come back yet. Since the previous evening. And then there was Beau's rent. Due to a number of things like his physiotherapist's bills and his income tax fund and the price of running shoes, he hadn't paid me any for more than a month, so I'd been rather looking forward to it, but once I'd paid the rates and the milkman and had my shoes mended there'd only been seven quid left, so I spent it on a bottle of vodka before it had a chance to vanish.

Now I could forget Sophie by getting drunk in the kitchen having one of my metaphysical twitches about the nature of money.

People think of money as though it were actually a collection of solid objects, or else as some vast and whimsically majestic abstraction like a cross between the Holy Ghost and the Theory of Relativity. But in point of plain fact it's a liquid; look at the way small quantities evaporate.

Beau came in and I gave him a drink and put this theory to him. He thought money was more like blood. 'I mean,' he said, 'people talk about being bled white. Things costing an arm and a leg. Don't they?'

'Of course,' I murmured, drink warming my brain with an expanding sense of wisdom and generosity. I nodded.

'Mind you,' Beau said, 'Freud thought it was shit.'

'Freud was a misanthropist.'

'Why?'

'For not being a revolutionary. The man had no world view at all. The logical outcome of his money as shit theory is that our lives are all ruled by some monstrous arsehole but he was quite contented with the idea.' I sighed. 'I just wonder if I'm ever going to be one of those people who has money that feels like their own,' I said. 'All I ever seem to do is watch it go past.'

Beau concurred with this view somewhat morosely, and began recounting a recent dream in which he'd been on a raft with a big pile of loose banknotes stacked up at the far end. He'd been able to hold them in place by not breathing, and kept seeing land get closer through the rolling waves, but then when the phone rang he had dived into the sea to answer it, and the money blew away.

'What bothers me is what it might symbolise,' he concluded. 'Supposing it's health? I'm not supposed to drink really.'

'Painkillers?'

'God no. I threw them down the bog. D'you know,' he said, 'I'd been totally wasting my time for *six months*? That arsehole of a doctor had been treating me for pains in the back of my head. What these actually derived from was a stiff shoulder which I had as a result of leaning forward to lessen the pains in my chest which came from a pulled muscle which had resulted from doing press ups while my back was out of alignment due to my strained knee.'

'Gosh,' I said. 'And he never realised.'

'He didn't *begin* to realise,' Beau said. 'And that's not the only thing...'

I settled back into a comfortable position for not listening to Beau and poured another drink. I wanted there to be no world and no Sophie, to be just a passive brain lapped and cossetted by alcoholic vapours and the familiar friendly tedium of Beau's eternal health bulletin. At the moment he seemed to be between cures.

It came to me all of a sudden that Beau's indefatigable search was not so much a pursuit of health itself as a health regime to *believe* in. In a few days he'd recover his optimism, find himself some other guru of the muscles and the bloodstream, throw away his running shoes and buy a rowing machine, a set of weights, a bale of ginseng or a sensory deprivation tank. This would set him on the road to recovery until bitter disillusion struck once more. Perhaps the entire modern world was like that – lurching from one miracle cure to another to alleviate the twinges in its soul.

'. . . in the end,' Beau was now saying dolefully, 'I just gave up. Let my system be pumped full of crap for the sake of temporary relief. But my *skin* was peeling off.' He stroked his forearm, once, with a look of squeamish solicitude. 'My head was buzzing all the time, I couldn't concentrate. And my *back* . . . Well, that's life,' he concluded. 'I mean the trouble with life is you have to live it. I may as well get pissed.'

'Go ahead.'

'Thanks,' he said, refilling his glass. 'It's this job.'

October and the Fringe were now nearly upon us. Beau was forever tearing around the place high on caffeine, smoking six cigarettes at once, screaming down the telephone and predicting disaster. This was by way of contrast with the winter which he had spent on the dole, flat broke and trying to relax from his exertions of the previous autumn, contemplating the twinges in his navel and predicting disaster. Beau was manic depressive really; sometimes he was depressed and sometimes he was manically depressed.

'Anyway,' he said as he said every year, 'this is the last time I'm doing it. They can find some other prick. Let's talk about something else. Where's Sophie?'

'She took a walk yesterday evening,' I said.

'So?'

'So she's still taking it.'

'Oh,' he said. 'Where was she going?'

'I never ask her things like that.'

'Oh.' After a pause he said: 'Why not?'

'I'm afraid she'll vanish.'

After another pause Beau said: 'Well I'd better go', and got up to do so. 'One of my imbecile directors wants to meet me in a pub which he thinks would be ideal for live comedians. So it's bound to be terrible. I'll see you.'

I poured myself another stiff glass of Slavonic ruin and yawned my legs out under the table.

I was already threatened by the empty kitchen, which stretched and spread to become an empty house, an empty street and town, an empty sea and world under an endless sky.

If Sophie didn't come back this was all there would ever be. It was one of the rules of passion, that foreign country I now lived in whether I liked it or not.

At least there was enough drink in hand to get blitzed out of my brain. And if this stuff wasn't sufficient I could throw caution to the wind and drag out the elderberry wine. I had a premonition of coming stark awake with a five o'clock hangover, and washed it away with a drink. The worst thing was that I wasn't surprised that Sophie had vanished.

It was inconceivable that I could be more to her than a human extension of the house, both of which she quite liked. She gave herself with abandon, but she didn't seem to care much what happened to her, so while this absolutely slayed me it didn't tell me anything. She was always *somewhere else*, a fugitive. I was sanctuary to her, pure sanctuary, and except to the old and the defeated, sanctuary is not permanent. If she hadn't gone now she was bound to go sometime so what was the difference?

The difference was I'd have traded the rest of my life to have her walk in through the door and stay till tomorrow morning.

How could there be such a thing as intelligent self-interest or philosophy and law when one's essential self was definable by this give-all depravity?

By now I had wandered into the living room: I found myself looking straight at my intended sculpture which sat on its plinth in the middle of the room like a lump of dead wood which had been worried by a passing beaver. I went over to pick up the mallet and chisel, then had an argument with myself about whether this was wise.

'I think I'd better sleep on it,' I said, patting the wood reassuringly and putting the tools down. 'I'll let you know in the morning.'

'Sleep on what?' Sophie asked.

My leap of surprise sent me right into the plinth and I nearly knocked over the whole shebang. 'Hello,' I said, steadying it. 'I was beginning to wonder where you were.'

'Oh.' She dropped herself into a chair. 'Well I'm here.'

'So you are.'

'Are you alright?'

'I'm pissed.'

I stared out of the window. I could see street light and a couple of ship's lights and a blurred reflection of myself. Well, here she was.

I could barely remember my wild despair, but she hadn't blown it away with bright trumpets. It seemed to have got covered over by an aching dullness. 'I missed you last night,' I said.

'Oh I'm *sorry*.'

She came up behind me and put her arms round my chest. 'I didn't mean to be that long,' she said. 'But – well – then I had to be.'

'I see.'

'You see it's . . .'

'No don't,' I said. 'I don't want you to explain.'

'Oh George. Look, sit down.'

We sat on the sofa.

'I have got this problem,' she said.

'You don't have to tell me about it.'

'Oh *alright*. I won't. You'll find out anyway,' she said. 'Why are you drunk?'

'As the fairly inevitable consequence of upwards of a pint of vodka,' I said. 'Why do you ask?'

'It isn't because of me?'

'Of course it is, you silly bitch.'

'You *shouldn't*.' She picked up my hand. 'You shouldn't. Really.'

'Why *not*? I mean this is ludicrous. Isn't it? Look at you – you're practically a child.'

'I'm not.'

'Alright you're not. I'm sorry. Look at me then. Creaking,' I said. 'Riddled with creeping cynicism, half remembered dreams, the fitful fag-ends of a pathological libido.'

'I think you've just explained the attraction.'

'You can't be serious.'

'Why not?'

'What's attractive about decrepitude, for Christ's sake?'

'Alright, the majority of older people aren't attractive,' she said. 'But when they are they are. So there. It happens all the time, darling.'

'Usually the other way round.'

'No. More usually this way round. Anyway,' she said, 'I'm saving younger men for my middle age.'

'Sophie, don't. I can't bear to think of your middle age.'

'Why not?'

'I'll be dead.'

She laughed, let go of my hand, found a cigarette in her bag and sat back smoking it, clasping her elbow. 'You know that was the first thing you said to me?'

'Mmn?'

'You announced that you were going to die.'

'Did I? I was pissed then too. It did seem crucially important,' I said. 'It still does. Death was trying to tell me something. But...'

'But what?'

'Well.' I swallowed. 'When I'm with you, all that stuff goes out the window. I don't care about death or anything.'

'But that's *it*,' she said. She twined herself over to lie half on top of me, and touched me lightly on the nose. 'You're beginning to get the message, George.'

# 15

Dugdale did a couple of *haute couture* half pirouettes on my office rug, camping it up to the ceiling.

'How do I look?' he asked.

'Astonishing,' I said truthfully.

He was sporting a black three quarter length mac with a distinct air of highwayman's coat, a floppy cream Byronic shirt and tight black trousers with an alligator belt.

'I've always wanted to dress like this' he confided, dropping himself neatly into a chair with a flourish of the skirts.

'It's funny how well it all suits you,' I said. 'You don't look like a middle-aged trendy at all.'

'I should hope not.'

'More like a well-heeled pimp really.'

'Oh but that's *good*,' he said. 'Seriously. I discovered quite late in life, George, that the best way to inspire business confidence is to dress like a smelly don. But if you want to dazzle people with your brilliance it is *mandatory* to look like a Peruvian ponce. Mandatory. I'm talking about the arts, mind.'

'I hope you go down well,' I said.

'Bound to,' he averred. 'I'll be giving my first address any day now. Had a little chat about it last night, with your dear wife. By the way, hasn't she got the most terrifying teeth?'

'Teeth? I can't say I've noticed.'

'You amaze me,' he said. 'They're so *pointed*. Anyway she was most helpful. She's an interesting character, isn't she?'

'Perhaps she is,' I said, never really having thought about it. 'Provided one sees her from a distance.'

'Well yes, I can understand that one wouldn't want to get too close to her. Those teeth...' He shuddered. 'But anyway...'

'Look Dugdale. Tell me. Do you have any opinion as to why this outfit should be so instantly prestigious? I mean why all the interest? I refuse to believe *le tout* Swansea has gone down with a case of poetry all of a sudden.'

'No of course it hasn't.'

'No. Alice said something to me about the value of neutral territory.'

'That's about right, I think,' he said. 'You see most provincial towns are run by a loose masonic gang with conflicting affiliations. They're not numerous enough to form autonomous power groups, and not small enough to bury their differences and get on with things like a parish council might, say. And this lack of a nucleus can be very frustrating to the ambitious, which is to say the majority. In any local government, ten per cent are sincere and half cracked, seventy per cent are in it for gain and twenty per cent have no idea why they're there since they're incapable of sequential thought about anything. The dominant seventy per cent badly need somewhere to bump into each other and stitch up little deals. And the other thing it offers is instant cultural kudos. Painlessly. But pretty soon people are going to find that it's not easy to join. Ally all that with civic pride and you have a potent mixture. But what I think may be most important of all, George, is that Thomas has reached a critical age. I mean the poor bastard's been dead just about long enough for the whole question of what he means to be up for grabs. You know the way everyone thinks George Orwell's work is a searing indictment of whatever they happen to dislike? Well rather like that, only less overtly political. It happens to all artists who are any good,' he said. 'Honestly, people howl sententiously about the Kremlin's habit of rewriting history, but *everybody* does it. All the time. It's an integral part of the power game, which is universal.'

'I see,' I said. 'So you think *le tout* Swansea wants to redefine Dylan Thomas in its own image?'

'Precisely.'

'Well.' I began looking through his file. 'I hope there'll be some fringe benefits in it for you.'

'Oh, no doubt there will.' He ran a fingertip along his eyebrow. 'Readings here and there,' he said. 'Lectures. Little programme perhaps.'

'Hmm. Well I've no doubt you're up to it. You'd better expect spite from some of the academics at some stage, though. I mean you've no qualifications yourself, have you?'

'Not as such,' he said. 'That's why I thought it might be wise to invest myself with a couple of degrees.'

'Oh.'

'Plus a short critical volume, unhappily lost to posterity and not much reviewed, but which did create rather a stir in Hampstead and Soho circa nineteen sixty.'

'Dugdale that's fraud.'

'I prefer the word tact,' he said primly. 'After all, they're expecting a mad professor. It would be positively unkind to offer them anything less. It's a simple matter of theatrical integrity. I mean would you play Puss in Boots in workman's overalls?'

'I've a feeling someone has,' I said. 'But – oh alright.' After all what did I care? I'd have been perfectly happy for him to go along with a bomb under his coat. 'Now, the important thing is this – if you want to avoid being done by the Social Securicor for failing to maintain yourself, it would be best if you could sign off for a few weeks and live on whatever you make out of all this.'

'I see,' he said. 'Well the trouble with that is, much as I can smell money in all this, I can't distinctly see any just yet. And I don't want to seem pushy. Softlee softlee catchee big fat cheque. You know?'

'Yes quite. The trouble is,' I said, 'that I actually told them you were taking up paid employment.'

'So string them along for a while,' he said. 'Tell them I'm enhancing my professional associative motility with a view to taking up a post commensurate with my unique interdisciplinary propensities. That's bound to floor them for a couple of weeks while they look for the dictionary. But while we're on that subject,' he said, reaching into his mac, 'Here are my bills.'

'Bills?'

'For my clobber.'

'I though the Social Securicor gave you a grant for some working clothes.'

'Sixty five pounds,' he said, nodding. 'And very useful too. It paid for my shoes.'

I craned forward over the desk, in breathless curiosity to see what sixty five quid's worth of shoe might look like.

I had to concede that they had a dashed elegant line. Made of gleaming white crocodile skin, they had well shaped raised heels, large flopover tongues and silver buckles. Altogether the sort of thing James the Second might have worn to work, had blue movies been in currency at the time and himself a star performer.

'You blew all the money on *them*?' I said.

'They were reduced,' he said. 'By great good fortune they happened to fit me. They were made specially for someone who died.'

'When they saw the bill I should think. Well, I don't know.'

'George I do wish you'd stop being so chintzy. This whole bloody thing was your idea. And you must realise that I cannot function without a bit of decent gear.'

'Sixty five quid for shoes is not decent gear money. It's Sybaritic.'

'It's peanuts,' he said. 'How much d'you suppose a Cabinet minister spends on shoes?'

'I really have no idea. But I do have a sneaking suspicion that Cabinet ministers make other arrangements than asking the Social Securicor for the money.'

'Of course,' he said. 'Like having fringe benefits and vast tax concessions. George, you must see that in taking this attitude you're abetting an act of gross discrimination against the working class.'

'Dugdale, since when were you working class?'

'Anyone,' he said portentously, 'without money, property or power is a proletarian, regardless of origins.'

'Including me?'

'Yes. Though in your position you might aspire to liberal escapism or *petit bourgeois* reaction, but I don't advise it. The lower middle class is detested from below and above.'

'So how come they're running the country and everyone thinks they're the cat's whiskers?'

'A passing phase,' he said, waving away the Thatcher government like a fly. 'Anyway let's get back to my bills.'

'Yes, let's.' I picked up the top one and looked at it. 'Good God,' I exclaimed. 'What was this for?'

'My mackintosh I think.' He leaned forward to see. 'Yes.' 'That's diabolical.'

'A snip,' he said. 'You feel the quality of this sleeve.'

'I don't want to,' I said irritably, looking through the other bills quickly. 'Hey, these are all from the same shop.'

'Theatrical costumier,' he said, nodding. 'He was most accommodating.'

'For these prices I should hope so. Why didn't you just get one bill?'

'Didn't want to give you too much of a shock,' he said candidly. 'Besides, I thought you might find it easier to feed them through one by one.'

'Through where? Dugdale, please try and understand that the Social Securicor gave you sixty five quid. That's *it*. It looks like I perjured myself blue to help you get that, as well. It puts me in rather an embarrassing position.'

'Balls,' he said callously. 'We both know perfectly well that you people are hardly ever held to account for anything.'

'Yes that's true in a sense,' I said, glaring back at him levelly. 'We're extremely white collar and protected and work in a grey area where we have so many dealings with the criminal classes that whatever our shortcomings we generally succeed in blaming them. And I must say that in this...'

There came a tap at the door. I shoved Dugdale's bills under my blotter and called: 'Come in.'

'Mr Waddin'ton you are runnin' be'ind,' Joan said, dumping on my desk a saucerful of pale cold coffee, surrounding a cup about a third full of the same liquid. 'You got Ritchie Pritchard out there. 'E've been waiting a good 'alf hour now. Does Mr Dugdale want coffee as well?'

'No,' I said. 'Mr Dugdale is just leaving.'

'Right then.' She sashayed out, which for someone as broad as she was tall was no mean accomplishment.

'Now where were we?' I pushed my coffee aside, spilling much of it on the desk. 'Yes. Look I'm afraid you're just going to have to deal with these bills yourself – wherever they are,' I added, searching ineffectually. 'I'm sorry if that presents you with a problem, but it cannot be greater than the problem of getting so much credit in the first place. Frankly I'm quite envious. How did you do it?'

'Quite largely by saying I could pay within seventy two hours,' he said.

'Dear Lord.'

'I didn't know you were going to be difficult.'

'Well you'll just have to extend your period of credit. That shouldn't be beyond your capabilities – you got it in the first place with an address at the dosshouse.'

'Oh bless you,' he said, laughing. 'I didn't tell him I lived at the dosshouse.'

'So what address did you give?'

'Yours.'

'*What*?'

'George. Please. Try to calm down and be a bit more rational about this, will you? Even if things should get so far as this man knocking on your door, you just seize him by the hand and say: "*Dugdale*? The bastard owes me money as well. Please let me know when you catch up with him." Or something similar.' He sighed. 'You really are singularly lacking in useful knowledge, if I may say so.'

'No you may not. Dugdale, let me tell you, if I get anyone dunning me at the front door, I shall be down that bloody dosshouse like a ferret to drag you out and ceremoniously cut your throat.'

'Alright, if you feel like that about it,' he said equably. 'Though you might be disappointed. I should tell you I'm moving somewhere a bit more commensurate with my new social position.'

'Yes you should.' I took out my pen. 'Where is it?'

'Care of Mukkarjee,' he said. 'The Shahgbhag, Alexandra Road. There's a couple of spare rooms upstairs there. Mr Mukkarjee's a literary man. We seem rather to have hit it off. Anyway George.' He stood up and tucked his new black pigskin briefcase under his arm. 'See you the same time next week.'

'Mghm.'

'If not before.'

'Not if I see you coming,' I said. 'Toodle-oo.'

I sat there for several minutes after he'd gone, stunned and gazing at his file for no particular reason. I even attempted a mouthful of coffee. Looking at his file a bit more closely, it seemed it was time to put in another progress report.

After the very minimum of hesitation, I wrote, 'Mr Dugdale has continued to show a most gratifying response to probationary counselling. He now displays a very positive social attitude, which is exemplified by a sincere and well planned search for employment, a move to less minimal accommodation and a marked change in his personal appearance. It really seems that counselling has afforded him the confidence to move among his intellectual peers where it is to be hoped that his considerable abilities as a communicator will take him further along the road to recovering his full economic and social function.'

I snapped the file shut and went out to fetch Ritchie, poor Ritchie whom I had left waiting for so long, nice open-hearted Ritchie who broke the law according to the rules and had the decency to get himself caught and sentenced. He was a bona fide sinner and part of my proper congregation, someone who actually needed me to help him recover from his last crime rather than abet him in the next one.

I smiled at him warmly and held the door open. I was feeling a bit off Dugdale altogether.

# 16

The room was very dark and I couldn't see Sophie anywhere. I hadn't particularly wanted to come to this party but for some reason she had insisted, though she wouldn't tell me why.

What light there was came through a doorway and from an orange shaded table lamp on the floor in a far corner, filtering through knots of people who all seemed at least twenty years younger than me, most of them squatting about the carpet discussing things. It reminded me of some village in Mozambique or San Salvador where everyone's out getting their consciousness raised by the local guerrillas. Out in the hallway a few figures were dancing absent mindedly to the sound of music from another room. I managed to find the drinks table and procure a plastic tumblerful of cider. I felt sweaty and uncomfortable; I wanted to take my shoes off and throw them away.

Someone came over and leaned his elbow on my shoulder with offhand drunken intimacy. 'Pathetic isn't it,' he said. It wasn't a question.

'What is?'

He made a gesture with his free arm, as though spreading corn about the carpet. Hung from his other hand, his drink spilled down my jacket. 'Ev'thing,' he said. 'I mean these people think they're the cure. Okay?' He slipped off my shoulder and staggered a little, spilling drink on his own self and flicking at it with loose ineptitude. 'But,' he said, leaning his face towards me. '*But*. They're the faghing *disease*.'

'I see,' I said. 'So what are you?'

'Me?' he said. 'I'm the Flying Doctor. 'Scuse me.'

He assumed forward locomotion by leaning forward like a felled tree and letting his feet chase his head. The fact that this propelled him out through the doorway was probably sheer luck. Whatever record had been playing now finished and another one began. Over by the window a girl made to get up and fell down again. More people started dancing and I felt more and more like a taut balloon.

I made a lunge for the door and ran straight into Sophie. She had been carrying some sandwiches which now got spread around the immediate vicinity and trodden on.

'Oh I'm *sorry*.'

'Oh . . .' She glanced at the now empty plate and put it on the drinks table. 'It's alright,' she said. 'Hallo.'

'Hello.'

'Hallo,' she repeated. 'What's the matter?'

'I just feel a bit . . . look, can't we get away from this mob a minute?'

'If you absolutely must,' she said after a short emphatic pause. She led me out into the hall.

'Who are all these people anyway?' I asked.

'These people are friends and acquaintances of me and Mark.'

'You simply must be intending me to ask who Mark is.'

'You're probably right.' She opened the door to a room off the hallway with nobody in it, and shut the door behind me as I followed her in. 'Mark's my partly ex boyfriend.'

'Oh.'

'Sit down.'

'Thankyou.' I did so.

'And this is his study,' she said. 'Have a drink.'

I clocked the room rapidly while she searched for a drink. Spick and span leftist graduate, I concluded. About thirty. Anal repression. Sublimated rage. Hysteria. Displays self esteem covertly by attacking other people's, probably in the name of principle. Might be dangerous. Might also be gullible if handled right. Sophie eventually found the bottle she was looking for – it was in a filing cabinet placed beneath a big wallboard marked off in squares and labelled PROJECTS – and poured me a drink.

'Cheers,' I said. 'I think. What is it?'

'Tequila. Mark's very into Central America just at the moment.'

'Oh.' I took a sip of tequila. It was that yellow variety which tastes like a compound of petroleum waste and *cucaracha* piss but is quite bracing if you can manage to keep it down. 'D'you think he'll mind?' I asked.

'Mind about what? You and me, us being in here or drinking his booze?'

'All three.'

'Mind,' she said thoughtfully, sitting on the arm of my chair and rubbing her cheek with her glass. 'You know I wonder if he's really got one. I don't think he'll have any clear idea whether he minds or not.'

'Why did you ask me here tonight?'

'That's a good question. Mark's been away,' she added. 'He got back on Monday.'

'Have you mentioned me to him?'

'No.' She sighed. 'The thing is . . .'

'What?'

'Well – the thing is I think I hate him,' she said.

'I see. Are you afraid of him?'

She shook her head. 'I'm more afraid of me. I used to be afraid of him. Mentally. But I think that's why I wanted you here. I'm less afraid of myself with you around. You're so above it all.'

'You're going to tell me how mature I am in a minute'.

'No,' she said. 'Not mature exactly. More kind of inwardly deadpan. As though whatever people do doesn't shock you.'

'Believe me,' I said. 'That's just incredulity. It probably looks similar...'

The door crashed open. For a few seconds nothing else happened, then the Flying Doctor was propelled into the room on his unsteadily twitching legs.

'Oho,' he said, rallying by the filing cabinet and catching sight of us as his gaze panned, without very much volition, about the room. 'Do I detec' the subtle nuances of adultery? I wonder. Or do I juss detec' the subtle nuances of adultery?'

'I should say you detected the subtle nuances of adultery,' I said, looking at him levelly and weighing him up. He was on the large side with a muscular physique softened by many kinds of self-indulgence – type of the Adonis Dipsophrenic. I'd probably be alright if I hit him first. 'Your instinct is correct.'

'C'ngracha *lashiuns*,' he said, cackling to himself and attempting to slap his thigh. 'Trouble with world today iz people have no style. Too mush fornication. Not enough adultery. I c'ngrashlate you.' Then, still savouring his own wit with short, hiccup like bursts of appreciation he staggered out again.

Someone closed the door from outside. I eased past Sophie's legs and stood up. 'That was Mark then?' I said, expecting him back any second.

'That? No,' she said. 'That was Alex. One of Mark's henchmen.'

'Oh?'

'He's a theatre company,' she explained. 'Mark is I mean, and that idiot's part of it. And do stop bracing yourself for fisticuffs, George. It isn't going to be like that at all.'

'Are you sure?'

'Yes.'

The door opened. A rather short man with a heavy, neat black moustache and eyes like an enraged rabbit put his head round it, looked at us as though he were looking for something else, said: 'Oh. I see,' and disappeared again.

'Now *that* was Mark.'

Mark reappeared in the company of Alex the Flying Doctor, to whom he was lending considerable assistance. Alex said 'Yes' and they both left. Then Mark came in on his own and closed the door.

He placed his fists on his hips and looked towards us although not straight in the eyes, creating an absurd but nevertheless unnerving effect of absent minded outrage. I fancied he was quivering somewhat, but he was also the kind of man who probably quivered anyway so this might not mean anything. After this pause had gone on quite a long time he seemed to jerk himself awake, then brushed past me with contained irritation and said: 'Excuse me, I want to find something.'

He began opening drawers in the grey metal desk, muttering with his lips.

'What are you looking for?' I asked, unable to contain the question.

'Mnh?' Still bent over the desk he looked round at me. Having conceded to himself that my query was not deliberately insulting he said: 'Oh, cassette player. Small one. Black, in a sort of leather case. You haven't seen it, have you Sophe?'

Sophe, I thought. *Sophe*. Dear Jesus.

She said: 'No.' She had her arms folded, weight on one leg, the other foot sketching small arc patterns on the carpet, hair trailing in her eyes as she looked at him with dreamy circumspection and a great deal else suppressed beneath it. Static electricity there was; you could have plugged the room in to the National Grid.

'I see.' He straightened up. 'The thing is,' he explained to me, 'I don't really like people coming in here. I work here, you see. We need to do some rehearsing. That's why I need the recorder, we always...'

'Mark,' Sophie cut in.

'Yes?'

'This is George.'

'Pleased to meet you,' he said. I supposed I'd better shake his hand.

'He's the man I'm leaving you for.'

Mark let go my hand, looked away, folded his arms, unfolded them and said: 'I see. Oh *there* it is,' he added, referring to the cassette recorder which he had spotted on top of a bookcase. He took it down and said: 'So anyway, if we could have free use of the room? Say within about two minutes?'

As he closed the door, Sophie hurled her glass after him. It smashed against the wall by the light switch.

'*Christ*,' she said. 'See what I mean?'

'Erm . . .'

'*Ooogh*, the sly little bastard.' She was beside herself. 'He does it to everything, everything, everything . . . As far as he's concerned it didn't happen, you see? He wipes out other people's experience all the time. Nothing exists for him but his own tight-arsed little fantasies. Look at this,' she said, beginning to pull open drawers in the desk. 'I'm going to show you something. Here we are.'

Having found the drawer she wanted she tipped its contents all over the desk top. 'This is me.' She held up a photograph of herself in police uniform. 'So's this.' Another one, in a white coat and stethoscope. 'And this.' Wearing nothing but a black spiky wig and a string vest, clutching a microphone and snarling. Each time she showed me a picture she ripped it across. Then she swept everything off the desk top onto the floor. 'Theatre of Conflict,' she said.

'What?'

'That was my life as an actress I was tearing up. Theatre of Conflict is the name of Mark's peripatetic little funny farm.'

'Careful, little bit of broken glass,' Mark's voice said as the door opened. 'Oh. You're still here.' He was followed in by the Flying Doctor, who now seemed as near unconsciousness as was humanly possible without being horizontal, and Sion Slugge, who was carrying a script tucked tight beneath his arm and smirking malignantly at nothing in particular.

'Dave decided to leave the company,' Mark said in an explanatory tone to Sophie, who presumably knew who Dave was.

'Really?' she said.

'Yes. So Sion said he'd give it a try and see how he gets on.' He leaned over the desk to plug in the recorder, careful not to tread on the things on the floor. 'Mmm,' he remarked. 'Bit of a mess.'

I saw Sophie wondering whether to hit him with a bottle. Then her shoulders took a spasm as if she were cold and she strode out of the room, tipping her head at me. I followed. I could feel Slugge's glutinous leer on our backs.

Sophie was standing in the hallway biting her lip. 'I'm going to pack,' she said.

The study door closed behind us.

'Want some help?'

'No. Could you stay here and guard things when I bring them down?'

'*Guard* them?'

'Won't be a sec,' she said. She was gone in a blur of slim legs up the staircase.

'Hi,' Sky Hendersen said, looming out of a doorway at me.

'Oh hullo,' I said. 'I didn't know you were here. I take it you know them.'

'Sort of,' he said. 'And I can smell free drink from a considerable distance. Is something wrong, George? You're looking rather strained.'

'In a way,' I said. 'Look, let's go outside.' There was a terrace and a sloping lawn, and a fine dark view of the bay.

'You were saying?' he said outside.

'Yes. It seems I'm in the process of eloping with Sophie,' I said.

'Oh.' Sky lay down on the lawn, then finding it rather damp stood up again quickly. 'I see. Well I must say I'm rather pleased about that. She's terribly nice isn't she?'

'Mm hm.'

'Mind you, she's a real fruitcake,' he added, 'but absolutely charming with it. And Mark's an arsehole. Have a drink?' He produced a bottle of whisky, about a third full, from inside his jacket.

'Thanks,' I said, impressed. 'Where did you get hold of this?'

'It's Alex's,' he said. 'He can never remember where he leaves the stuff after about eight o'clock in the evening. He must be on two bottles a day by now. That's since he met Mark and joined Theatre of Subsidy or whatever they call themselves. You know, George, you want to be careful.'

'What of?'

'Mark. He's dangerous.'

'You're kidding.'

'I'm not.'

'But he's so repressed.'

'That's the point,' Sky said. 'He's a middle class psychopath. They all are. Why d'you think Sophie's so loopy?'

'I do wish you wouldn't keep saying that,' I said. 'I don't think she's loopy.'

'Don't be so gallant,' he said. 'You know perfectly well what I mean. Why does she have this vague, wayward manner as though she's always hearing faery voices? She does it to get through life, the way some people get stoned all the time.'

'I like that air she has,' I retorted. 'I think she's like that anyway.'

'And some people get stoned anyway,' he said, spreading his hands. 'Defence mechanisms don't create new traits, they exacerbate existing ones. Don't they teach probation officers psychology . . . ?'

'About two more trips,' Sophie's voice said.

I looked round. By the front door were three suitcases and a round, open basket of clothes and books. I said: 'That was quick.'

'I was half packed already.' She went inside again.

I gave Sky the whisky back. 'I think I'll fetch my car,' I said.

It was parked about four or five streets away up the hill, outside my place; it took me less than five minutes to get back.

Something was wrong. As I ran up the steps I could see Sky struggling with someone by the front door. Alex. He kept taking wild swings at Sky, who parried by pushing him since he was too drunk to be taken seriously. Slugge stood off to one side of all this as though deputised to see fair play. As I reached the group, Sky caught Alex's face with the heel of his hand and sent him sprawling backwards into the front doorway, tripping over Sophie's basket.

There came a flash of flame from the middle of the lawn. I hadn't noticed Mark, who had been busy tipping out one of Sophie's cases and pouring paraffin over it. He gave a nod of satisfaction to the fire and then actually walked right up past me to get another case from the doorstep.

Tense as he was there wasn't the least hint of embarrassment in the way he did this. He was moving like a clockwork rat inside some piece of tunnel vision logic where doubt had been scored from the dictionary. I grabbed his shoulder and shouted: 'What are you *doing*?'

'She can't take all these things,' he said reasonably. In the half light of the doorway his eyes were big as saucers. 'She can't possibly. She doesn't need them.'

Sophie appeared with a full cardboard box and said: 'Oh God.'

'You know what we agreed about this,' Mark said to her. 'You just buy things and buy things and there's no satisfaction. So you buy more things.'

Sophie ignored him. She was helping Sky repack the upset basket of books. Alex appeared to be unconscious and Sky had dragged him out of the way.

'It's just going to go on for the rest of your life if you don't break the habit now,' Mark said. 'Isn't it?'

He pulled free of me. I caught him by the collar and sent a punch, not very cleanly, into the middle of his righteous features. Then I stamped on his foot and managed to land a good one in his solar plexus, at which he dropped the case and lay in a foetal ball on the terrace, gasping.

Sophie grabbed up an armful of things. 'Let's just *go*,' she said.

'Right.'

Sky helped us down to the car. Slugge watched it all, and as I came down with the last case he moved over to Mark and began helping him up. On the lawn, Sophie's things were still blazing merrily. I got into the car and slumped behind the steering wheel. I was shaking.

'Christ.' I rested my head on the wheel. '*Christ*, what a circus.'

'Look I hate to rush you,' Sky said from the back seat, 'but I really think we'd better get out of here before the Filth arrives.'

'Good idea.' I let in the clutch and drove away as though taking off from a blag, and spun left up the breakneck steepness of Constitution Hill, tyres bucking and squealing as they grabbed at the damp cobblestones. I let Sky out at the top and we drove to my house and shifted all Sophie's things into the hall with a sense of hurry, as if we were being pursued. Then I shut the front door with a glad sigh and she sat down on the stairs, elbows on her knees and head in both hands. She was laughing.

'*Honestly*,' she said.

Not quite sure how to interpret her laughter I put my arm round her. 'Did you lose anything important?' I asked.

'No,' she said. 'That's the funny part. I don't really give a damn about things. Oh sure, I like them, and I tend to get things that I like. But after a while I'll always quite happily give them away or something. And that's what Mark couldn't stand. It drove him mad. You see ...' She found some cigarettes in one of her boxes, and lit one. '... Mark has a terrific neurosis about possessions. That's one reason he's quite unfit to share his life with anybody – he'd have His and Hers bog paper given half a chance. And his response to this is to attack possessiveness in other people, whether it exists or not. He had me convinced that I had some chronic materialist compulsion, absolutely convinced. Used to give me abstruse, interminable lectures about sensual delusion which he'd got from some shabby little self-improvement manual written by a Buddhist Japanese businessman. Don't you hate good people?'

'Er...'

'I do,' she said, not really bothered whether I did or not. 'I loathe them. Except you.'

'What makes you think I'm good?'

'Dunno,' she said slowly, looking at me through one eye. 'Perhaps the fact that you're rather naive.'

'Oh thanks.'

She laughed. 'You're not a professional good guy anyway,' she said, 'and they're the ones I can't stand. But shall I tell you what I really like about you?'

'Well?'

'The fact that you think you're real,' she said.

# Part Three

# 17

'This town,' Dugdale said, 'sprawl, chapter of happy accidents, Welsh Alexandria which is not in Wales, and not English, and which definitely isn't part of Europe, began down near the docks in a tired but still breathing district of shipping offices and old wharves, which is now almost an island bounded by the sea, the river and the Oystermouth Road. I don't exactly know when it began, but you can see the seventeenth and eighteenth century reflected in a few fine buildings down there...'

The room, full of grubby councillors and culture punters, seedy solicitors, businessmen of tax marginal intelligence and pale nonentities who had been dragged along because their wife or somebody else had told them to come, was rapt and silent as a circle of small children. I had not before been aware of the melodiousness of Dugdale's voice; pitched out to this public speaking level it had a subtly hypnotic quality like distant music.

'There is something about those buildings,' he said, 'which is not mainstream British architecture. There's no Jacobean clutter, no Queen Anne whimsy, nor even the perfectionist classic modulation of Bath, Clifton or the Regent's Park. What foreign influence there is seems to have come straight from the sea and not through the constricting medium of fashion. The ironwork balconies are delicate and pleasing, the symmetry is impeccable, but the proportion is something all its own; masculine, mercantile self-confidence in the best sense. The exotic ideas the builders saw fit to adopt came to them straight from Amsterdam, Lisbon, Naples or Marseilles as directly as the goods they unloaded, and were theirs to do what they pleased with.

'Some of this bold spirit seems to have gone on well into the nineteenth century. Above shop level down Walter Road and Mansel Street – that broad drag where estate agents, solicitors and loan sharks lurk together like some latterday medieval guild – stand buildings which are like and not like Victorian houses anywhere. The difference is now harder to define, but in the way they've done the upper windows, or in the pitch of the roof, or just in the expansiveness of the whole there is a sense of casual substance which is good to see. There are buildings in Penzance which give you that feeling, and it could be that some facet of the climate has expressed itself in stone: Swansea is just inside that Western Seaways region where you suddenly hear less of the shrill, flat sounds of Britain on the breeze and sense the chords of an Atlantic music just out of hearing, broad and hypnotic like the summer light. All up the breakneck cobblestones of Constitution Hill stand worn, once wealthy terraces which face due south, so that the houses bask blindly in the sun all day like cats. And a lot of the streets of that style and period have that same daft gorgeous feeling.

'And so we can see,' he said, 'that in the more comfortable districts, the angst and toil of the Industrial Revolution – that black clad age which now in its turn lies to the other side of twilight – were played out on a background which looks very different in spirit from what merely happened. And still the western breezes pour their benediction on the seaward parts of town, so that the uneasy gregariousness of Wales is transformed into something happy and benign. Inside the covered market, thrown up after the war like some cheap, slap-happy nonconformist cathedral, Gower families stand selling vegetables and shellfish in the falling light from high windows, and you want to linger without buying very much, wondering what it is about the place that gives you such a lift.

'But elsewhere, as the town grew or expanded or exploded, the usual mean streets poured in like porridge, around factories and ironworks long since sunk back into the poisoned ground so that the streets remain for no apparent

100

reason, mile after ring road mile on the way from the town to the sodden valleys of the hinterland. They are very Welsh streets in everything but their suburban concentration, as if some lunatic giant playing God had picked up a lot of villages and crammed them down together by the coast, and perhaps the genius of the Industrial Revolution was just such a lunatic giant. But change of occupation notwithstanding, his effect on people has been nil: you feel no urban spark here, none of that magic anarchy of cities which can fire the birth or doom of civilisation. From Hafod to Llansamlet, down the Carmarthen Road from Waun Wen towards Llanelli and Gorseinon, out in Port Tennant, Bonymaen, St Thomas or a dozen other weary chunks of everywhere and nowhere, out of the gossip and huddle of shops and street corners and loud, dark bars, the same eyes peer that looked on the dark age or the iron age or the age before that, obsessed by the same inner landscape of suffering and death, within a low horizon bounded by work and money and a world where the artefacts of the twentieth century lie around with all the permanence of autumn leaves. Sometimes the timelessness of Wales can be so oppressive that you scream for any kind of change as a relief...'

No one else could have got away with such a remark. Of course it caused a stir but this was deliberate; he wanted to wake the audience just enough as he began to focus on his subject.

'Now by the time,' he said, 'that Dylan Thomas's father was screaming for relief, and had embarked on the excruciating journey from peasantry to the lower middle class, he was able to buy a house which looks custom built for the purpose, as in fact it was: from about that time on, Swansea houses have looked very like their contemporaries anywhere, and it could be that this drab universal trend is exactly linked to the modern delusion that a private destiny can be pursued by anyone if they take the trouble to address themselves to a course already laid out for them in society. It was certainly that abortive impetus of his father's which sent Dylan on another tack, outside society and slanting halfway back towards his cabbage background, by which he transfigured his father's bitter failure into the majestic ruin of himself and the vast enlargement of the English language...'

Alice was tugging at my sleeve. Having failed to get rid of her by frowning I eventually gave in and followed her out into the hall. She shut the door carefully behind us and we tiptoed along to the kitchen, where she closed the door again.

'Well what d'you think?' I asked. 'Good, isn't he?'

She nodded, leaning back against the fridge with her arms folded. 'The only thing is,' she said, 'I'm just wondering if perhaps he's not a bit too good. He seems to have a capacity for getting at the truth, which could be disastrous.'

'He also has a facility for deception which is at least equal to it,' I said. 'But I warn you against trying to influence him too directly. He only tells lies on his own terms.'

'Really?'

'Yes. You might get him to hand out some line or other if you managed to persuade him it had been his idea, but I doubt if you're clever enough for that. But I also think you're worrying unnecessarily. People like him – you saw it. He's clicked. So from now on they'll listen to him when he's saying something they agree with, and when he isn't they'll either disregard it or pretend he means something else. It's the same with pop stars, politicians – you name it.'

'You know it's grossly unfair of you, George,' she said, 'but you sometimes turn out to be a deal less stupid than I generally take you for. And I do like to have a clear picture of people. But okay, perhaps I'm worrying too much. He should do very nicely.'

'What have you got lined up for him anyway?'

'Mm?'

'In the way of, oh – lecture tours or whatever?'

'Lecture tours? I really don't know.'

'Oh. But I understood... *Look*, Alice, when you were trying to con me into doing it, you distinctly mentioned a paid lecture tour.'

'As a possibility,' she said. 'Which it remains. But just at the moment it's the Affiliation which matters – the ground-work. Anyway you got out of it neatly so why the concern? Where did you meet him anyway?'

'In a pub. I just feel a certain responsibility.'

'Well,' she said, 'if Professor Dugdale does want to earn

102

himself some extra money he'd better be pretty circumspect about it. Demonstrable amateur status is terribly important to an organisation like this, for the simple reason that everyone that matters is in it for self-advancement and we don't want this to be obvious. And the very last thing we want from our distinguished speaker is the stench of poverty. He's *not* poor, is he?'

'Good Lord no,' I said with a light laugh. 'He has – oh, a modest private income I think. But I mean he has great ability, and knowledge of his subject, and he's putting himself to a good deal of trouble. That there should be some sort of payment sooner or later seems no more than fair, that's all.'

'Oh *please*, George,' she said. ' "Fair" – that word went out with Beatle haircuts. Anyway this is *the* thing to belong to and he's jolly lucky to be here.'

'Alice.'

'What?'

'You're such a revolting cow, I'd like to stuff your head in that fridge and tan your arse with the handbrush.'

'*Oooh*,' she said. She went red. 'But d'you think there's *time*?' she asked, chewing her lip and glancing at the door.

'Figure of *speech*,' I said, back away. 'Alice – let go of me. *Alice*...'

# 18

'With his sock,' Delderfield said. 'I'm afraid so. One of yours I believe, George.'

'Yes...'

'Of course there'll have to be a, er, whatsit called...'

'Inquest.'

'Yers.' I could hear him belching down the phone. 'Pop into my office later, would you George? I'll phone the prison in the meantime and get the, er...'

'The SP.'

'Hmm?'

'The details,' I said.

'Yers. Details.' He never said goodbye.

I leaned back in my chair, stretched extravagantly and groaned at the ceiling. It was one of those days when being a Bailiff and Official Dog Catcher for Her Majesty's Penal Racket was less of a cushy number than usual.

It seemed I had been wrong in supposing that prison might be a less harmful environment for Charles Edward Andrew Phillips than his mother. Unless one could postulate that he was better off dead, or that he was just as likely to have topped himself in the same period while living at home, though it quickly became apparent to me that both these arguments were invalid on the grounds of sophistry. However, it was possible to say that the concept of moral responsibility did not apply, or that in any case it didn't lie with me, but neither of these arguments did a bit to alleviate the aggressive depression which took hold of me.

Ergo, I said to myself – I was now pacing the room and hitting myself on the head with a copy of *Police News* which Joan gets from some mysterious source and leaves lying around the place – ergo, either I am just being silly, or someone was actually to blame for his death and I haven't worked out who. This is to say I would dearly love to get hold of somebody and smash their head against the wall.

Beware the sophistry of violent indignation I then said to myself, but it was too late – Phillips's mother was already in the frame. It was ignoble of me but I then paled, wondering if she would be called, and would recount the gleeful way I had looked forward to putting him away. Oh God, Oh God oh God.

'Dear Mrs Phillips,' I said aloud to an imaginary typist. 'What *am* I to say to you? You must be wondering, as indeed I am wondering, how it was that your son came to quit his life by means of his first and last original act i.e. choking himself to death with a prison issue sock. I think we had better forgo considering the psychological significance of his choice of method since in prison this is necessarily limited. Inmates are also under some strain, especially in the early stages, so that

104

their normal state of mind becomes deformed or even totally deranged. Thus his circumstances do not permit of an objective judgement, though I cannot resist the passing comment that perhaps his choice of suffocation arose from an unconscious yearning for your presence, that might be some comfort to you and it might not.

'What might be more instructive would be a consideration of the whole course of his life, though here again I can only illuminate fitfully and offer little which might seem helpful. In view of my qualifications, connections, experience, air of authority and regular salary this may surprise you, but let me hasten to assure you that I am by no means exceptional in my profession. Indeed, and this may seem arrogant, I would assert that I understand the causality of crime at least as well as anyone in the judiciary, police force, legal profession or social services, which is to say that aside from a certain instinct as to *what* people might do, when it comes to *why* I know absolutely piss all. I differ from my colleagues only in that I will occasionally admit it.

'You see I'm sure you would like it if we could offer some explanation of your son's demise but we're simply not equipped. We've all been trained on Freudian ideas at third and fourth hand. Since we lack the stature and the intelligence to understand them properly, the net effect of this has been to teach us that no one is really to blame for anything. Thus our natural petty inclinations to praise or blame are taboo and we are permitted only a lot of rather volatile theorising. We will consider your son briefly and agree that we might have expected just that sort of thing from someone of his background. There will even be a certain academic satisfaction in this, as of a problem which works out nicely, or a crossword solved.

'But what do *I* think, you may ask, I myself as a private citizen of the world and a furtively superior individual? Well to begin with, your son's death is not a tragedy. A horror possibly, even a catastrophe, but tragic it ain't. Mrs Phillips I see your son by the thousands, not only in my office but the streets. They lope into the world with that sly, hopeless leer on their faces and they go out the same way. They snigger at life and in return it kicks them. The ones who grow old develop a defeated look but otherwise remain essentially the same. They are products of their background as your son was a product of his, of which you, if I might say so, were a vital and destructive part.

'Now according to the received wisdom of social psychology, Mrs Phillips, you're not to blame for this either, since you are a mere product of *your* environment, but I think I am about to rebel against this orthodoxy. I've felt it coming over me for years. Of course the impotence of our outlook is perfectly suited to our position, since we are universally hated and despised by the police, the judiciary, the prison service, the legal profession, the criminal fraternity and the general public, all of whom would doubtless massacre us in a body if we tried to say anything positive, but I'm doing this for my own satisfaction purely.

'I will never forget the pity and revulsion which always churned in me as I came to the street where you live, principally because the world is full of just such streets so I shall always be reminded of it. I don't know which was worse, your spick and span front garden or the factory at the end which, according to the goblinesque laws of finance and public demand, was built to produce things which were once essential but which are now either superfluous or turned out by people in Taiwan or South Korea for three pounds a month, a rice allowance and generous free advice about the apocalyptic benefits of capitalism. In such a world as yours, Mrs Phillips, there are only three real choices and they're all pretty dour.

'I will deal with the one I myself made first, since in point of fact I don't find it very dignified. Escape through betterment. One becomes a teacher, businessman, bland entertainer, office manager or what have you. Or of course a Bailiff and Official Dog Catcher to her Majesty's Penal Racket. The psychic cost of this will be a permanent sense of dislocation, which has never worried me a lot since I was dislocated from the beginning.

'The second choice is perhaps the hardest, or certainly the most obviously gruelling. This consists in saying to hell with it, you are a factory worker, or the wife of a factory worker. Life is bloody well about factories and you fight like the devil to make sure that a factory worker's life is worth living. You

106

stick at absolutely nothing and if you've any sense you'll go on to take over the factory, turn social mores on their head and take over the government too while you're about it.

'And the third choice is escape on one's own terms. You become an artist, a gambler, a snooker player, your own sort of entertainer. Or you become a criminal. Of course the vast bulk of my clients are people with too little sense to lead normal lives, but it has always struck me that a significant minority are people with too much, and this is without counting the people I never see because they're too clever to be caught. Your son of course belonged firmly in the inept category. He made no kind of decision at all but merely grabbed convulsively at things he hadn't a hope in hell of keeping, and thought he could always retreat behind your omnipotent refusal to allow him any responsibility for anything.

'But as for you, Mrs Phillips, what did you do? You neither got out nor stayed put. Rooted firmly in the street itself, you turned your plump back to the world and set about turning the house into a bank manager's dream home from Slough, Hendon, Bexley Heath or Basingstoke. Anyone within reach was a bit player in this cannibalistic fantasy. Your husband, plucked from that homogeneous, thought proof, woman hating crowd of goodfellows from the world of the workingmen's club where everybody ages fast but no one ever has to grow up, will doubtless have been chosen for his tameable qualities. Wheedled, buttered up, threatened and cajoled, alternatively irritated sexually or starved, sat in the corner with the living room carpet stretching like Siberia between him and what he dimly remembered as freedom, it will not have been long before his already weak personality became, to your triumph, disgust and disappointment, so much putty in your hands. I believe I saw him once, a haunted man in slippers wheezing back from the coal bunker predicting rain, inflation or the Last Judgement.

'And this is what you made of life, Mrs Phillips, and you have the incredible fucking temerity to be shocked by the fact that your son, a piece of flotsam barely differentiated from your own sick fantasies, decides that enough is enough and does away with himself. No doubt in many ways things were never easy for you and you could have done with a lot of things including, although it is deeply unfashionable to say so, a good fuck once in a while. And no doubt the fact that you didn't get one is just as much the fault of your husband and the whole chapel ridden, porn obsessed, flesh hating culture you both sprang from. *Nevertheless*, Mrs Phillips, on sober consideration of every social, genetic, economic, existential and political facet of your life, and because the truth is hard for the simple reason that it *is* the truth and there is no escape from it – *J'accuse*, Mrs Phillips. *Je t'accuse . . .*'

I don't know long Joan had been standing there, and thus if she had overheard some of my soliloquy or merely come in to have me whirl round and go: *'Je t'accuse'* at her. Her attitude gave me no particular clue.

'Mr Waddin'ton you've got Mr Dugdale and Ritchie Pritchard out here,' she said. 'At the same time. Talkin' to each other. It is well past time to see both of them. A lady has been trying to tellyphone, Mr Delderfield wants to see you, you 'ave left yiwer phoan off the hook, look, and your coffee 'ave gone cold.'

'Not gone,' I said. 'Remained. Please tell the lady to go away, Mr Delderfield that I'll be up in five minutes and Dugdale and Ritchie to come in.'

'What? Both together?'

'Just so.'

'Ridic'lous,' she said loudly to herself, going out. 'E've only got one chair.'

'Then they can sit on each other's knee or something.'

In the event they both sat on my desk while I lay back on the rug with my eyes closed.

'Do tell me,' I said, 'that things are going well for both of you. Ritchie – you are getting up in the mornings, refraining from arrest and discharging your Community Service Order?'

'Ah,' he said. 'And norronly that, I . . .'

'Please,' I said. 'That'll do nicely for this afternoon. Dugdale – you're getting up in the mornings, charming the Dylan Thomas Memorial Affiliation into a cheese soufflé and keeping the Social Securicor happy?'

'Yes, yes and no,' he said. 'Actually I do have something of

108

a problem with the Social Securicor, which I was hoping we might discuss.'

'Oh dear.' I sat up. 'The thing is I just haven't time this afternoon,' I said. 'Is it important?'

'Yes.'

'How important?'

'Very,' he said. 'D'you think you could see me for a drink after work?'

'Oh I'd love to, but...'

'I'll pay.'

'Really?'

'Really,' he said. 'With real money.'

'Well in that case,' I said, standing up to indicate the conclusion of probationary counselling for the afternoon, 'the Blue Dragon. Five thirty three.'

They jumped off the desk in unison and left. My phone squawked.

'George, where are you?' Delderfield asked, not a very intelligent question if taken literally. 'I've been waiting to talk to you about this, er...'

'Phillips?'

'Quite. Pop up, would you? And we can...'

He was slouched over his fat green desk top which, as ever, was quite innocent of paperwork. There was nothing on it but a phone, an open packet of pork sandwiches, his elbows and a flask of coffee.

'What a good idea,' I said.

'What?'

'Bringing your own coffee. Doesn't Joan mind?'

'Of course not. George stop asking silly questions and sit down, would you? Now then. This, whatever his name is...'

'Or was.'

'Ers,' he said, stuffing about half a sandwich in his ample features. 'But can one say that? In a way it still is his name even though he isn't there. Curious.'

'I suppose we're going to get it in the neck,' I suggested.

'Get it in the neck? Why should we?'

'Well, we did put him inside.'

'Of course we didn't, you fool. The law did.'

'I suppose so,' I said unhappily. 'But I do feel I might have

109

tried harder to keep him out, you know, given him another go at his Community Service Order. But then he was a very disturbed boy. Perhaps he'd have killed himself even if we'd kept him under our care.'

'Then we *might* have got it in the neck,' Delderfield observed. 'Good thing he was put away.'

'When are they holding the inquest?'

'Soon, I should imagine.'

'But . . . I mean don't they want me to go?'

'Of course not. What for?'

'Well . . . I don't know. I was his Probation Officer. I've been dealing with him. For some time. Aren't they interested in his state of mind?'

'And haven't you heard,' Delderfield asked, dusting his greasy fingertips with a handkerchief, 'of prison psychiatrists?'

'Frequently,' I said. 'And never in very flattering terms. They're the bum end of a profession I don't think a lot of at the best of times. In any case – Christ, I'm *involved* with this. Responsible.'

'Your responsibility,' he said, 'ended when he went through the gate. Try and understand this, George. Prison governors are intensely possessive of anything that happens within their precincts, their staff even more so. And I mean the boy was out of our juris*diction*. Good God this is *elementary*. If he'd killed himself while under our care then we *might* have had something to account for. But even then, for you to be called to account he'd need to have done it on a Community Service project under your direct control, preferably with a piece of Probation Service equipment which you had carelessly left in his charge.'

'Such as what?' I wondered, rather intrigued by this line of thought.

'Such as . . . *I* don't know . . . a telephone cord – stapling machine . . .'

'*Stapling* machine?'

'Yes – you might have left him in charge of a stapling machine, then he might have gone off and . . . stapled himself to a railway track or something. This is all perfectly beside the point. The thing is he died in prison so from our point of view it's quite straightforward. And even from theirs. People in prison have no rights, to begin with, which tidies things up a great deal from the outset. He was in a cell on his own, no one attacked him – "blah blah while of unsound mind". Or something.'

'And . . . they won't want to call his mother or anyone?'

'I shouldn't think so,' Delderfield said. 'I mean would you? You mustn't get emotionally involved, George. It's a mistake and it isn't like you. Perhaps you're not eating a proper diet. Now listen, I really want to talk to you about something else.'

'Oh?'

'Mmngh.' His fat fingers formed an arch like an inflatable Gothic portal, meanwhile his lips flapped gently together while he squinted at a spot in the air beside my left knee and wondered where to begin. 'This, ah, man of ours,' he said. 'The, um, literary critic. Or whatever he is.'

'Dugdale?'

'Mmngh.'

'What about him? He's good, don't you think?' I said. 'A good speaker.'

'Oh, excellent, yes. Fine. I, ah, I thought his name sounded faintly *familiar*. I've been looking through the, er . . .'

'The records?'

'Yes. He seems to be one of your clients, George.'

'Well – yes,' I said. 'He is. Why?'

'*Hrrmngh*. "Why?" the man asks.'

'I *see*,' I said. 'You mean somebody might . . .'

'Quite so.'

'Oh – but they've no access to our records.'

'But they read *newspapers*. They have *memories*. Some of them are lawyers.'

'Nobody's said anything to you so far, have they?'

'No. And he does seem to be something of an asset,' Delderfield said. 'But he'd better be prepared to pack his bags if anyone does.'

'Alright,' I said. 'Well I didn't mention his record to you before, because he did seem so exactly right. But I can see your point really – I mean it could be a bit embarrassing for us.'

111

'"*Us*"?' Delderfield said. '*We* won't be embarrassed, George. You might, conceivably. But I don't know a thing about it. This conversation is not taking place.'

# 19

'I don't *like* being specially investigated,' Dugdale said. He shuddered. 'It isn't *nice*. It's also cripplingly expensive. Do you realise the bloody man cut off my Securicor allowance just like *that*, pending *my* submission that I'm a clean, deserving case?'

'I'm afraid they do that,' I said. 'Like the Income Tax. They have the technology; it's called a red pen.'

'They amaze me,' he said. 'They simply amaze me. It's this Byzantine imperial whimsy I can't get over. I mean there they are one minute buying me a nice pair of shoes. Next thing they're telling me to piss off and starve in the gutter. One feels *exactly* like last week's courtesan. But what's the *reason* for it?'

'Well you did apply for a clothing allowance on the basis that this was going to help you get a job,' I said.

'Did I?'

'Yes. Or I did mainly, on your behalf. So naturally Pollock was curious as to whether you'd started it yet.'

'I see,' he said. 'I see. But I'm not getting *paid*.'

'Did he believe that?'

'No,' Dugdale said. 'That's what I found so insulting. He started muttering darkly about concealed earnings and prosecution. And *then* he made another attempt to get me to become a lavatory attendant in Blaen y Maes or wherever it is.'

'That's amazing.'

'Isn't it?' Dugdale said. 'I think he has a reverse Pygmalion complex.'

'What amazes me is that the job's still going,' I said.

'If you ask me,' Dugdale said, 'the lavatory doesn't exist yet. Somebody's got a government grant to build one, provided they can get me to work there. The whole deal has been fixed up by some secret Whitehall department created by the Tories.'

'D'you know, that wouldn't altogether surprise me,' I said. 'But anyway, I'll sort Pollock out for you. And you can appeal, you know, and call me as a witness.'

'Really?' he said. 'Before whom?'

'A panel of one lawyer, one businessman and one trade unionist usually.'

'I see . . . George I wonder if this is paranoid, but what if the lawyer or the businessman . . .'

'Are members of the Memorial Affiliation?'

'Quite.'

'That is a point,' I said.

'I thought it might be.' He sighed. 'One way or another I've quite a lot to lose there. There really are some golden opportunities in this lark.'

'So don't appeal,' I said. 'Leave it to me. In any case the Social Securicor very rarely excommunicates anyone for ever. If you can hang on for a couple of weeks . . .'

'Oh I'm sure I can.' He produced some money and waved it at me. 'Look at this.'

'I was wondering how you were buying the drinks,' I said. 'Where did you get it?'

'Aha,' he said slily, putting it away again. 'There's lots of ways, George.'

'Dugdale . . .'

'No no. Above board activities. Or nearly. Maybe having my Securicor cut off was a good thing. It puts one on one's mettle. D'you know I was talking to Ritchie this afternoon, and it seems he runs errands and does odd jobs for some man, which I must say sound remarkably remunerative . . .'

'What sort of jobs? What man?'

'I don't know. But the point is, the man's looking for someone who can – oh, write a decent letter once in a while. Answer the blower for a few hours a week. He's evidently in some way of business and wants to point himself up market a bit . . .'

'So that's what you've been doing, is it?'

'Not yet, no. Oh, you mean this money? Ah,' he said, tapping the side of his nose. 'Now this was another form of fiscal enterprise altogether. And I think I might let you in on this, George. D'you ever gamble?'

'I do punish my wallet from time to time,' I said. 'Not a lot.'

'I suppose if I were to tell you I'd found a means of winning regularly you'd think I was mad.'

'I should personally telephone the white van,' I said, nodding.

'Oh ye of little faith.' He pulled his money out again. There did seem to be an awful lot of it. 'What's this then?'

'Luck.'

'System.'

'Oh I *see*,' I said. 'Like James Bond.'

'George . . .'

'Well I'm sorry, but if it really is a system, how come everyone doesn't do it?'

'Stupidity and masochism,' he said briskly. 'Your average punter is exactly like your average criminal, and I don't need to tell you anything about them. And why is it that the police are generally stupid? Because they don't need to be intelligent to succeed. Crooks obligingly convict themselves,' he said. 'It's the same with bookies and gamblers.'

'So that's the sociology,' I said. 'What's the system?'

He drew out a piece of paper, sketched out five columns and started rapidly filling them with numbers – all sorts of stuff about odds and aim to win and accumulated stake and gaming tax. '. . . and on the sixth race,' he concluded, 'you win.'

'Why the sixth?'

'Alright the third,' he said. 'The seventh. The first even. It makes no difference. The point is you've won.'

'But what about all these losses?'

'Even after subtracting them. This is the whole point of it.'

'Are you sure?'

'Of course I am. Look for yourself.'

I looked. In spite of vast internal friction, I really had to concede that the figures made sense.

'It's so simple really, isn't it?' I said.

'Recipes for success always are,' he said blithely. 'The hard part is getting human nature to conform to them. I can guarantee that that method will treble any given sum in about three days.'

'Alright.' I gave him ten pounds. 'Treble that.'

'With pleasure,' he said. 'Shall we say Saturday evening?'

'Come to dinner. You can bring it with you.'

# 20

'How old are you anyway?'

'Twenty three.'

'That's ridiculous,' I said. 'When I was your age you didn't exist.'

'And when I'm your age neither will you. So there's only now.'

'This is everything.'

'It is,' she said, perhaps not meaning quite the same thing as me.

'You know, I can still remember my childhood vision of the future,' I said. 'It was something like the Great White Way, wending off timelessly to a golden horizon.'

'And?' she said, settling her head into my shoulder. Her body felt like the darkness of the room come alive, lazy coils of darkness on which we were both floating.

'And – well, there was a spot just out of sight. Just over the horizon there was something poetic and erotic, and the sunlight fell softly like rain – all that kind of thing. This was the essence of all my looking forward to growing up. Then from time to time since I did grow up I've woken up and realised that the magic sunny place was still over the horizon and it was time I got there. But now,' I said, 'well, for the first time in my life I'm standing in it.'

'George how *sweet*.'

'It's true. Only I've been thinking. I think when I was a child everybody had some sort of similar feeling. For the most part they were going to grow up disappointed but they still at least started life with this hope.'

'So?'

'So I wonder if people still do. It isn't the kind of thing you can do surveys about.'

'No,' she said drowsily.

'It was maybe a kind of innocence,' I said. '*I* don't know – there was a feeling in the air. I don't notice it nowadays. It could just be because I'm old of course. But the air seems to have gone flat. It's full of bleeps and twinges. Sometimes I worry about it. Suppose the unconscious mind is affected by radio signals?'

'*Radio* signals?'

'The brain is organic electricity. I defy you to prove me that it *can't* be affected by radio signals. Perhaps the unconscious mind actually picks up programmes,' I said. 'Imagine it. Imagine if Jung had been born fifty years later – there he is, dabbling away looking for symbols in the collective unconscious, comes up with the Jimmy Young Show. It doesn't bear thinking about. But I wonder if you know the feeling I mean, from your own childhood?'

'Ummm . . .'

'I imagine you had a happy one?'

'Why?'

'I just do. Did you?'

'Did I . . . ?' she said. 'Alright I admit it – *well* . . .'

'Yes?'

'Well the thing was it was *de rigueur* to be happy in our family so we could never be quite sure if we were. Then when I was about nine my father buggered off and a lot of bailiffs and people came to take away the furniture, so then things got very fed up for a while and my brother got a golf ball stuck in his throat and nearly choked. But then we quite quickly started feeling better. I felt guilty as hell about this for a while because I thought it meant I secretly hated my father but that wasn't it. It was just such an incredible relief to stop pretending to enjoy life all the time that we cheered up.'

116

'And was that the last you saw of him?'

'Oh no. My mother inherited some money quite soon after that and he used to turn up and borrow some.'

'And she lent it to him?'

'Oh yes. They were still very amiable and messy together. Actually I think they still loved each other but things had just got tired because my father could never make life work out. Money and that. Like we never had any, and my mother's relatives used to come round and slip her fifty quids which she couldn't refuse and he hid under the stairs.'

'What did he do for a living?'

'It wasn't a living,' she said. 'He wrote poetry.'

'Oh.'

'It seemed to consist of drinking bottles of wine and groaning. When I was little I thought that's what poetry was.'

'He sounds very like somebody I know.'

'If you mean the distinguished Prof. Dugdale,' she said, shifting, 'he is.'

'*What?*' I sat bolt upright. 'Dugdale's your father?'

'Why d'you think I've been staying away from the Dylan Thomas Dismemberment Society?'

'I had wondered.'

'I make all sorts of excuses,' Sophie said. 'Haydock Williams must think I'm having it off with somebody. Which of course I am.'

'But this is terrible,' I said. 'And how does he come to be here?'

'He's always had a tendency to show up. Especially since my mother died. He just tracked me down to Swansea one day, conned Mark out of about thirty quid, which was rather funny, and then – well, he seemed to like the place. One kept seeing him around.'

'But I mean, do you say hallo to him? In the street?'

She laughed. 'Usually,' she said. 'But not invariably.'

'He must be a bit of a liability.'

'Yes of course he is but one can't dislike him. I mean can one? I tend to stay out of his way and get other people to keep an eye on him. But since you've got him I can relax, George.'

'Oh don't say that,' I said. 'Don't *say* it. But you mean he's always after you for a bit of the family money?'

'Oh no. My brother's got all that, or what's left of it. Why d'you think I work?'

'I thought maybe you were one of these people who like to prove themselves.'

'By typing letters for Haydock bloody Williams,' she said, hitting me. 'Christ.'

'I'm sorry.'

'I should hope so. I just thought I'd better do something when I started thinking about leaving Mark. But I *don't* go around thinking happiness is a warm job, that's all. The bloody thing only lasts six months anyway,' she said. 'It's one of those schemes this cowboy government has for concealing the unemployment figures. But I really don't think I'd bother to work if I was rich.'

'Bit crummy of your brother to have all the money, really.'

'Oh, don't blame Hugh,' she said. 'There isn't much money anyway, and he absolutely hated getting it. It all came from some very establishment uncle of my mother's who insisted Hugh should inherit and go to public school and all the rest of it. It all made him absolutely miserable and he became a left wing homosexual.'

'Is that so bad?'

'I think so. He always joins these very macho cliques who think he's a perverted bourgeois scumbag. That's how I met Mark,' she said. 'Theatre of Conflict were playing at this pub in Islington and they had Hugh up on the stage and beat him up. It was when they were beginning to experiment with audience participation.' She yawned. 'So there we are.'

'Yes. Actually I've got him coming to dinner on Saturday,' I said.

'Who?' she asked, alarmed and incredulous. 'Mark?'

'No no. Your distinguished Pa.'

'Oh that's alright,' she said, nestling into my shoulder again. 'I can go out somewhere.'

# 21

'George what *am* I to say to you?'

'Ah, it was only a tenner,' I said. 'Forget it.'

'But it's the *principle*,' Dugdale said. 'I persuaded you to part with money on what turned out to be a bum scheme.'

'I thought that was how you normally made your living.'

'Not from you. Anyway in this instance I believed it myself.'

'Perhaps that was your mistake.'

'Possibly. The annoying thing is,' he said, 'that it was just a mathematical error. You see there are six dogs in every race, so I thought you could just back one trap number until...'

'Spare me the details please,' I said.

'Oh alright. The trouble is it really is insuperable if backed by a vast sum of money.'

'You mean if you've got so much that you don't need any more you can always win some?'

'Quite.'

'Well that's money for you,' I said. 'How long have you been doing this anyway?'

'Just recently. I guess I was lucky at first. Why?'

'I wondered.' Actually I was wondering how many similar calls his wife had taken and if that's what had killed her.

'George you *don't* imagine...'

'No of course I don't,' I said. 'You're not that kind of con man.'

'Thankyou. I mean I have kept the losing slips if you want to...'

'No of course I don't. Just forget the whole thing. I'll see you tomorrow.'

'Mmn?'

'For dinner.'

'Oh, under these circumstances I don't...'

'Nonsense. And you'll be all the more in need of a meal by the sound of things.'

'I suppose I will,' he said in a weary tone. 'Alright, thanks. I'll see you.'

But then on the other hand, I thought, gazing at the dead receiver, it was *after* he left her that his wife died. He affected life so drastically that one's system had to undergo a massive distortion of itself to accommodate him. So inasmuch as he had anything to do with it, she had probably died of withdrawal symptoms.

# 22

'Coffee,' Beau said. 'Mnnghh.' He seemed to float across the kitchen suspended on invisible wires of attenuated nervous ectoplasm, then as he took the cup from me and drank his movements solidified; he had bought a temporary lease on solidity.

'How's life?' I asked, never a question to throw at him carelessly.

Beau considered it while he attached a cigarette to his face. 'I've forgotten,' he said. 'Got a match?'

The cigarette was half consumed before he added: 'Creating the biggest thing since the Edinburgh Fringe is not a form of life really. It isn't even existence. I *do* everything but I'm *not* anything. You know?' he said. 'Shit gets thrown at me and I deploy it. If I can't function I panic. If I can I still panic, because there's so much to do.'

'Oh.'

'I mean there's less than three weeks left till we open,' he said. 'The printers haven't delivered the programme, half the events will have nobody to do the door. We haven't found anywhere to hold a club yet. Nobody's rung me back for a block licence for street performances. One of the venues has to shove in about six fire doors in three days or it's got no theatrical licence. Unless we hear from the Arts Council in about the next ten minutes my wages are going to run out bang in the middle of the whole thing. Otherwise things look pretty good.'

The phone rang. Beau was positively twanged out of the

room to answer it, running now on wires which were made of wire and all but visible. 'It's for you,' he said, coming back slowly.

'Hello,' said Alice. 'George you've been rather naughty, haven't you? You've sold us a dud prof.'

'I *gave* you a good speaker,' I said. 'Honorary professorship was his idea.'

'Whereas his criminal record was common knowledge to both of you.'

'*Caveat emptor*,' I said. 'And may I repeat that I made nothing out of the whole thing.'

'So bloody what?'

'Oh nothing. How did you find him out anyway?'

'He shouldn't have called himself a prof,' she said. 'Not with all those academics about. You know how petty they are. And I mean these things are a matter of record. Someone looked him up.'

'Who?'

'Actually I believe it was Sion Slugge,' she said. 'But then he told one of our real profs and he told everyone else. After that, well, we sort of checked up a bit further and then . . .'

'Don't tell me,' I said. 'Delderfield volunteered to check our records on the offchance.'

'That's it. He just rang me,' she said. 'How did you guess?'

'Clairvoyance.'

'He's not overly pleased with you at the moment.'

'How tragic,' I said. 'I suppose you want me to find someone else, or is this another attempt to rope me in?'

'No and bloody well no,' she said. 'So sucks to you. As luck has it we've got ourselves a real prof.'

'You mean one of those dirge besotted male spinsters from the local English Department?'

'No I don't. I mean an eminent little philologist from the Midwest, reeking of prestige and hungry archives and money.'

'I didn't know American Universities were still handing it out.'

'Most of them aren't,' she said, 'but his department's backed by some rich industrialist or other.'

'Rich? You mean a cruise missile manufacturer?'

'Could be,' she said. 'Actually I think it's a security firm – anti theft devices, handbag sized napalm packs. I forget exactly. Anyway, he's on a visiting lectureship somewhere, and doing a thesis. *He* actually wrote to *us* wanting to join the party.'

'Good Gawd – I suppose a Swansea address is enough to make you seem authentic,' I said. 'What's his name?'

'Holloway.'

'Alright Alice. Have a happy time with Holloway,' I said. 'Was there anything else?'

'Yes, as it happens. My roof's leaking.'

'I'll tell you what to do then.'

'What?'

'Mend it.'

When she rang back I left it. The fact that the phone went on seven full minutes meant it could be no one but her. I had practically to nail Beau's foot to the floor to stop him lifting the receiver. Sophie staggered downstairs just as it stopped.

'My God,' she said. She was dressed in a sheet. 'It gave me the most *shattering* early morning dream. I thought everyone was out.'

'I'm sorry. It was my partly ex wife and we were freezing her off.'

'Oh.' One of her eyes was glued down. She rubbed it and slumped into a chair. 'Is there any coffee?'

I put the kettle on. 'Doing anything today?'

'Matter of fact yes,' she said, yawning. 'Haydock Williams has asked me out in his boat.'

'His *boat*? Why?'

'Possibly to try and feel me up. I'll have to see. The thing is I just can't resist boats.'

'I didn't know he had one.'

'He's just got it,' she said. 'It's called the *Polly Garter*.'

'It would be. D'you want me to come?'

'Alright – good idea.'

The phone rang. Crouched in his chair Beau looked up at me pleadingly, like a greyhound begging not to be barred from the track. I tested the psychic emanations; it didn't seem to be Alice. 'Okay,' I said.

It was Dugdale, for me.

'Look George, I'm not going to be able to make dinner tonight after all,' he said. 'I'm going to be busy.'

'Fine,' I said. 'Doing what?'

'Minding my own business, if I might put it that way.'

'I am your Probation Officer, you know.'

'Oh excuse *me*. Well then George, as a sop to your professional pride, suffice it to say I shall be gainfully employed.'

'No, I'm afraid it doesn't suffice entirely.'

'Oh *Jesus*. Look, I shall be doing something for Ritchie's man. Okay? Something terribly innocuous. I believe he wants to get into a golf club or something. He's had the verbal nod but he has to write a formal letter and the dear chap can't even spell. What the hell did you think I'd be doing, robbing a post office?'

'Alright, I'm sorry. Look while you're there, I've had a rather terse note in response to my pursuit of Pollock and I'll be seeing him on Tuesday.'

'Uhuh?'

'Also, a difficulty has arisen with regard to your eminent speakership at the doings.'

'What difficulty?'

I told him.

'Holloway,' he said. 'May his balls calcify. May his anus impact each time he farts. Oh well, George, I have other fish to fry. Thanks for telling me.'


# 23


'Oh,' Haydock Williams said. 'George. This is a surprise, boy.'

'You don't mind?' I asked. 'I thought I'd come along in case Sophie drowns. She can't swim, you see.'

'Drowns?' He pulled off his blue denim cap and slapped the cabin roof. '*Drowns*? She's safe as 'ouses.'

'Houses don't float,' I said, running an eye over the *Polly Garter*'s patched, sea-weary lines. I know just about enough about boats to be able to distinguish one from a bus, but anyone can spot a piece of junk. 'Where did you get it?'

'Her,' he corrected me. 'Off an old fisherman, since you ask. Used to run trips right down the channel and beyond. Of course if you don't wish to come aboard you needn't. But you are quite welcome, in spite of the fact that you were not invited.' He turned to busy himself with a chart laid on the dashboard of the open-backed cockpit.

'Oh no, I'd love to,' I said, overdoing my placatory tone since I resented having to use it. 'You mustn't take my deprecations seriously. It's an old sailors' custom to say rude things about a craft.'

'Really?' He looked round at me.

'Yes, to ward off bad luck,' I said. 'It's like the taboo on whistling, saying "pig", carrying a white handled knife or pissing to windward.'

'Oh,' he said in an interested tone. 'Now let's get this straight. You don't whistle, you don't say . . .'

'*Shut up*,' I said. 'You're aboard, remember.'

'Oh ah,' he said. 'Thankyou George. That could have been nasty.'

'Yes it could. If you should feel the need to refer to pigs at any time,' I told him, 'say four footed friends.'

'Right,' he said solemnly. 'Four footed friends it is. Though why a sailor should need to discuss them I can't imagine.'

'Oh you never know,' I said. 'One of them might live on a four footed friend farm in hills somewhere. Then one day he feels homesick and wants to talk about it, and the next minute *khavoohm*, a squall blows up and the boat goes down with all hands. I've heard of fishermen being flung overboard for saying pig. You can say Macbeth if you feel like it though,' I said. 'Unless of course you're holding an inboard play.'

'But not Piggy Macbeth under any circumstances,' Sophie cut in. 'Look, can we just get aboard the bloody thing?'

'Yes of course,' Haydock Williams said placatingly. He held out a hand. 'Ladies first.'

'Not at sea,' I said, determined to have the last word. This might have been fortunate anyway since he had neglected to tie the boat at the stern, so that as I stepped down I found myself doing the splits above a sudden yawning of oily water and my own truncated reflection. Haydock Williams had grabbed my arm, and by hurling himself into the gunwales somehow managed to bring me aboard on top of him. The graze on my leg was only minor but he seemed rather winded. I threw Sophie a line and she looped it round an iron bollard and flung it back. Thus we got the stern pulled back against the quay and she got herself aboard: the tide being full there was only about a two foot drop. After a lot of fumbling and farting with the starter, and Sophie's spotting at the last minute that we were still tied at the bows, we were under way. Haydock Williams nosed out down the walled river estuary at what seemed to me an alarming speed, squinting through the windscreen and scowling with concentration.

Ahead and to starboard were quite a lot of small craft around the lock gates to the new yacht haven, behind and to port the outer limits of the decaying commercial docks, where moorings in the open river were older and considerably cheaper. The yacht haven was a council-backed scheme I had always thought mad. It had seemed to me like a cargo cult runway, a piece of sympathetic magic put together under the illusion that King Farouk's ghost was going to show up and start chucking money overboard. But lo and behold, the place was no sooner built than it had filled up: it seemed there was still plenty of money around somewhere; perhaps the sea was where the rich nowadays hung out, the better to protect themselves from burglary and revolution. At any rate they had swept in from the briny like Vikings, and the South Dock area had gone from a mud and corrugated iron wasteland of shifty car breakers and small factories processing sulphur and bone meal, to a spick and span wasteland of clanking aluminium masts on a wide variety of boats which all had the same aggressively sterile air of Swiss bank accounts. I wondered if Haydock Williams had voted for the scheme or against it.

There came a small indrawn gasp from Sophie, and I looked up to observe that we were now actually sweeping through the middle of the yachts and cabin cruisers and yachtettes near the yacht haven dock; the prospect ahead was a forest of masts with yellow oilskinned figures leaning off them like monkeys but swearing rather more violently. Haydock Williams's tongue was stuck so far out through his teeth that it could be seen in half profile: Sophie and I clasped hands as he wrastled full pelt with the wheel as though at the dodgems, a manoeuvre which created a vast wash so that everything we passed was set rocking with a hectic metronomic motion which made it even harder to avoid things. Quite a lot of people looked wet and somebody took a swing at us with a boathook. At one point there was a small yacht written right across our bows; however with a great swerve we succeeded in only grazing it and cannot have injured anyone since the crew had all got well clear when flinging themselves overboard at our approach. And then all of a sudden there was open water again, and we made way peacefully down beside the concrete wall of the South Pier while nautical curses faded, gradually behind us.

'Bloody people,' Haydock Williams said. 'Supposed to keep to the bloody right.'

'Are you sure?'

'An old rule of the sea,' he said, shaking his head sorrowfully. 'Shouldn't be allowed on the water, people like that. A boat is not a new toy.'

The next few minutes passed without incident, except for our getting a bit closer to an incoming tanker than I would have liked so that we shipped about a gallon from the propeller wash and a bucket of slops just missed me in the stern. Shortly after that a tugboat pilot shouted something to us which probably wasn't Good Afternoon, but I couldn't see what it might be about. The swell hit us as we rounded the end of the concrete pier to broach the open sea, and Sophie and I moved forward under shelter of the cockpit since every wave we hit was soaking us.

'This is the life,' Haydock Williams said hopefully. 'There's a cabin through that little door by there if you want to get comfortable. We'll be through this choppy patch in a minute or two.'

We staggered through into the cabin, which was right forward and would have held four seated people with their knees touching and their heads going through the ceiling only occasionally. It was nice to have the wind and spray muted but the smack of waves on bow was considerably louder in here and started to frighten me.

'I wonder if he's got any drink,' I said faintly.

Sophie found a bottle of rum in a cupboard and we took a swig each. The motion changed, from up and down crashes to a sideways slithering compounded by abrupt shuddering jerks which left my stomach lining wrapped around my ears. At one point I was looking down vertically on Sophie as I braced my feet against the far bulkhead. Nevertheless I was not much alarmed by this until I saw that she was. She struggled out of the cabin as soon as she could.

'For Christ's sake steer *into* it,' she screamed. 'You'll turn us over.'

Clambering out behind her, I saw her fighting with him for control of the wheel. '*I'm* the bloody skipper,' he was shouting, at which she landed a lucky punch; aided by the boat's rocking it flung him clear, and she grabbed the wheel and eased us round so that the waves came straight on to us. Up and down crashes resumed, and wetness. The bigger waves looked about ten feet high.

'I'm sorry, Mr Haydock Williams,' Sophie said as he got to his feet. 'But you were about to kill us.'

'I've never heard of such an action,' he said dejectedly. 'I could charge you with mutiny, you know, and lock you in that bloody cabin on bread and water. That is the law, my girl.'

'Yes I know it is,' she said with a lack of embarrassment which worked placatingly. 'And if you had them handy you could put me in irons as well. But honestly, how much sailing have you done?'

'I've been on fishing trips regular,' he said evasively. 'Right down as far as Cornwall sometimes. On this very boat.'

'In other words none?'

'Not at the actual helm, so to speak, no.'

'Please believe that I've done quite a lot,' she said. 'And what you have to do is hold this course and hope for the sea to drop a bit. Throttle back a little – like so – but no more. And keep a good look out since we are in the shipping lanes

127

and it's high tide. Would you like the wheel back?'

'Yes,' he said, and promptly started to throw up over the side, so that Sophie kept control of the boat anyway. I was sick myself, though I seemed to recover quite quickly.

Not very long after that the weather calmed as though a clamp had been put on it. I was amazed at this but Sophie explained that it was not at all uncommon. The sun bloomed and the motion of the sea rolled slowly. Warmth beat through towards my shivering bones and a blue aspect took over sea and sky. The transition was dreamlike; complete physical absorption in the moment left my mind floating happily and I began to see why people did it.

Sophie was aiming a course westward down the channel, handling the boat with an offhand competence which was lovely to watch. There was still a certain swell but she knew how to ride it, sometimes slicing obliquely at large rollers so that we climbed up their forward motion like a surfboard.

'How far were you thinking of going?' she asked.

'Well . . .' Haydock Williams stirred himself. His complexion had lost some of its formaldehyde green tint and was returning to rough pink but he had been motionless for some while, reclining beside me in the stern while his stunned metabolism picked up after the dual trauma of mutiny and vomit. He now appeared to have come to terms with things, if a little wanly. 'I thought it might be nice,' he suggested, 'to pop in at Laugharne. Perhaps have a drink or two at Brown's Hotel. That might round the trip off nicely.'

'What about the estuary?'

'Estuary?'

'Yes. You see, Mr Haydock Williams, Swansea being a seaport, small craft can get in and out practically any time. But at low tide the estuary at Laugharne is miles and miles of mud. What's the draft on this boat?'

'Draught?'

'Probably about six foot,' she answered herself. 'And that's cutting it fine. By the time we arrive we might get in if we're lucky, but it would be about three o'clock in the morning before we got out again. That would mean long cold hours of boredom at exactly the wrong time of night, unless of course we found one of those nice little pubs where it is always opening time, in which case we'd all be too drunk to sail back.'

Haydock Williams was stroking his chin. 'That's bloody smart thinking,' he said.

'It was elementary,' Sophie said to herself, shaking her head at the windscreen.

'Hell of a girl, isn't she?' He slapped my knee. 'Does more than type letters and make the bloody tea, I can tell you.' He got to his feet, bending his knees a couple of times to test them out. 'Now who's for a tipple?' he asked.

He disappeared into the cabin and there was the sound of cautious obscenity and rummaging.

'If you're looking for the rum,' Sophie called, 'it's probably on the floor.'

'The floor?'

'Yes. I'm afraid we had recourse to it during that short episode when the boat was sinking. Then everything got rather thrown around and it became impossible to keep hold of it.'

'Oh ah. Here it is.'

'Still in one piece?'

'Yes, yes,' he said, coming out with it. 'Top on tight and everything. I don't blame you at all. You did the right thing.'

He meant by opening the rum, though this was really his way of accepting Sophie's takeover of the boat without saying so. He had got some metal beakers and poured us all a drink, spilling some on my ear as he lurched back into the seat beside me.

'Bottoms up. (Sorry George). Well this is the life I must say,' he said. He raised his beaker to the strengthening sun. 'Why do sailors drink rum, I wonder?'

'Sailors drink anything.'

'You know what I mean, George. Why does it have this seafaring association?'

I shrugged. 'The West Indies?' I said. 'Pirates? Captain Morgan?'

'Ah, you got it,' he said. 'Half Barbados is descended from Captain Morgan.'

'Really?'

'I think it's Barbados,' he said less certainly. 'Course, you

129

know where the West Indian lilt comes from, don't you?'

'No?'

'Wales, boy. Cor, have you ever wanted to be a pirate, George?'

'Not since I was about ten.'

'Think of it,' he said, as though I had simply said yes. 'The wild blue yonder full of plunder, rum in the night and all the bloody women you can catch hold of when you reach port. There was an innocent gusto in those days, George, you can say what you like.'

'I don't know that Blackbeard firing off pistols under the dinner table epitomised innocent gusto.'

'Ah, I've worked for people like that,' he said. 'When I was younger. Dinner with the boss. Not that they actually fired pistols at your feet, of course, but you could see they wanted to. My whole point though, George – if we lose the sea we've lost everything. I don't mean the navy and the impregnable bloody island and all that stuff. Cos we know – they got rockets now come blat out of the sky like that, you got no chance. But I mean . . . look, out there somewhere used to be a lightship. One of my uncles worked it all 'is bloody life. This channel was thick with men would keep an eye on you, and right round the coast of Britain the same. Like seafarers in trouble help one another, don't matter if they're Russian or Chinese or what. They got automatic lights now.' He shook his head. 'It's not the same. I don't mean just for the sailors – it's not the same for us, ashore. It means we are gradually losing the feel of the sea from our blood. And that's what we've always been good at. Welsh, English, Cornish, everybody. That's all I'm saying, George.'

'Mmn, I agree,' I said. I agreed.

'Things,' he said. 'It's an age of things. The more things make life easy, the more we exist for them instead of the other way round. Funny, isn't it? Dylan would have hated it of course,' he said. 'See the reason I wanted to call in Laugharne today – we can have outings. Select I mean, just a few of us from the Affiliation. And guests. I can paint this boat up, get an awning. Picnics . . .'

'It sounds fun.'

'Fun? It's an education, boy. We have got to establish

Dylan Thomas as a serious literary figure.'

'He already is.'

'Ah, but you know what I mean, George. His reputation. All this muckraking. You know these people you bump into – "Oh, so and so, met him one night and he was pissed as a rat. Kept saying bum all the time." Or: "Dylan Thomas grabbed my wife's tits/pinched a pair of my shoes/was sick on my brother/still owes me five quid/pissed behind our piano." That isn't the kind of thing we want,' he said. 'Bloody gossip.'

'Most of it.'

'All of it. And those people that's still got IOUs from him – well. Worth a good deal more than the original loan, I'll be bound. Signed ones particularly.'

'I suppose rhyming IOUs would be worth even more.'

'Indubitably. No, we want to forget all that stuff. And look what he's done for Swansea if we only had the sense to see. Still,' he said, 'we're on the right lines now. And this Professor Holloway – Duw. *Delighted*, he is. He's delighted with us. And the connections he's got, well. We could write a blank cheque, George, in a manner of speaking.'

'When's he coming?'

'Week after next. He's only over at Bristol or somewhere. It's his vacation at the moment. But he said he wants to be right with us, everything we do. Term time and all. Him and his wife are coming.'

'We're off Rhossili,' Sophie called. 'I think I'll turn back now.'

'Right. Good girl. See that, George? That's the Worm's Head. That's in "Who do you wish was with us". And that beach is the one Extraordinary Little Cough runs right the way along – remember – and Brazell and Skully take no notice. And you see that house by there, right by itself above the sands at the end of that path? It's an old vicarage. Dylan was thinking of living there once. But I don't think it would have suited him.' He chuckled indulgently. 'Too far to the bloody pub.'

# Part Four

# 24

'But you *don't* have to *show* them to me,' Beau said. 'This is an *open festival*.' He made a gesture of exasperation like lifting a boulder above his head and flinging it down. '*You* find the gallery, *you* hang the pictures, you pay us a tenner and *we* put you in the programme. I am *not* here to *judge*.'

'Oh I *see*,' Sky said. A lot of his paintings were dotted about my living room, some of them framed. 'I'm sorry.'

'Oh it's alright,' Beau said. 'Half my bloody directors don't understand what we're supposed to be doing so why should you?' He sat down and a little of the tension left him. He was living at full manic stretch now, subsisting on rice and coffee, smoking six cigarettes at once and hearing the phone in his sleep, which sometimes actually was the phone in his sleep. He massaged his scalp wildly as though able to rearrange the brain beneath into a less uncomfortable figuration, and looked up. 'Have a good day?' he asked me.

'Routine.' I put down my briefcase and yawned. 'Told a few people to be good, locked a few people up, attended two boring and entirely futile meetings and wrote a couple of largely fictional progress reports. How about you?'

'Ooaaagh.' He stretched and rolled his eyes to indicate that words failed him. 'Some guy's been phoning you up,' he added.

'Who?' I asked. 'Sky – I like that one.'

'Dunno,' Beau said, 'but he sounded pretty annoyed about something.'

'Do you?' Sky said. 'Really?'

135

'Yes.'

'That's the one I nearly ripped up.'

'Good thing you didn't. Did he leave his name?' I asked Beau.

'Bassett.'

'Never heard of him. Listen, Sky, I want to show you these.' I led him into the back half of the living room where I now had half a dozen pieces in various stages of completion, lined up on a table.

'Uh *huh*,' he said, perusing them thoughtfully. 'And how many of them are finished?'

'None of them.'

'Correction,' he said. 'Those two are.'

'Are you sure?'

'Positive.'

'I was going to smooth them down and give them harder edges.'

'That's because you're repressed,' he said. 'Believe me, you'll ruin both of them.'

The phone rang and Beau was catapulted out into the hall to answer it. 'It's him,' he said, coming back.

I went out to get it. 'Hallo?'

'Mr Waddin'ton, is it?'

'Yes?'

'It's your partner I wants really, burr I don't suppose 'e's there.'

'My partner . . .?'

'Ah. Dungwood or some bloody name.'

'Dungwood? You don't mean Dugdale by any chance?'

'Right. Now tell 'im, not to forget. This is Bassett speaking. Charlie Bassett.'

'Not to forget what?'

'Look,' he said wearily. 'I'm a man of my word. Tha's no bull. I don't wossname people, I means it. When I say a thing that's it. Right? So don't give me no bull neither.'

It was the word bull which gave me some clue how to proceed. Clearly this was a type who would only be blindly enraged by any further protestation of ignorance. If he had the fixed idea that I was Dugdale's partner I should just have to concede to this fiction if I wanted him to tell me anything else. But partner in what?

'The trouble is,' I said circumspectly, 'that we have so many dealings, you see. I believe he did mention your name the other day but I can't remember what it was in connection with, exactly.'

'That's better,' he said. 'We're beginnin' to talk some bloody sense now. The connection is – I got the rights.'

'Rights?'

'That's it. Sold 'em to me, he did.'

'Now these are...?'

'The Dylan Thomas rights,' he said, as though this were obvious.

'I see.' The slightly firmer ground I had thought myself standing on was wiped out. 'The rights to what, exactly?'

'To Dylan bloody Thomas. They're mine. Anyone else wants a piece of the action got to talk to me. Okay? I got the receipt I 'ad off 'im,' he added. 'In my hand. Now. For forty quid cash. So I can settle this thing in court or outside court or any fackin' where you want it.'

'Forty pounds,' I said weakly. There was no other comment I could think of.

'Ah. Plus about six pints of strong lager and four brandies. I'm not on about that. Tha's juss 'osspitality I threw in, like. But you juss tell Dungfield if 'e tries dealin' with anyone else direct there'll be trouble. With a big T. And tha's no bull. You ask anyone up yere about Charlie Bassett an' they'll tell you. When I says a thing I means it.'

'Fine,' I said. 'Splendid. Where would that be, exactly? Do we have your address?'

'Don't start playin' clever buggers wi' me,' he said. 'You juss make sure Dungvale don't forget.' He rang off.

Very bemused, I wandered back into the living room and sat down. There must have been something odd in my expression because they were both looking at me.

'Something the matter?' Beau asked.

I nodded faintly. 'Dylan Thomas,' I said.

'Eh?'

'I haven't much of a clue either. All I know is Dugdale's just conned somebody again and used my name in the process. God, I'm going to have to do something about this. I

137

mean what does he think the Probation Service *is*? He uses it like it was an answering machine, an uncle with bottomless pockets and some kind of a demented extras agency for con men.'

'You mean he keeps giving your name to people?' Sky asked. I nodded. 'Described me as his partner.'

'Christ. Look there's something else going on here,' he said. 'He's trying to drag you in.'

'How?'

'Well look, he was nicked wasn't he? I mean that's how you know him. It was the first time he'd been caught out. He'd been going on all his life blithely conning people – *he* was writing the script all the time. You see? But now the *law's* trying to write the script, represented by you. So he wants to assert himself by getting you into his play.'

'I think you might be right,' I said. 'In which case I'm going to have to drop him in it. Or else he'll drop me.'

'It looks that way.'

I sighed heavily and dragged out my address book. '"Care of Mukkarjee, The Shahgbhag",' I said, putting it away again. 'I think I'd better go and see the bastard. You don't feel like coming along?'

# 25

The door of the Shahgbhag was dark green, peeling and very firmly closed. There were several bell pushes which did not appear to work, a rusted knocker and a letterbox choked with official envelopes. Rapping on the wood with my knuckles was painful and ineffective; the hallway behind might have been packed with kapok for all the sound it made.

'Sod it, there's nobody in,' I said.

Sky shook his head. 'Somebody clocking us from upstairs.' He pointed.

On the first floor, a dark face loomed uncertainly from behind a grimy net curtain. He saw me, ducked back, hovered and came forward again, perhaps reassured by our appearance. Evidently this was Mr Mukkarjee. He nodded, raising his eyebrows in a gesture of invitation. Sky returned this, which seemed to provoke encouragement. Mr Mukkarjee went through a leeringly ostentatious dumb show of eating, in response to which Sky nodded and shrugged. Mr Mukkarjee then gave us a V sign and disappeared.

'Well that's nice, I must say,' I said. I made to cross the road.

Sky grabbed my arm. 'He meant wait two minutes,' he said.

Sure enough the door was starting to creak open. Unseen at first, Mr Mukkarjee's head bobbed shortly into view at the front end of a bow of welcome, and we squeezed past him into a tiny hallway smelling of turmeric and mildew. Once the front door had been closed again it was hair raisingly cramped and almost completely dark: Sky was standing on my foot, some kind of sharp protrusion was sticking in my back and the only light in the place came from Mr Mukkarjee's teeth.

'Welcome,' he said, making me jump considerably. He seemed to be compensating for the gloom by speaking at the top of his voice. 'Now if I can squeeze past you two gentlemen perhaps? The door of the restaurant is over here...'

All three of us then concentrated on the task of manoeuvring Mr Mukkarjee to the other end of the cupboard sized hallway. A quite extraordinary number of things seemed to be stored there, most of them with abrasive edges. We started to make some sort of progress once I managed to stand back on top of a wooden box. Mr Mukkarjee was then able to lunge forward, tripping over a broom, and grab me by the balls.

'Oh, excuse fingers, I am most frightfully sorry,' he said, giggling slightly with embarrassment. 'I was looking for the doorknob. Ah.'

A door opened and we all fell gratefully into the restaurant itself. Sky seemed considerably less shaken by the ordeal in the passage than me; perhaps it reminded him of home.

'We thought at first you might be closed,' I remarked. I took out my handkerchief to mop the back of my neck; sweat seemed to have broken out all over my skin.

'Oh no.' Mr Mukkarjee waved vaguely around the restaurant, empty but for two or three sauce bottles and a small swarm of flies which hovered hopefully by a greasy beaded curtain leading to the kitchen. 'We lock up to be on the safe side. The hooligan element and so on. But customers are welcome,' he said oglingly. 'Do sit down.'

'Thankyou. We didn't actually come for a meal, I'm afraid.' I thought it was about time I confessed to this.

'You don't want curry?' I could have wept at the hesitantly disappointed tone; it was not inconceivable that he needed to sell a meal for the price of some cigarettes.

'Not really. We came to see Dugdale.'

'*Oh.*' It was as if, in Mr Mukkarjee's soul, the optimism switch had just been flipped on again. 'You must be the publishers,' he said rapturously. 'Doctor Dugdale is out, I'm afraid.'

'Not the publishers as such,' I said, finding myself unable to let Mr Mukkarjee down completely for a second time. 'Not the ones he might have mentioned, anyway.'

'But different publishers, yes?'

'Not entirely.'

'But you do have a certain connection?' he offered.

'I have a certain interest, let's put it like that.'

'Oh good.' Mr Mukkarjee rubbed his hands, not the least bit put out; he seemed quite at home with this convoluted method of bargaining for the truth. Having come here to sort Dugdale out, the first thing I found myself doing was another bit of perjury on his behalf. Sky was right – he was dragging me into a twilight zone where I had no identity but what his whim allotted me in random conversations with other people. He didn't bend the truth so much as assassinate it. I started sweating again.

Mr Mukkarjee had sat down at the table with us, with the tensely deferential air of someone ready to disclaim this course of action the moment a better one was suggested. Sky was playing with a chili sauce stain on the plastic tablecloth,

140

shaping it into what looked like quite a promising nude; meanwhile the vibes from Mr Mukkarjee's quarter became steadily more stifling, a mounting pressure of words pushing on some worn but tight clamped gasket of reserve. A fly bounced off his glasses and he smiled at me weakly. 'Soon we shall have a cup of tea,' he announced suggestingly, this statement being the basis and the outcome of his inner struggle. 'And perhaps a nice literary chat.'

'Yes,' I said, desperately trying to reach him. 'How nice. Yes of course.'

'Oh good.'

The silence resumed. I didn't think I could stand much more of it. Mr Mukkarjee was fidgeting now, perhaps about to spring off to the kitchen to serve us up a nice literary chat with prawn curry and poppadoms. It occurred to me that since it was dinner time I might as well order a meal anyway: we launched into speech at the same instant.

'As a matter of...'

'Don't you think...'

'Sorry. Do go on.'

'No, I'm *so* sorry. Please.'

'No I insist,' I said. 'What were you saying?'

'Well.' He smiled apologetically. 'Don't you think too much fuss is made about T.S. Eliot, that was all.'

'Oh.'

'A profoundly ungenerous bastard, if I might say so. Dugdale calls him the High Anglican Messiah. "No man shall come unto the father but by me, and since he doesn't talk to me what chance have you got?" Good God alive, what a bloody character.'

'Who? T.S. Eliot?'

'No. Dugdale. The last of the bent umbrellas.' He chuckled. 'We were chatting the other day,' he explained, 'about world topics and national characteristics and so on. I observed that Dugdale was a most atypical Englishman but he denied it. "Me?" he said. "I'm as English as a bent umbrella." Isn't that delightful?'

'Yes...'

'God blimey but what is happening to this country nowadays?'

141

'Well...'

'You know what I think? This is not a popular opinion but –' He lowered his voice. 'Women prime ministers are fatal. Look at Mrs Ghandi – least said soonest mended. And Thatcher is exactly the same. She is a skinhead in a blue wig. But have you noticed the way they always have to build new countries?'

'Er...'

'Not content with the old one, they have to chuck it away and build a new one in its image. Good God, this is like murdering Duncan, digging him up in the morning and telling him to eat his damn breakfast.'

'Yes, I see what...'

'You know when I first came to Britain? Nineteen sixty six,' he said. 'To London. I wanted to be a literary bohemian. Isn't that silly? Soho, Tavistock Square. Oscar Wilde, Dylan Thomas, E.M. Forster. All gone by that time. Finished. And the whole of the West is suffering from despair. But. The next thing I know – whoosh, despair is successful. All aboard the bandwagon. Kaftans, joss sticks, meditation. John Lennon on a lotus flower contemplating his penis. I am in a hall of distorting mirrors walking backwards. But you are wanting your tea.'

'Oh, that's...'

'I will tell you one thing though.' He stood up. 'Despair is no longer fashionable. Now, the British think they will attain eternal life by painting their arseholes red white and blue. Pardon my candour but this is a fact. I wrote a blank verse satirical poem on the subject the other day, which Dugdale was generous enough to find promising. Just one moment.'

He vanished through the bead curtain like a mongoose, and a conversation in muted but emphatic Hindi began coming through from the kitchen. The other voice, presumably the cook's, sounded as though it had just been dragged from a nice refreshing kip under the table. Sky glanced at me and exchanged a facial shrug, wearing his usual look of tired inscrutability, as though life were a spectable he found rather pleasantly tedious. He had abandoned the nude now, and was diluting the chili sauce with vinegar to produce a misty landscape of hills and clouds.

Mr Mukkarjee reappeared to announce with some triumph that tea would be along immediately. 'I wonder if you've read Salman Rushdie?' he added.

'Er . . .'

'Masterful,' he said. 'He can write the trousers off anyone. A wide range of influences, of course. Sterne, Rabelais, Joseph Heller. Henry Miller. Oh, good God. But look, are you sure you won't have a meal?'

'Well . . .'

'I mean,' he said. 'For the publishing profession, such a thing would of course be on the house. I hope you don't find the offer too obsequious.'

'Not at all.'

'Fine. I shall be honoured.'

'Actually, I was just thinking of ordering a meal anyway.'

'Oh, I wouldn't hear of it,' he said, striving valiantly to keep the despair out of his voice. 'No no no. This is on me.'

'Well.' The sense of guilt was excruciating. 'Thankyou.'

'However,' Mr Mukkarjee said testingly. 'Perhaps you could oblige me by giving me some change?'

'Change?'

'For the cigarette machine.'

'Oh of *course*.' I dug into my pocket to pile silver on the table.

Mr Mukkarjee reached forward to take the coins he needed between finger and thumb, smiled at me and just prevented himself running to the cigarette machine on the wall. As he fed coins into it he began hurling phrases towards the kitchen, and curt, mutinous monosyllables were volleyed back at him. Finally there came the sound of a pan hitting the stove from an apparent height of about three feet, and he smiled with satisfaction. He could of course have unlocked the machine and taken cigarettes any time he wanted; I supposed that like most of the chronically poor he vacillated between mad extravagance and massively self punitive ordeals of restraint which were just as illogical. On his way back, he collected a tray of tea from the kitchen.

'Allow me to be mother,' he said, settling happily back into his chair like a broody chicken. The teapot was of battered aluminium and the cups and saucers matched only inasmuch

143

as they had all once been the property of hotel chains. The tea was the colour of Ganges mud and very nice if you like that sort of thing which I do. Mr Mukkarjee passed the sugar and wondered if we didn't feel that Bernard Shaw was altogether too cerebral to be seen as a true artist. He added that it was difficult to take seriously a man who had kept his cherry till the age of twenty seven, then went on to speculate that his air of total certainty about everything might indicate that he had the mind of an adolescent virgin till the end of his life. The more I thought about that remark the truer it seemed and the more I was aware of the contrast between the substance of Mr Mukkarjee's *bons mots* and the gusty, childlike eagerness with which he delivered them. I supposed this was symptomatic of his own virginity, which was social; he had spent years having his best conversations with himself since he had never achieved the *milieu* that he wanted. This made him highly vulnerable and I was growing more and more annoyed with Dugdale for taking advantage of it. But Mr Mukkarjee thought he was a gentleman.

'A real gentleman should have a whiff of decadence, don't you agree?' he asked. 'He should be a bent umbrella. Have a gasper.' He unwrapped his packet of Park Drive with loving solemnity and pointed it towards us. Sky took one. 'He has other gentlemanly characteristics too,' Mr Mukkarjee said indulgently. 'For instance, not paying his bills.' He lit up.

'Oh dear.'

'Oh, it's of no importance,' he said airily. 'I'm a literary man myself. And he will make money, I can see that. Not the big time perhaps, but sufficient for rent, a few meals, what have you. Shirts.'

'Shirts?'

'He appears to borrow clothes.'

'Oh.'

'It doesn't matter in the least. In him, I can see, this is a kind of asceticism. Possessions – what are they?'

'Quite.'

'However.' He took in about half a cigarette in one long seething draw, and continued speaking with his breath held. 'I am concerned about him.'

'Why?'

'He has no business sense.' He beamed at me and killed about six passing flies in a cloud of smoke; it even seemed to be coming out of his ears. 'No get out there and knock 'em dead. He cannot promote himself.'

This is quite true in a sense. Dugdale might conceivably sell the Guildhall to a passing Aráb but he didn't have long term schemes to promote himself as such – his very destitution testified to it.

'I mean,' Mr Mukkarjee went on, 'who is this Bassett?'

'What?'

'A moment.' He got up in response to a growl from the kitchen, and shortly returned with a tin tray laden with saffron rice, poppadoms, chutney, vegetable curry and a meat curry which was a very dark red. *'Bon appétit,'* he said, ceremoniously removing from his arm what was either a tea towel or a floor cloth and dusting our plates with it before laying them down. He served the food himself, with some reverence, dividing a massive quantity between us. 'Do wade in. This is my own special recipe,' he said fondly. 'A rather warm vindaloo. I thought you might appreciate it.'

'You aren't joining us?'

'I have eaten.' He settled down happily to spectate.

I am still willing to swear that I could taste the first forkful before it touched my lips: at any rate it was instantly apparent that 'rather warm' testified to Mr Mukkarjee's love of English understatement. Or perhaps the meal itself represented a serious attempt on the part of the cook to kill us off before going back to sleep. The whole thing was made six times more excruciating by the necessity of giving Mr Mukkarjee vicarious pleasure while we ate.

'Good?' he asked eagerly.

I managed to say: 'Mmhh,' through my inflamed and quite possibly bleeding lips while Sky, who had actually swallowed some, gave a kind of muted death rattle, nodding his head. His normally deadpan features were as near being animated as I'd ever seen them.

'Have some chutney.' Mr Mukkarjee pushed it across and we fell on it in the hope of a cool taste. However it proved to consist principally of chillis and ginger with perhaps a smattering of snake poison. At first I had felt as though my taste buds were being systematically pulled out by the roots but now they were being obliterated wholesale. It was no longer possible to distinguish between the tears and the sweat which flowed down my face, and when I tried to wipe them away there was some curry sauce on my finger which burned my cheek.

I began very nearly to hallucinate; the most persistent impression was of being trapped in a small iron walled cabin in a burning ship, my brain slowly melting in the ubiquitous, steadily increasing heat. This nightmare was compounded when I reached for a poppadom to find it contained pepper, though by now it didn't seem to matter a hell of a lot. Anything a bit less abrasive than the curry would have been welcome. Broken glass for instance.

'But my God,' Mr Mukkarjee said, throwing up his hands. 'You are not drinking anything. We must have a noggin.'

'Noggin of what?' Sky wondered feebly as he dashed off.

'Any bloody thing,' I said, a remark which proved premature.

Mr Mukkarjee came back with three small glasses and an unmarked bottle of a clear liquid which was very faintly yellow. He gave each of us a brimful measure and stayed on his feet to knock his own back, downing it in one.

It turned out that Sky had been under the same hopeful misapprehension as me, that it was some sort of white wine. Had they still been working our noses might have told us differently, of course. We both followed suit.

It was very like trying to put a fire out with a can of petrol. I actually blacked out for a few seconds and came round thinking seriously about my heart. Mr Mukkarjee was standing there with bottle poised, radiating hospitality. I will own that at this point I was mean enough to wonder fleetingly if he might be some kind of malicious prankster – perhaps a latterday Thuggee. I put my hand over my glass rather firmly.

'I wonder if you've read *Fahrenheit 451*?' I asked.

It took him a second or two to get it, then he obligingly roared with laughter. 'You find it a little strong?'

'Strong?' Sky said. 'Christ. What *is* it?'

'It keeps a lot of people in Bombay very happy,' Mr

146

Mukkarjee said evasively. 'I've no licence but –' He flapped a hand contemptuously. 'This is a private party. To hell with them.'

'Something non alcoholic would be just as welcome,' I ventured.

'Yeah, like a bucket of water,' Sky said. 'Mr Mukkarjee, I really don't want to sound pushy but I think I'm going to die in a minute.'

'Oh my God, of course.' Suddenly galvanised by anxious concern Mr Mukkarjee rushed off to the kitchen, traded a few insults with the cook and shortly rushed back with a jug of iced fruit juice. I poured myself a glass and Sky seized the jug in both hands and drank about half of it; a slightly undignified struggle then ensued as I got it back to secure the rest of my share. After about three more jugs we began to feel relatively human. Mr Mukkarjee poured himself another noggin and sat down. 'I should have realised,' he said, raising his glass. 'This stuff is a little bracing when you aren't used to it.'

'How about the curry?' Sky asked him. 'Are you used to that?'

'What – *this* curry? Oh good God.' Mr Mukkarjee chuckled helplessly. '*I* don't eat *that*,' he said.

'No?'

'God bless your socks no. That stuff is hot enough to singe the hairs off your arsehole. *Nobody* in India likes it like that. But.' He tapped the side of his nose. 'I know the English taste. People come from miles around for my warm vindaloo.'

'What, you mean twice?'

'Oh, innumerable times. A lady journalist from London,' he said lasciviously, 'comes here to have it with me every time she is in Swansea. Pardon my *double entendre*. You know about this book of Dugdale's, of course.'

'Book?' I asked.

'His critical biography of Dylan Thomas. *The Fox in the Wave*. A good title, from one of Thomas's unpublished poems.'

'I didn't know there were any.'

'Well, an unfinished poem rather. You'll find it in the back of some biography or other. Dugdale's book will be *much* better. A biography of the works themselves, with the incidents of his life merely peripheral. I tell you, you are in on the ground floor of something good.'

'I suppose we are,' I said, realising that the only way out of this appalling fiction was forwards and that I now knew just how Macbeth felt about his wife. 'I shall be quite interested to see the manuscript, I must say.'

'Oh, there's no manuscript to look at yet,' he said. 'Not as such. But we have discussed the concept exhaustively. It is brilliant, I can tell you. The whole thing is in his head. He said he never puts pen to paper without taking a commission.'

'Right,' Sky said. 'Someone loses money every time he opens his mouth.'

'Er, yes,' Mr Mukkarjee said. 'But if you ask me he is talking to the wrong people. Why Bassett?'

'Why indeed.'

'This is what I was telling him. Bassett knows no one. Dugdale sells him the *world rights* on such a book for forty pounds. *Forty pounds.* I was telling him – why not ask me? I could have got you forty pounds just like that –' he snapped his fingers ' – if you had asked me. But now Dugdale's hands are tied. He cannot collect from anybody else.'

'I wouldn't put money on it,' Sky said.

'What? Yes, well, money is the thing isn't it?' Mr Mukkarjee said. 'Dugdale must deal with America. Direct. The Dragon Press, Abertawe Associates,' he said dismissively. 'What are they? The kind of people Bassett can come up with. They will print it up badly and sell about five copies to members of the Dylan Thomas Memorial Affiliation. I told him – we may as well bring it out ourselves. Pay the printers and bang – world rights. And I am designing the dust jacket already,' he said proudly, beginning to delve into his pockets. 'A moment.'

He began covering the table with a riot of unpaid bills, scraps of recipe, VAT demands, miscellaneous coloured photographs torn from magazines, and copies of probably unpublished letters to the press. ('Dear Sir, Accustomed as I am to the ineptitude of planning departments ...' '... The blatant hypocrisy of such a speech would be risible were it not inherently so tragic, or perhaps that word lends dignity where it does not rightly belong. In dreaming of rivers of blood, Mr Powell is having nightmares about himself . . .')

I began to feel I could relax a little. The whole thing was certainly a nuisance, but separating people from money on the strength of an unwritten book was not, except for a proven illiterate, an act of fraud. Unhappily this was not entirely the point.

'Ah, here we are,' Mr Mukkarjee said at length. He unfolded a piece of paper and held it close to his chest for a moment, saying: 'First I should explain to you that I am rather a noted calligraphist.'

'Uh huh?'

'So what you are going to see is not quite what it appears to be. It is in fact a copy of a reconstructed, original, and undiscovered poem by Dylan Thomas.'

'Oh.' I began to smell a rat. I'd been smelling them all evening, but I had an inkling that here at last was the real rat, the rat of rats, Mr Big, the rat we'd all been waiting for, rather than just another small time rat with a red herring in its mouth.

'And this is what makes the book so *hot*,' Mr Mukkarjee whispered, utterly misreading my expression. 'You see we *just* use the poem on the dustjacket. Say *nothing* about it in the text at all. Wait for some bright spark to notice it and *then* watch the fireworks. A literary scandal. Worldwide interest. Questions in Parliament.' His eyes gleamed. 'I can see it vividly.'

'Yes.' I could see it even more vividly, if anything.

'Just this on the outside, then, with the title written across it.' Mr Mukkarjee at last turned the paper towards us and showed me what I'd been dreading. Judging from memory, it was a hair raisingly accurate facsimile of a Thomas work sheet, by which I mean it erected small hairs up the back of my neck; the handwriting was precisely caught. The words I already knew. 'How should my wellspring cat/Electric lard within a mottled tomb of cancer/And the shouts of praise/Forsake etc.'

'Good?' he asked.

'Unfortunately, yes.'

149

'What?'

'Very. This seems to be a photostat copy.'

'Oh yes. Dugdale has the original. My original, shall we say. The *original* original is somewhere else entirely. You know that no one has ever seen it?'

'Very few people anyway.'

'Well quite. But do let me tell you a little of the history of the poem itself.'

'Yes please.'

'Well.' Mr Mukkarjee lowered his voice. 'This woman,' he said, sketching a shape in the air with his hands, which in conjunction with his sneeringly conspiratorial expression I took to mean unscrupulous and lewd, probably fat and drunk into the bargain. 'She is still living. Somewhere in Herefordshire. Thomas gave her this poem at an early age, subsequently forgot it and was never able to get it back. Can you believe that she paid him three flagons of brown ale and a ham sandwich? She liked to make him beg, you see, though she is stinking rich. Absolutely bloody stinking. The poem hangs, to this day, framed, on the wall of her private chapel. When he was young they had an infatuation. She used to make him dress as a priest and stand before the altar declaiming poetry. Meanwhile she lay on it in various guises. Sometimes a policewoman. Sometimes a schoolgirl, and so on. One can readily imagine the rest.'

'Don't tell me,' Sky said. 'They had a Satanic communion service with ham sandwiches and brown ale.'

'*Exactly*,' said Mr Mukkarjee. Then he frowned. 'But you must have been speaking to Dugdale already.'

'No no,' Sky said. 'Just guessing.'

'Oh ... Well yes of course, they did do some rather extravagant things. Pouring the brown ale over her naked buttocks, and so on.' He giggled. 'By that time, you see, quite a lot of ritual undressing will have gone on. Good God alive.' He rubbed his hands together vigorously. 'The *richness* of human nature. Anyway...'

'So how did Dugdale get hold of the text?' I asked.

'This is the bit I am coming to. *Real* poetic justice. The wheel of fortune comes around. The woman has a daughter...'

'This wouldn't be Dylan's daughter by any chance?' Sky asked.

'*Possibly*. No one knows for certain. And, as the girl grows up, there is much hostility between her and her mother. At the same time she is a real chip off the old block, you know, a right kinky little raver. And. When *she* grows up...'

'She and Dugdale...'

'Are *having it off* together. Precisely. You are way ahead of me again. This is how Dugdale learns about the poem's existence. So. One night when her mother is in a stupor, the girl steals the key to the chapel, copies down the poem, gives it to Dugdale and there we are.'

'Yes,' I said. 'Here we are.'

Mr Mukkarjee put away the poem in his pocket. 'But I'm afraid you may be too late.'

'So am I.'

'Dugdale is already gone to London to rustle up some publishers. I lent him the fare.'

'*Oh.*'

'I thought that perhaps you might be the first wave,' Mr Mukkarjee said. 'Still, perhaps you do still have an interest in a piece of the action. Yes?'

'Er...'

'In this case I must tell you right away to put it on the table.'

'What?'

'Money.'

'Oh I see.'

'I mean,' he said. 'Dugdale and I have decided. No one is going to take us for an arsehole any more. Enough is enough.'

'Yes. Yes quite.' I felt terribly sad. Mr Mukkarjee had fed us and confided in us for the same reason he had let himself be taken in by Dugdale: social starvation, the need to believe in something greater than the dour reality of loneliness and failure. Now he was doing his hard-nosed entrepreneurial number as a sop to his image of himself as a dynamic operator.

He mistook my silence for cunning and said: 'Look. I'm not asking you to say how much money you want to put up, at this juncture. Just to remember that a piece of the action is going to cost. But there will be plenty of action, let me tell

151

you. A lot of people will be getting it *right* up the arsehole.'

'Yes. Yes I can just picture that.' I stood up.

'Oh, but you're not going?'

'I'm afraid I really must. Thanks for dinner, it's been really . . .'

'Oh, not at all.' He shook our hands. 'You are most welcome. I'm not just a businessman, you know. I'm far more interested in literature and good conversation. But perhaps you'd like to call and see Dugdale when he returns.'

'I can't wait.'

'Excellent.' He nipped in front of us to open the door. For some reason it was a lot easier getting out of the place than getting in; perhaps there were two doors. 'Call in a few days' time,' he said, beaming at us as we left. 'We'll get out the grog and make a night of it. *Au revoir.*'

The door slammed and was elaborately locked. Sky looked at it, looked up and down the booming, windy street and the streams of traffic passing with a homicidal swish, gazed briefly at his shoes and looked up at me.

'Oh dear,' he said.

# 26

'Oh dear,' said Dugdale. He dabbed at his sweaty cheeks with the sleeve of his culture-bashing mackintosh. 'Do we *have* to use that word?'

'What word?'

'Fraud. It's so aggressive. Coarse. So lamentably unsubtle.'

'Nevertheless I think you'll find,' I said, 'that the Director of Public Prosecutions is reasonably fond of using it. He's a man of lamentably coarse, unsubtle and aggressive habits. Like locking people up.'

'What? Oh, but I mean *surely* . . .' He rocked slightly in his chair, the other side of my desk, luxuriating a little hesitantly in his tenure of this portion of the safe, congenial, unlocked up world, waiting for me to endorse his image of himself as emphatically not really a member of the criminal classes. I decided to put the knife in.

'You know that look old cons get?' I asked him. 'The drawn, blank face, the grey skin? The deep-etched downward lines beside the mouth? Some hold out against it longer than others, but once it's stamped on their faces it's there for life. It comes from being tucked up in a tiny cell in an atmosphere of hatred, sodomy, religion. The smell of lavatories. Not knowing when some other con's going to turn nasty, or if six screws are suddenly going to burst in and bounce you around the cell for some breach of prison etiquette three days ago. And hopelessness. That's the main thing – complete hopelessness. The crushing of the soul. You see in my opinion, any prison sentence becomes effectively a death sentence after a certain point, but the length of time it might take for this point to be reached varies widely. It depends on temperament, resilience, age, all sorts of things. I'd give you an outside limit of about six weeks.'

'Yes I see.' Dugdale gazed wanly at the desk, as though on the blotter there were a crystal ball which had only now, after a lifetime of obscurity, cleared to reveal the nature of his sins. This made me feel so exactly like Badger reprimanding Mr Toad that I wanted to laugh.

'You'd better give me a full account of what you've been doing.' I pointed my pen at him and slipped the safety catch. 'Precisely what you've discussed with whom, and how much it's cost them.' I drew towards me a sheet of paper with the HMG logo at the top; these do tend to impress people with a sense of gravity.

'Yes of *course*,' Dugdale said. 'What a very good idea. Where shall we start?'

'Anywhere you like. Whom did you see in London?'

'London?'

'Oh *Dugdale*.'

'I did make a few phone calls to London,' he offered. 'But when I thought about it, actually going there didn't seem necessary. Except to satisfy Mr Mukkarjee's romantic inclinations.'

'Not to mention clobbering him for the fare.'

'That too,' he conceded, as a sop to my lamentable vulgarity in mentioning it. 'But he thinks it's smoky London paved with poems, you see? Even though he's been there. The other image is stronger than mere experience. He probably pictured me travelling up in the lavatory, like Samuel Bennet in *Adventures in the Skin Trade*. Getting conned into the bath by Polly Dacey. The whole thing.'

'Samuel Bennet was nineteen,' I objected.

'Is,' Dugdale corrected me. 'The character is timeless.'

'Well anyway – so you boozed the fare.'

'Some of it,' he said. 'I should hate you to get it wrong. I mean you're issued with that paper under oath or something, aren't you?'

I looked at him sharply but he fazed me off. 'Yes, that's true in a sense,' I said. 'Every sheet must be accounted for and I can't destroy one without written permission from a judge.' I wrote DUGDALE in a large hand at the top, underlining it twice. 'Now the first thing,' I said. 'Did anyone in London bite?'

'Bite?'

I sighed. 'Have you separated anyone in London from any money?'

'Oh no. No. Not money as such.'

'What's as such mean?'

'It means as such. One publisher did express a tentative willingness to pay money.'

'In the event of what?'

'Delivery of my critical biography,' he said. 'I've been planning it for years. Didn't Mr Mukkarjee mention it?'

'Yes, but was that all?'

'Yes of course.' He seemed genuinely puzzled. 'George, what do you mean?'

'Look, Dugdale, I know what Thomas's handwriting looked like. I've seen pictures of his worksheets. Mr Mukkarjee's calligraphy is certainly uncanny and what he showed me the other day frightened the life out of me.'

'... *Oh*,' he said. '*You* thought...'

'I sure did.'

'*Honestly*, George. But that's simply for the dustjacket.

154

Surely Mr Mukkarjee told you that too.'

'Oh yes,' I said. 'He also told me about a private chapel in Herefordshire and some woman having her bum anointed with brown ale. So what am I supposed to believe?'

'Look,' he said. 'No one is going to be asked to believe the poem's genuine.'

'Except Mr Mukkarjee. He thinks the brown ale woman has it on the chapel wall.'

'An expedient fabrication,' he said. 'The thing is – you remember that evening when we had dinner at Sky's?'

'Very vaguely.'

'Well, before we came to write the poem, you might recall that Sky and I had a long argument about the nature of originality. And since then I've been thinking about it. That's the key to the whole book. The mere existence of that poem on the dustjacket will demonstrate both Thomas's originality *and* the fact that originality is imitable once it's been brought into being.'

'And no mention in the book of Hereford, or buttocks or brown ale?'

'Positively none.'

'So what do you tell Mr Mukkarjee?'

'Anything. Mrs Brown Ale Bum forged it herself, only she's powerful and litigious so we can't mention it. Or what have you. Unless you insist that I disappoint him with the truth.'

'No, I . . . suppose there's no need.' I found I had been sketching a hanged man. He rather resembled somebody. Me. I overscored it heavily. 'What I do insist you do,' I said, 'is pay him back the fare money.'

'Tenfold,' Dugdale said. 'Provided you'll let me get on with things and stop holding me back. I might remind you George, that I now have no income whatever.'

'*Alright*. But there are things I need to know. For instance, who's Bassett?'

'A problem,' Dugdale said. 'I think we're going to have to buy him off. How do you know about him?'

'I spoke to him on the blower. And I must say he didn't strike me as very buy-offable.'

'Perhaps not.'

'And while we're on the subject I *don't* like being described as your partner.'

'I'm *sorry*, George. It's just that I haven't got a phone.'

'There is also a somewhat obvious psychological explanation,' I said. 'But I think I'll leave it out.'

'Is there? Well anyway – Bassett, since you enquire about him, is Ritchie's man, for whom we both now perform small services from time to time. In many ways I find him a rather endearing figure and he has the right attitude to drink.'

'You mean he buys one round after another?'

'If you wish to put it that way, yes. And he has, like so many people turn out to have, a keen interest in Dylan Thomas. Now since my critical biography has been uppermost in my mind recently, we got to talking about it. And since Bassett likes to make money, is adventurous, knows a printer, and since I'm always in need of money, well – the next thing I knew I'd signed.'

'For *forty quid*?'

'That's just for an option,' he said airily. 'But it was only after *that* that I mentioned the whole thing to Mr Mukkarjee, and discovered his wonderful flair for handwriting, and we thought of this promotional dustjacket and the pair of us started getting bigger ideas.'

'So – does Bassett know Mr Mukkarjee at all?'

'Shouldn't think so. Why?'

'He was very wound up about something. Seemed to think you might be making deals behind his back.'

'Oh. Oh dear,' Dugdale said. 'Well perhaps I mentioned the whole thing to Ritchie or someone. Yes I believe I did.'

'That was less than discreet,' I said. 'So you've got Bassett on your neck. What's the nature of this contract you have with him anyway? What does it actually say?'

'Er, it gives him the option on any original and unpublished work by or about Dylan Thomas that I might have in my possession.'

'*By* or about?'

'Yes.'

'And it's original *and* unpublished. Not *or*?'

'Correct.'

'But you dated the contract?'

'No I didn't,' he said. 'It's just a sheet of paper.'

'So if you do produce a book and it's published elsewhere, the contract's void?'

'Precisely,' he said, smirking inscrutably.

I sighed heavily, screwed up the sheet of paper and threw it in the bin.

'You forgot to ask the judge.'

'*Shut up*, Dugdale,' I said. 'Just pick up your briefcase and your devious brain and piss off, will you?'

# 27

'No,' Pollock said. 'I'm sorry. We are not at liberty to take that view at all. We must, where circumstances indicate, presume earnings. It is then up to the claimant in question to disprove this. If I were to believe every Tom, Dick and Harry with a hard luck story I'd be out of a job.'

'That would be awful.'

'Anyway there is this other clause, Mr Waddington,' he said, a gratifyingly stung look on his cheap, bullyingly ambitious dial, leaning forward uncertainly for emphasis. It was wonderful to watch his discomfort as he did this: knowing he was due I had come in early with a tenon saw in my briefcase, and taken half an inch off the two front legs of the chair; he'd been sliding and lurching ever since he sat down. 'And this clause states that if a person perform for another any service for which that other person might normally expect to pay, appropriate benefit will be deducted anyway. And you can't tell me lecturers usually work for nothing.'

'D'you seriously mean,' I asked, 'that if one man out of a job digs the garden for another one, and gets his windows cleaned in return, they could both lose money?'

'If they made a habit of it, yes,' he said, folding his arms. Since his feet were braced akimbo to restrain his sliding bum he looked like a Cossack dancer with piles. 'Cases have been known.'

I was speechless. Reason was clearly powerless against such gloating illogicality, gleaned with sly facility from one ministerial broadcast after another: how easily types like him crawled out of the woodwork with a little encouragement. I wanted to pick up the glass ashtray and smash it into his face.

'But since it appears that this, er, lectureship of his is finished,' Pollock went on, 'then in due time, provided this is established, he'll be able to make a fresh claim.'

'And thus become eligible for one of your rehabilitation camps?'

'Quite possibly, yes.'

'Alright thankyou,' I said, not looking at him. 'Your remarks are noted.' I allowed a pause to develop and looked up. 'Run along, sonny. If I were you I'd either get a real job or give up working altogether. That is all.' I looked down again and busied myself casually with Dugdale's file. I heard Pollock trying to start up his voice in reply; finally he said 'Right' in a strangled tone and left the room.

I felt better. Insulting people is in any case one of life's vastly underestimated pleasures. I closed the door behind him and got out my tenon saw. Two erasers under the front legs had sufficed for those visitors who were not Pollock, but it was time to even up the chair again.

'Five thirty two, Mr Waddin'ton,' Joan said, bustling in. 'And I want to – *what* are you doin' wi' that *chair*?'

'Isn't it obvious?'

'Sawin' pieces off it,' she said. 'With a saw. That is Home Office property.'

'Perhaps you'd like to send these slivers of wood to the Home Secretary with my compliments,' I suggested. 'That bloody chair has been wobbling for weeks. Until such time as somebody discovers money again and they start buying new furniture, we must all do the best we can.' I thrust my briefcase under my arm and made to leave.

'And wharrabout that mess on the floor, look?'

'That will give the cleaners something to do.'

'Any'ow you can't go yet,' she said as I reached the door. 'There's two gentlemen to see you.'

158

'Gentlemen? Who?'

'*I* dunno. From the medical profession. And I'd be obliged if you would conduct business with them *outside* the premises. It is now very near five thirty five. I have a meal to prepare. My mother is a woman of regular habits and she's not well.'

In the outer office were two goons wearing white coats, white paper caps and gauze masks.

'George Waddington?' one asked, indistinctly through the gauze.

'Yes? Who the hell are you?'

'Please come with us.'

'I'll accompany you to the door,' I said, incredulity wrestling with mild alarm. 'We all have to leave the building.'

They walked either side of me down the steps into Mansel Street. I began to think I was hallucinating. At the kerb was a white Commer van with 'SANITY PATROL' in big red letters on the side. At the pavement they each grabbed an elbow.

I started struggling. The van's rear doors were opened from within and I was pushed back to sit on the tail, lashing out blindly with my fists and feet. I'd dropped my briefcase and one of them picked it up and threw it in the van.

Joan passed, not five feet away, with a large shopping bag, peering around the van to find a gap in the traffic. Stolidly intent on crossing the road she glanced in my direction once, registered fleeting disapproval and was gone.

They managed to get my feet, so I was swung round right inside the van, then they piled in on top of me and the doors were slammed. Someone jumped in the driver's door and we started.

Pinned at the bottom of the heap, I managed to get my teeth into a hand. There was a cry.

The other one said: 'You are George Waddington. You live at 69 Matabele Road. Your existence is an illusion. You are an insane person and we are going to cleanse your mind.'

I began to recognise the voice. I feigned exhaustion till I felt their grip relax, then I got a hand free and clawed at the nearest face mask.

Sometimes one's National Service is useful. My unarmed

159

combat instructor always said that with real hard nuts you go for the body and cause injury, but your average assailant was much more worried about his face. And these were not real hard nuts.

'Ow!' Slugge said. He reeled back and pulled off his face mask, clutching his torn cheek.

Alex made to pin me down again but I got a knee into his nuts, hard enough to roll him off me momentarily.

'Perhaps an injection is in order,' Mark said. He was driving. 'A little tranquilliser. We are trying to help you, George. You'll see it our way in the end.'

Slugge was fumbling with a medical kit. I got a hand in his face and slammed his head into the van wall. Alex lunged for me again and I dodged him, grabbed a small fire extinguisher from its clip and brought it up into his stomach. Then as we pulled up at some lights I rabbit punched Mark with the extinguisher and he slumped forward.

I grabbed his hair, extinguisher in the other hand. It was a small $CO_2$ spray made of cast iron.

'If you don't open the doors now,' I said, 'I'm going to pulverise his skull.'

'Let him go,' Mark gasped. 'Just let him go.'

I kept the extinguisher till I was out on the road, then exchanged it for my briefcase and beat it. The traffic had started up again and I nearly got run over.

I was right out along the Oystermouth Road by the beach, opposite Singleton Park. I straightened my tie and started checking myself for bruises, of which there didn't seem to be a lot; they had been far more inhibited about causing injury than I was. It gradually became easier to breathe normally. After a couple of minutes a taxi came past, and I got it home.

Sophie was there, draped over the bay window sofa. I got out some elderberry wine, poured her some and drank two glasses myself before I felt capable of recounting my adventure.

'Oh dear,' she said. 'It must be their latest thing. I am sorry.'

'Why are you sorry?'

'I just am. I feel it must have happened because of me.'

'So do I. What do you mean by their latest thing?'

'They do that kind of thing,' she said. 'As I told you. They have odd notions about audience participation.'

'You mean they go around virtually kidnapping people without getting arrested?'

'It used to surprise me as well,' she said. 'But not any more. Of course people generally know they're supposed to be taking part in a theatrical event, whereas you didn't. But they'll take all sorts of crap. I think they feel chosen. And if you train a camera on them there's no limit. You could get them to walk into a gas chamber singing the National Anthem if they thought it was going to be on television. Of course from Mark's point of view, he's teaching people valuable lessons. Sometimes they go around being security forces, picking people up for suspected terrorism and grilling them. Or they'll pretend to be the IRA questioning traitors. They take people out and shoot them.'

'What?'

'I mean pretend to shoot them, of course. It's all to do with expanding people's awareness. This latest thing of theirs must have to do with the political implications of insanity, and what do we mean by sane, and all that kind of thing. That injection will have been harmless of course.'

'Not if an air bubble got in the spike,' I said. 'They could kill people.'

'Tell that to the Arts Council,' she said, yawning. 'They think Mark's the cat's whiskers.'

'I thought the Arts Council was skint,' I said. 'They must be the last subsidised theatre group in the country.'

'They are, practically,' Beau said, making me jump. He had been stretched out invisibly behind an armchair, trying either to meditate, calm down or straighten his back. 'That's why we can hardly get any money out of them. Theatre of Conflict are putting something on in the Fringe, as a matter of fact.'

'Oh?'

'Mmh. Some convoluted version of *Under Milk Wood*, incorporating his original concept of it as 'The Town That Was Mad'. The programme copy's a load of pretentious crap.'

'So it sounds as though they've started rehearsing,' Sophie

said. 'George, there's someone on the doorstep.'

'Who?'

'Dunno,' she said. 'He looks rather like a bookie.'

The letterbox rattled just as I reached the front door.

'Bassett,' Bassett said. His feet, check trousers falling loosely over well made shoes, were planted with care. His arms hung loose as if available for any contingency and his head loomed slightly forward from his thick shoulders. He was partially drunk, or punch drunk, or this stance was his habitual demonstration of his approach to life and he didn't realise it was overdone; I took all this in very quickly. 'An' I wants Dinsdale,' he added.

'You mean Dugdale?'

'Ah.' He made no move to thrust past me, but somehow this suggested confidence rather than lack of it.

'Well I'm afraid,' I said, 'that Dugdale doesn't live here. You might have been misinformed.'

His right arm began very slightly swinging, eloquent of an ability to grab me by the throat any time it wanted. He was waiting for me to go on.

'To begin with,' I said. 'I'm not in fact his partner. I'm afraid he misled you.'

'Then who . . .?'

'His Probation Officer.'

'Oh.' He backed off a bit. He didn't exactly move; it was more as though the whole of his skin contracted slightly. Then he recovered and said: 'You sure?'

'Of course I am.' I produced my HMG identification. This time he did move. His feet shuffled.

'Well, I dunno,' he said. He sighed and shook his head, glanced round at the sea and back again. 'So this guy's a total bloody con artist.'

'Oh no, not entirely,' I said. 'To the best of my knowledge he really is writing a critical biography of Dylan Thomas.'

'He never said nothin' about probation,' Bassett said. 'What's it for?'

'Shoplifting,' I extemporised. 'But I really shouldn't worry. A contract is a contract. It guarantees you some share of whatever eventually happens.'

'But tha's not the point,' he said. 'I 'ad a printer lined up

162

and everything. An' I mean we know – stuff to do wi' Dylan Thomas is worth money nowadays. People are interested. *I'm* interested.' He tapped his chest. 'If I could juss purrit into words by Christ the book I could write. An' this Dungdale is an educated man. Well – it seemed ideal. But then 'e starts carryin' on, talking to people all over the place. 'E's gunna do this thing with the bloody book and that thing – publish it in London, all sorts of stuff about some bloody poem. Never said nothin' to *me* about no poem. Point is *I* got a contract with 'im,' Bassett said. 'So *I* wants to know wha's goin' on. That's all I'm sayin'.'

'I think the best thing you can do is go and talk to him.'

'Course it bloody is. Tha's why I'm standin' yere.'

'Try the Shahgbhag, Alexandra Road,' I said. 'He has a room there.'

'Thank you,' he said, leaving. 'We're beginnin' to talk some bloody sense now.'

I shut the door and stood in the hall chewing my lip, replaying the conversation in my head. Aggressive people who are impressed by one's semi-legal status tend to have one thing in common. Form. I got out my address book and phoned an old colleague of mine, a retired police sergeant called Joe Crunch who lived up in Waurn Wen somewhere, in a dark rambling house full of boxing trophies, dry rot spores and grandchildren. It took three of these, in relays to bring him to the phone.

'Bassett,' he said, wheezing and bellowing and churning the name around like a plug of tobacco. 'Bassett . . . now that does ring a bell.'

'Not quite sure where he lives,' I said, 'but I imagine it's somewhere out your way or beyond.'

'*Oh*. That's it. I got 'im now. Charlie Bassett.'

'That's him.'

'Been going straight for years, boy. Got a nice little business. Scrap iron, roofing contracts, a bit of undertaking. Got sons working for him and all, see? *Very* quiet and above board. For years. Used to be a hard man, mind.'

'Really?'

'Oh ah,' Joe said. 'Terrible. Then he finished up doing a ten in Parkhurst and that changed 'im. I was on that case, I remember. First time we'd really managed to nail 'im, see? Shook 'im up, like.'

'What was the charge?'

'Manslaughter. Coudn't prove intent, see George. Well fair enough too, maybe this other feller did come after 'im. Fair play to the man. There was rivalry involved somewhere, that was obvious. And this other feller'd broke in, see? Charlie was in the 'ouse. Makin' a sandwich in the kitchen. Killed 'im with the breadknife.'

# 28

Mr Mukkarjee got beaten up. I felt dreadful about it because it happened as a direct result of my telling Bassett where to find Dugdale. The trouble arose partly because he didn't, which promoted a feeling of irritation which was greatly compounded when Mr Mukkarjee called him a bullnecked philistine pig.

He was still visibly proud of this epithet, clinging to it to try and compensate for the smashed crockery and the bruises on his cheek and the fact that he was now without a cook. Evidently the cook had reacted to Bassett's presence by hiding in a cupboard, and afterwards they had had a vociferous argument which ended either with the cook's being sacked or walking out. At any rate he had now gone, minus a fortnight's wages which Mr Mukkarjee didn't have anyway. There had been no customers for three days. Mr Mukkarjee gave me a cup of tea and sat the other side of the table with an air of subdued introspection, a pair of glasses mended with Elastoplast balanced on his swollen nose, reading a back number of *The Sporting Life* and frowning thoughtfully.

'Do you ever gamble, I wonder?' he asked me.

'No,' I said emphatically. 'Not any more.'

'I see.' He rubbed his forehead and leaned forward to sip

some tea. I wondered if he had any cigarettes and whether to offer to buy him some. 'But you know it seems to me that one should take a sporting go, somehow,' he said, sitting back and folding up the paper. 'I mean all this clinging on to a squalid little bit of security is all very negative. I feel I should have been a far more adventurous fellow. All my life. But I have hoarded my small pence of experience and my little bit of an income, dreaming about transfiguration through art, and so on. All this is very enervating. Do you have any ambitions of that sort, or did you ever?'

'Sculpture, as a matter of fact,' I said. 'I've always wanted to sculpt. Actually I've just started.'

'This is interesting.'

'Is it?'

'Oh yes.'

'I don't know that it is,' I said, sighing. 'It just feels dead. I feel more dead than one of my bits of wood at the moment. Perhaps it's better just to dream.'

'Oh no it isn't,' he said with feeling. 'This is what I have been realising. One must act. This will either lead on to something or kill off the dream. Both these things are better. Unresolved dreams are poison,' he said. 'Sheer poison.'

'Perhaps you're right,' I said. 'Listen – Dugdale hasn't been trying to persuade you to gamble, has he?'

'Good God no,' Mr Mukkarjee said. 'It was me that persuaded him.'

'Oh I see.' I laughed.

'This is funny?'

'Of course it is,' I said. 'He lost. It serves him right. He's always talking other people into things.'

'I see,' he said ponderously. 'I see. But he would not have lost if he had listened to me properly. Look here.' He searched through the paper for the page he wanted. 'This horse,' he said, tapping its name in the list and showing it to me. 'Pogson's Little Fancy. Thirty three to one. It won that race. I *knew* it was going to. They had been holding the damn thing back all through the Flat Season, then suddenly they let it go. I knew it. Dugdale cannot properly have understood my system.'

'No,' I said. 'He was backing greyhounds.'

165

Mr Mukkarjee winced; turf snobbery runs deep.

'But what system is it?' I asked. 'You mean an ability to pick outsiders?'

'Oh no no no. That's just a little gift of mine,' he said. 'A system is basically a means of increasing one's stake to cover losses, and so on. Mathematics pure and simple. The horses you choose to back are another matter entirely. Of course the better you are at choosing them the more you win. Or the more *often* you win.'

'Forgive me if this question's intrusive,' I said. 'But if you're good at it why are you poor?'

'Because I can handle everything except myself,' he said, smiling. 'Two pounds on a horse and I get palpitations. I'm afraid it might affect my judgement. So I pretend. This is what I mean, why I castigate myself for being unadventurous. I note everything down, what I might have staked on what horse, and then wins or losses when I read the results. Do you know that last Handicap Season I won forty three thousand pounds?' he said proudly. 'And that's starting with a fiver. Oh, dear oh dear.'

'But Mr Mukkarjee that's awful,' I said. 'And are you sure you didn't cheat?'

'Positive,' he said. 'I'm very conscientious about it. That's the really awful part.'

'And you started with a fiver?'

'A fiver. I backed a few long shots, mind you,' he said. 'With real money I doubt if I would have dared.'

'All the same, you know how to win. Look, you really must do something about this.'

'But what?' He spread his hands, palm upward, in a gesture which reminded me of Hindu sculpture. 'They are cutting off the electricity next week,' he said. 'I am due in court soon to discuss the rates. I have enough unpaid bills to redecorate the restaurant. I have twenty two pence in my pocket. I know because I counted it half an hour ago. So *what* am I to do?'

'You're being negative again,' I told him. 'You yourself said just now that one must act and either kill the dream or succeed.'

'So perhaps I can sell the tables and chairs,' he said with wistful sarcasm. 'How much d'you think they'll fetch?'

'About two quid,' I said. 'No, that's obviously no good.' I was trying to think of a way to give him a little money without this being obvious. 'Look,' I said, taking out my wallet. I put a fiver on the table. 'Half each, right? I mean you can pay me back by giving me half your winnings for the first week if you like.'

'Oh no. No,' he said, shaking his head. 'This is quite out of the question. What if I were to lose?'

'I wouldn't care. Mr Mukkarjee I *insist* you take it. You've nothing else to hope for. Don't you see? Please don't think Dugdale represents any sort of a way out. He'll bring you nothing but trouble.'

'What?' he said, bristling. 'What do you mean by that? Please explain.'

'Dugdale's a con man,' I said. 'I couldn't bear to tell you the last time I came. And I've nothing to do with publishing whatever. I'm his Probation Officer. I called this evening because he didn't show up for his weekly appointment and I don't know where he is.'

'Neither do I. I haven't seen him for two days. I imagined he must be hiding from Bassett. But good God, d'you mean he's a criminal?'

'Not exactly, no,' I said. 'That's what makes him such a bloody nuisance. Out and out crooks have the virtue of being predictable, even trustworthy within certain rather obvious limits. It's all a matter of professionalism. I've no doubt that Dugdale is quite sincere in his intention to produce the definitive critical biography, though I don't know how high I'd rate its chances of being published, or its chance of selling much if it were. But the thing is that halfway through it all he'll get talking to somebody else and some other scheme will pop into his head.'

'I have noticed,' Mr Mukkarjee said, nodding. 'He is a rather inspired bullshit artist.'

'He's not slavishly addicted to the truth, no.'

Mr Mukkarjee sat back and thought about this. Behind his battered features thoughts were realigning themselves like the digits on a fruit machine, perhaps producing some new digits altogether. He was emerging from the immobility of shock and humiliation to some kind of decision. 'And I suppose,' he

167

said, 'he wrote this damn poem himself or something?'

'Something like that.'

Mr Mukkarjee chuckled. 'It's damn good anyway,' he said. 'Good luck to him.'

'And what about you?'

'Yes. Well. Indeed. That is more difficult,' he said.

'Mr Mukkarjee you can't just give up,' I said. 'That'll mean they've won. The red white and blue meanies, Bassett, Mrs Thatcher – everybody. You're going to die in the end anyway. In the meantime you must pick up that money.'

'Oh no I cannot,' he said, shrinking away from it. 'I cannot possibly.'

'Well I'm not putting it back in my wallet.' I stood up. 'Look.' I tore a sheet out of my notebook and wrote down my address. 'Here's where to send the winnings.'

'If there are any,' he said, holding his head in both hands and gazing apprehensively at the money on the table. 'I might get an attack of the jitterbugs, walk into the damn bookie's shop and back the wrong horse.'

'Not if you pick them beforehand and start cautiously,' I said. 'And as I said, I don't care. Please take it.'

'You know, I am very touched,' he said. 'Very very touched ... Alright. God *damn* it. Nothing venture.'

'Precisely.'

He put the money in his breast pocket, carefully, as though it were delicate or hot. Then he smiled broadly and stood up to pump my hand. It was very affecting. 'Good *God* yes,' he said, his blood now practically boiling with enthusiasm. 'I must go and get an up to date *Sporting Life* and study some damn form. I really am most grateful.'

'Don't be.' I made for the door. 'It might affect your judgement.'

'Oh yes,' he said, coming to let me out. 'I must guard against the jitterbugs. Perhaps a little grog before I step into the bookie's.'

'Give some to the horse.'

'Yes.' He laughed. 'Or indeed the bookie. This is a splendid thing you have done,' he said, pleasingly eager for me to be gone so he could begin studying form, perhaps put on a pin-stripe suit and polka-dot tie while he was about it.

'Splendid. *Au Revoir.*'

I walked off thinking how easy it was to be someone else's lucky star, impossible to be one's own.

Ritchie was out. Sally wasn't quite sure when he'd be back, but thought probably in about twelve months' time.

'Oh *no*,' I said. 'But I saw him this afternoon. When was he nicked?'

'Later on, must've been,' she said. 'Come in a minute.'

'I'm really looking for someone else,' I said. 'I wanted to ask Ritchie about somebody called Bassett.'

'Bassett?' she said. 'Don't mention that bloody name in yere. That's why Ritchie've been done.'

'Oh?'

'Ah. Siddown,' she said. 'Ritchie was nickin' things for Bassett and passing them on. For money. I told 'im,' she said, shaking her head. 'I bloody told 'im.'

'What sort of things?'

'Expensive ones. Cameras, tape recorders, video. Right out of 'is league, see?'

'Good God alive. So that's what he was doing for Bassett.'

'No, not entirely,' she said. 'He run a few errands as well, like. Done a bit of hobbling with the roofing and that. But then Bassett's on to 'im to nick things. Well. The money was handy, Mr Waddin'ton, I don't mind confessin' that to you. But I was on at 'im all the time to pack it in.'

'I hope Bassett's been arrested too.'

'No,' she said.

'But you will be giving evidence?'

'I'm scared to, Mr Waddin'ton,' she said. 'Honest. And that don't mean they'll believe me any'ow. There's no proof, see. They never talked to each other when I was around. I never saw 'em pass money or goods or nothin'.'

'Do you have any idea where he lives?'

'No.'

'This all looks pretty bad,' I said. 'If I'm going to appear as a character witness I can't make dark allusions to Bassett if there's no other evidence to back it with.'

'Well that's too bad,' she said. 'It's juss too bloody bad. He can serve 'is time and tha's it. Thank God I'm not bloody pregnant.'

I had to admire her primitive stoic honesty. Nobody else in her position could have faced it so well. The living room of the flat already testified to an implacable capacity for enhancing life at its most direct level. Some fresh paint, a carpet, unobtrusively comfortable armchairs, a picture or two. The place was a human dwelling now.

'D'you know if he's been asked to cough to a TIC?' I asked.

'Wha?' Sally said; I'd dragged her out of some train of thought or other.

'Have they tried to con him into thinking things'll be easier for him if he asks for three hundred previous offences to be taken into consideration?'

'Oh ah, they did,' she said. 'But 'e 'aven't. Not so daft as he looks, is he?'

'No. So what was he pulled for today?'

'Coupla video tapes it was.'

'That's not too bad then. Though with his record . . . I'll do what I can, though it may not be much. Has he got a lawyer?'

'Ah,' she said. 'A good one. I got on to 'im. I got the legal aid forms and all.'

'That's good.' I stood up. 'I've got to go now. I'm sorry about this.'

'Why?'

'Because I like you,' I said, breaking every rule in the book. 'I like Ritchie as well.'

'Bloody waster.'

'You live with him.'

'I can't 'elp my nature, can I?' she said simply. 'Twelve months, Duw. I'll go out of my cowin' mind.'

'So I'll see you in court.'

'Yeah, I 'spec so,' she said wearily. 'Tara.'

The lift being buggered as ever I took the staircase, eloquent of the scatology and psychopathology of tower block folk art. The basic theme of this was that one faction was going to kill another one on the basis that they ate shit. Otherwise people had written their names in huge letters, as though afraid that without this magic they would disappear. On the outside walls of the block, the same hands had with marginally more care daubed up messages of support for Her

Majesty on the occasion of her Jubilee, and wished all the very best to Charles and Di. There was something obscene and offensive in these faded sentiments, like the details of a tacky affair dragged through a divorce court so that you wondered why the participants had bothered in the first place. I abruptly abandoned my search for Dugdale and drove home pursued by a weird and misanthropic melancholy: I went straight to bed.

Sophie climbed in at about midnight and woke me up. She drew me out of a dream like a genie being charmed from a bottle, into a warm and hectic conversation of body language, lifting me up and obliterating me with her customary careless grace. In the drifting glow afterwards some image from my dream came back to nag me with a half seen dread. It seemed to be a snakeskin. I found myself thinking about the years of wasted life strewn behind me like takeaway cartons. The sense of oceanic luxury evaporated.

I sat up on my elbows. There had been no new dawn in my life. Just Indian Summer, one of Death's little jokes.

My fidgeting had pulled Sophie into wakefulness and she lit a cigarette.

'I wonder how long it'll be before you leave,' I said, stroking her back.

'Oh, come on George,' she said, choking on a mouthful of smoke and pulling away from me. 'Shut up,' she added. 'Just shut up.'

'I'm sorry,' I said. 'I can't help thinking about it sometimes.'

'Well, take a cold shower or something. I mean *I* don't know, darling,' she said, turning over to face me. 'What the hell did you have to ask me for?'

'Some self destructive compulsion perhaps.' I put my arm round her and cradled her head. 'Who knows? But you're not going to stay for ever, are you?'

'What's for ever mean?'

'It means till death.'

'Yes I know,' she said. 'But the death of what?'

I said: 'Ah', since clearly she had said everything. Perhaps it would be best if I died, tomorrow, now, in her arms in about ten minutes' time. Then we should still be attached, and my ghost could be usefully employed watching over her. She had age after age of life to get through, with Christ knew what horrors to supervene around her. She was the really tragic figure and I was just some sort of clown. She had a charm and vital power which raised the level of life around her but brought her nothing: she was just blowing through, carried on some dark inner wind to perdition.

'I dunno though,' she said languidly. 'I do have little contingency escape plans I suppose.'

'Like a bank robber?'

'Sort of.' She shifted against me and reached over to stub out her cigarette in the ashtray by the bed. 'It started when I was living with Mark,' she said, settling back again. 'Since then I've always had a fund and kept my passport handy.'

'Ready to go where?'

She shrugged. 'Paris,' she said. 'Barcelona. Where do people go? Though as a matter of fact, George, for the past few weeks I've rather enjoyed *not* thinking about taking off anywhere.'

'I'm sorry,' I said. 'Forget I mentioned it.'

'I can't, can I, now that you have? But the problem – shall I tell you what the problem is?'

'Mm hmn.'

'The problem is I doubt if I could choose between one place and another.'

'But you're not afraid of life being different, surely?'

'No,' she said. 'I'm afraid of it being the same. Of all the cultural differences people talk about being so much wallpaper.'

'I wouldn't worry about that,' I said. 'I've only been abroad a few times but the differences are amazing.'

'To you maybe,' she said. 'Your viewpoint's different. You grew up in a world I never saw – don't you see? That's what you are. It's what I like about you; you think you're real.'

'Thanks.'

'But people don't, now,' she said. 'Haven't you noticed? There's no such thing as ordinary life any more. It's just something else to get nostalgic about, a time when there was hope and a vital and tangible world which people thought they could take over by being socialists and making it all work out. Like those prewar photographs of Swansea you see in the Industrial and Maritime Museum,' she said. 'That's all gone now. For ever. Everywhere's just a suburb of somewhere else.'

'But that doesn't mean one can't rail against it.'

'It doesn't mean *you* can't. But that's what I mean. You're about a quarter century older than me. Look,' she said, 'when I was a child I was happy most of the time. I mean I loved my parents and they loved me and all the rest of it. But everything was sad. Things never quite connected. Feelings. By the time I grew up I knew what it was. I'd been raised in a museum. But *you* weren't, because when you were a child it wasn't a museum. That's why you think you're real.' She ran a finger down my chest, wrapped herself into my shoulder and yawned luxuriously. 'The world you rail against is me,' she said. 'It's my inner landscape.'

# Part Five

# 29

'Well I must say,' Alice observed. 'This is looking positively cosy.' Hands folded on the kitchen table in front of her, cradling her tea, she looked around with innocent, bright malice at all our improvements. These were a blind on the window masking the back yard, some herb jars, decorative recipe posters, a washing up rack, a lined dustbin in place of the cardboard rubbish box in the corner and one or two other things. 'Did you do it, dear?' she asked Sophie, raising tea to her mouth and looking wide-eyed over the top. 'Are you one of these insatiable, restless domestic souls who *has* to get things right?'

'Of course she isn't,' I said, flushing with annoyance. 'Does she *look* like a domestic soul? As a matter of fact it was Beau. He had insomnia; he was terrified to close his eyes in case the phone rang.'

'Really?' Alice said. 'Dear Beau. How is he?'

'Ill.'

'What with?'

'Don't ask me,' I said. 'Don't ask him either. Anyway, I thought doing something to the kitchen might calm him down a bit. He wanted to paint it lemon yellow at first but I put my foot down. He said it was good for the kidneys and the pituitary gland but I threatened him with eviction. So he painted his room lemon yellow instead. It looks absolutely foul. D'you know what your ulterior motive was in coming here this evening or are you playing things by ear?'

'George, that remark was offensive.'

'Good,' I said. Sophie left the room. 'Alice, of all the things you unreasonably continue to expect from me, you surely don't include politeness.'

'You two must be fucking like stoats,' she observed, sipping tea again. 'You're getting cocky.'

'Would you like me to take you by the scruff of the neck and fling you out through the front door?'

'Yes I should quite enjoy it, but it would prevent my discussing what I came to talk about.'

'So there was something.'

'Alright yes. There was. Look, where the hell is Dugdale?'

'I wish I knew. At least I think I do. At the moment,' I said, 'there's a warrant out for his arrest for defaulting on a Probation Order, vague but sinister threats of prosecution by the Social Securicor, also not inconceivably an economy package contract on his life.'

'Oh.' She sighed and massaged her temples with her fingers.

I said: 'Anyway, I thought you were all miffed off with Dugdale.'

'We are,' she said. 'We think he's a rotten little crook and we're miffed off with you as well for foisting him on us. At least this is how we felt until the other day. But Professor Holloway feels differently.'

'Oh?'

'Mm. And of course Professor Holloway means dollars and prestige. He's the Dalai Lama – his whim is our command. And he's *terribly* keen to get in touch with Dugdale. He can hardly talk about anything else.'

'Did he say why?'

'No. That's the annoying thing. He's being quite unspeakably cagey about it. And none of us was able to tell him anything. The best we could offer was that you might be able to help. So now he wants to meet you.'

'So you want me to see Holloway?'

'Please,' she said. '*Please*, George. I'll never, ever ask you to do anything else.'

'Can I have that in writing?'

'No.'

# 30

'And this is my wife Eugenia,' Professor Holloway said. 'But she prefers "Gina".'

'Really?' I shook her hand.

'Of course,' she said. 'Can you imagine being called Eugenia Holloway? You'd practically rupture your throat. I nearly made him change his surname as a condition of matrimony.'

'Yup,' Holloway said. 'But then we came up with Gina . . . You call me Stan, George. What'll you have to drink?'

'Oh . . .'

'A scotch maybe.'

'Alright.'

'And I'll have another half of mild and bitter,' he told the barmaid.

'That's four,' his wife said.

'We sure are enjoying Swansea,' Holloway told me, speaking on an indrawn breath and shaking his head thoughtfully as he leaned on the bar waiting for the drinks.

'Really?'

'Oh, let me tell you. We walked up Cwmdonkin Drive today. All by ourselves. I was shaking. And the *park* . . .' He had pushed a hand under his gold framed glasses to rub something from his eyes. I realised it was tears. To my surprise this was rather affecting. 'That shelter,' he went on, recovering and paying for the drinks, 'with the quote from "Fern Hill"?' He shook his head again.

'There used to be another one,' I said. 'Wooden.' We sat down. 'It was in "Patricia, Edith and Arnold". But it got demolished.'

'I know. And what some campus would have paid for *that*. Still, he does seem to be finding honour in his own country now. At last. You people are doing a great job. Cheers.'

'Cheers. And you – I mean is this a mutual interest?' I asked Mrs Holloway politely.

'Well, I think you could say that Thomasology is basically my obsession,' Holloway answered me. 'But she goes along with it.' He winked. 'It keeps me out of trouble.'

'Yeah,' she said in her deep Atlantic drone. She had those dark American good looks which middle age so often bakes into a mask. 'It's better than poker or masturbation or collecting stamps. But I do take a certain interest I guess.'

He smiled indulgently. Both of us had thrown quick glances about the room to gauge the effect of her very audible remarks. We were in the Cheerioh Bar of the Dogfish, Swansea's nought point four star hotel, actually rather enjoyable for its strained, scuffed plush air of better days and the tensely deferential eye it kept on those to whom it now looked for its survival.

'What's the matter?' Mrs Holloway asked, picking up our thoughts. 'Don't they have masturbation in Swansea? I thought the place was riddled with it.'

Holloway giggled.

'He thinks only men are allowed to be outrageous.' She wrinkled up her nose and pinched his cheek, stood up and picked up a magazine and her handbag. 'At heart he's a pig. Well boys, I think I'll leave you to it.'

'You're not coming with us?' I asked.

'Are you kidding? To hang around greasy bars watching old men die over the dominoes? I've got some letters to write.'

'Don't wait up,' Holloway said with suppressed happiness.

'Oh I shan't. But if you're ill in the morning I'll nail your balls to the bedframe. Night.'

'Let's have another one before we go,' Holloway said, taking my glass. 'I'll have a pint this time. You know this really is some vacation. And you know there's this arts festival, the Swansea Fringe? Somebody's doing an avant-garde version of *Under Milk Wood* which we *really* want to see. And there's going to be a late-night drinking club, for all the performers and everybody, for the whole fortnight. It's going to be right here in the hotel where we're staying.'

'I know,' I said. 'They couldn't find anywhere else. The man who runs the Fringe is my tenant.'

'*No*. Wait till I tell Gina *that*.' He swigged carelessly at his full glass and spilled some on his mac. 'Shit.' He flicked at it. 'Ah, what the hell.' He leaned back in his seat. 'I guess this place is a bit chi chi,' he observed. 'I'd have preferred to stay

180

somewhere a bit earthier, but ... What did Dylan say? He didn't like carpets because you couldn't spit on the floor?' He chuckled and drank a lot of beer quickly. 'Have I got something to discuss with you,' he added quietly. 'Wow.'

'So I gather.'

'We'll save it till later, George. If that's okay with you. It'll keep for another hour or so. It's kept for a long time. I'm going to the john.'

As he got to his feet it was difficult to know if he was somewhat unsteady on them or merely wanted to be. At first he had surprised me by being so like my preconception of him as to be uncanny. Of middling age and height, with neat thinning hair, a neat face and neat clothes on his body, pale and spotless and put together according to specification, he had quite lacked both the repulsiveness and the glamour of the human. Now, he was rapidly developing an unbuttoned look. His beerstained coat had come open to reveal a hidden paunch, and he thrust out his lower lip as though to help him navigate the room.

He was away long enough for me to order another whisky and drink it, and when he came back it was evident that he had spent his time in the lavatory mussing up his hair and dragging his tie askew in front of the mirror. He thrust his hands in his trouser pockets, coat flung wide, and winked at me.

'Give me some cigarettes, would you darling?' he asked the barmaid. 'Got any Woodbines? I only smoke occasionally,' he added, opening them. 'You want one?'

'I don't.'

'Well George.' He put a Woodbine in the side of his mouth and lit it with a match which he dropped, still burning, on the carpet. I trod on it. 'Come on,' he said, slapping my shoulder. 'Lead the way. Show me the real Swansea.'

## 31

'Hotel rezdent,' Holloway said. '*Course* I can get a drink.'

He did too. My reservations on the matter had had to do not so much with the time, as the fact that he had entered the Cheerioh Bar on hands and knees. He now made it to his feet and not without skill slanted himself forward and permitted the bar to break his fall. 'Two scotches, sweetheart,' he said. 'Funny licensing laws they have in this country anyway.' He fell backwards into a chair. 'George I have to thank you,' he said. 'That was one hell of an evening.'

'A hell of an evening,' I said, intending a somewhat more literal meaning which was lost on him. 'It was.'

'Mmngh.' He slipped into a partial doze and I removed the Woodbine from his lips before it set fire to him. There was a large quantity of drink thumping around my bloodstream, productive of nothing but a thick head which I supposed was the result of the necessity of my staying sober since one of us had to. We had stuck to the venerable old brown seedy pubs of which happily there were still one or two, and at first he had been suitably impressed enough by his surroundings to be fairly quiet, sitting on the bench visualising Dylan coming in this very bar trying to get one on the slate, eavesdropping on conversations and trying to recite 'The Force that through the Green Fuse Drives the Flower'. I think the change in his behaviour happened soon after a discussion about what precisely Dylan would have drunk, with which I eventually grew exasperated and said he drank anything he could lay his hands on. It was shortly after that that I had cause to remark on the funny colour of Holloway's mild and bitter, which turned out to have been mixed with a large Pernod.

The fight he tried to start was not so much of a problem since no one took him seriously, but I will own to being rather annoyed when a little later on he grabbed my arm and said we had to get the hell out of here because he'd just pissed in the passage. At the place we fled to we got nearly as far as the bar when he threw up on the floor, and at the next place we managed to buy a drink but were not able to drink it because Holloway told the landlady, fifty five if she was a day and with a husband as enormous as herself, that she could keep the change if he could fondle her tits. After that I was a little sharp with him and he fell into an alcoholic sulk, suddenly careening towards his knees in the street and being difficult to steer along. He had not yet broached the great exciting topic which was on his mind. Perhaps he suspected that my curiosity about it was the only hold he had on my company, which by this time was perfectly true. I had thought he must be out for the night now but I was wrong. He opened his eyes and said, quite clearly: 'George. I am going to tell you something perfectly incredible.'

'Go on.'

'What d'you suppose an original poem of Dylan's might be worth? I mean one that nobody had ever seen?'

'Er . . .'

'Telephone numbers, George. I want to show you something.' He reached into an inner pocket.

Heart thumping, I sat there waiting to see another copy of the worksheet of 'How Should My Wellspring Cat'.

Therefore I got a deep shock when he put the paper in my hand, which bit deeper as I read on.


# 32


Dear Professor Holloway,

Following my phone call of the other day, I enclose a photostat of one corner of the worksheet. You will I hope understand that I cannot let even a copy of the whole text out of my keeping at this time.

Of course if this poem is what I think it is, it will indeed be the most exciting thing to happen to either of us. At the same time I quite endorse your inclination to be sceptical, which does you credit and certainly accords with the high academic reputation which has preceded you here. I've been in a great quandary for some time wondering who to confide in; I suppose I feel a bit like an amateur archaeologist who dreams the riddle of Linear B script and wonders who he is going to get to believe him. Perhaps this sounds silly, but when I heard you were coming to Swansea it was as if you had been sent; I at once set about looking you up in Bristol and phoning you.

Now – the Swansea house where the poem was found (yes, *found*) was bought a year or so ago by a painter in his thirties with a family, with whom I became friendly. The previous owner having died, the house had passed to her son, a professional soldier with no need of a residence, who therefore disposed of it as a negotiable asset. Most of the movables were of course thrown away or sold, but when the Hendersens moved in there was the usual clutter of old papers and half rolls of wallpaper and plastic lampshades, old bills, photographs and disinfectant bottles left behind in corners and the bottoms of cupboards. Luckily the Hendersens are not the sort of people to throw all this away outright, and they scavenged through it to keep what was useful or interesting. It's lucky too that Sky Hendersen has a certain interest in poetry. I don't know how this affects you, but it certainly makes my hair stand on end to think that one day when they were burning rubbish in the grate, his wife Charlotte was about to throw the poem on the fire when Sky, *who happened to be looking over her shoulder*, was caught by a phrase and took it from her for a closer look. The more he read the more intrigued he became, and knowing my interest in Thomas he showed it to me.

To say I was excited is an understatement – the feeling I got was not unlike an electric shock of horror. There was no doubt in my mind that I was looking at the worksheet of a Dylan Thomas poem which the most exhaustive search could not turn up in any of his collected works. In other words an original. I was at once inclined to see it as an early work: though his idiosyncratic use of language is already quite developed, a certain looseness in the form suggests to me that it predates, though perhaps by as little as a few weeks, that wonderfully precocious flowering when much

184

of his very best work was written. This is a *vers libre* poem of four fourteen line verses, untitled (of course he usually just used the first line) and unhappily, as I said, not signed. But then it is not quite finished; the last two and a half lines are left out. Phrases clearly intended for them are jotted around the margins of the worksheet, and armed with these one can attempt to construct the end of the poem, as I have.

Generically, I would place the poem between 1931 and 1938. As you are probably aware, in about December of 1930 he wrote an unpublished poem which begins: How shall the animal/Whose way I trace/Into the dark recesses/Be durable/Under such weight as bows me down. This is widely regarded as the precursor of the mature work, written in 1938, with the title How Shall My Animal (Whose wizard shape I trace in the cavernous skull/Vessel of abscesses and exultation's shell/Endure burial under the spelling wall etc). The poem I have begins: How should my wellspring cat/Electric lard within a mottled tomb of cancer/And the shouts of praise/Forsake the succour of oblivion's womb. I see it as standing midway between the two poems, and in fact I have corroborative circumstantial evidence which has enabled me to pinpoint it as closely as early 1934.

The first thing I did, faced by the puzzle of how the poem came to be where it was, was to check the Hendersens' deeds to see who was living in the house during the 1930s. Quite simply, from 1932 to 1981, the house was owned by a family called Dando. It is one of those traditional neighbourhoods where people stay a long time in one place, often with their relatives nearby. However grandmother Dando was the last of her family in that street; the rest are all now scattered or dead. Luckily a neighbour has lived there since 1926, and can remember that from then until the war, the head of the household was Fred Dando, an unemployed steel worker who later became a merchant seaman. They had five sons, who all now seem to be dead except the youngest, from whose agent (they never met him) the Hendersens bought the house. As far as this neighbour can remember, the eldest son followed his father into the Merchant Navy and was drowned in a submarine attack. The three youngest were still at school during the 30s, the very youngest (also called Fred) being just a toddler. Another son became a policeman and yet another was to join the Merchant Navy. But it is the second son, called Bryn, whom the neighbour remembers best. She calls him 'a real bad lot, a terrible boy', always in and out of trouble for fighting, insulting behaviour, drunkenness, and petty theft. She vividly remembers old Mrs Dando's grief on hearing at the end of the war that Bryn had been killed in a brawl in a Glasgow bar soon after his release from prison. Apparently Bryn was Mrs Dando's favourite son, though he was always quarrelling with his father. You and I, with some knowledge of psychology, will not be surprised by this.

Naturally I started wondering how on earth a Dylan Thomas poem could have ended up in such a household. In early 1934, when Dylan was nineteen, the Dando household will have looked like this:

> Mr and Mrs Dando
> Eldest son, about 21
> Bryn, 19 or 20
> Son, about 11
> Son, about 7
> Young Fred, about 3.

Now there is something about the tone of the family which does not dispose me to think that Dylan might have known any of them as a friend. Of course Dylan's precocity often made him older friends, but Mr Dando, an unemployed father of five? I doubt it. Again, the eldest son is an unknown quantity, and all sorts of people do end up as merchant seamen, but again I doubt that Dylan would have known him. Anyway, why on earth should Dylan give a poem to a friend, or to anyone except a publisher or someone who knew a publisher? In fact, I have good reason for supposing that our connection is Bryn, and that Dylan did not intend him to have the poem at all.

My source for this can be found on page 106 of the British paperback version of the biography of Dylan by the Swansea born journalist Paul Ferris. In the middle of describing a letter from Dylan to Pamela Hansford Johnson (later Lady Snow but at that time a girlfriend of Dylan's) the author breaks off to say: 'Thomas began this letter on Wednesday 9 May (1934). He was still writing it on Sunday, 13 May, after, he said, an incident on Saturday night in "the deserted smokeroom of a seaside pub" where three "repulsive looking young men" cornered him and made him hand over cigarettes and money.' Think about that. It seems clear to me that Dylan had the nearly completed poem, written, as he then wrote, on exercise book paper, stuffed in his wallet, and the way it's folded is certainly consistent with that assumption. It is not actually stated that Dylan's wallet was taken, but can you imagine three thugs *not* taking someone's wallet once they had gone to the trouble of cornering them? I think we can safely surmise that they did, and that the wallet ended up with Bryn. I certainly don't think that he kept the poem intentionally, rather that he decided to use the wallet as his own, took out all the things he didn't want and flung them in the back of the nearest cupboard.

There is another lucky factor here. The house is that old-fashioned type of workman's terraced cottage with a lot of *built-in* cupboards. Had the poem gone into a wardrobe or chest of drawers it would of course have moved out with them. The Hendersens think it was in one of the fireside cupboards in the front, parlour room, among memorabilia like old holiday snaps, bingo cards and funeral notices. We must then assume either that no one remarked on it for nigh on fifty years, or perhaps that Mrs Dando, her grief-distracted brain thinking it be something by Bryn, kept it as a memento of her errant son.

So there we are. All we have to ask ourselves is why Dylan never mentioned the loss of the poem to anybody. It is my contention that in veiled form he mentioned it for much of the rest of his life, and that it certainly left a deep scar on his unconscious mind, but more of that later.

I look forward eagerly to meeting you, when we must decide what to do,

Yours sincerely,
Laurence Dugdale.

# 33

It was my own reaction which shocked me more than anything. This was a high example of Dugdale's powers of fabrication, and to quote his own words the feeling it gave me was not unlike an electric shock of horror. The whole business of the poem had, like its supposed author, taken a quantum leap out of the realm of provincial misbehaviour into the big and transatlantic and dangerous. Perhaps even into history, which most of us spend most of our lives merely observing inaccurately. And this squiffy little academic git would be the vital link, so blandly confident in his credulity, perhaps because unconsciously he knew quite well what power his credulity might have.

'I don't know what to say to you,' I said truthfully.

'Can you find Laurence Dugdale for me?'

'Possibly, but...'

'The man's vanished.'

'I know,' I said. 'Look...'

'It's the weight of this secret on him,' Holloway said. 'I'm frightened the poor man might explode.'

'Professor Holloway...'

'Stan.'

'Stan. Listen...'

'I want to see this poem.' He leaned forwards. 'I wanna *see* it. You find Dugdale,' he whispered. 'Please. This means *everything* to me. Everything. Can you understand that?'

'I think so.' I was going to have to find Dugdale anyway, and I realised there was no point in trying to tell him anything else at the moment. 'Okay,' I said. 'I'll have a look for you.'

'Attaboy. Tell him we'll all have a drink together.'

'I can't wait.'

'Then we'll *shake* the world,' he said. 'Boy oh *boy*.'

I went to the bog. As I came back I heard him arguing with weary petulance with the barmaid, who was trying to close the grille over the bar, and on impulse I turned around and left.

The streets were empty and wide and dry, dusted by moonlight which was strong enough to shine through the sulphurous gloom of the lamps. My footsteps echoed crisply past the dark shops. Had I been in a reflective mood I might have wondered why, since I was so keen to put a stop to everything, I felt suddenly so high, with that clean and primitive intoxication which belongs properly to success. I was talking to myself too.

'Jesus Christ,' I said.

# 34

'Jesus Christ,' said Sky. He removed a Teddy bear and a plate of cold porridge from one of their dining room chairs and sat on it rather heavily. 'Well, I don't know.' He massaged his face. 'You can't help admiring the way he's done it, can you? You know what I think? He's a cynic with a passionate desire to believe in things. His life is one long hopeless search for someone as gullible as his alter ego.' He started laughing. 'He really deserves to be ceremonially shot for this, though.' He yawned. 'I wondered why he wanted to see the deeds.'

'You mean all that stuff about the Dando family is true?'

'Broadly, yes. That's a good touch of course. The best lies are always interwoven with the truth. I wonder what gave him the idea in the first place.'

'I just wonder where he is.'

'Oh, out in the garden I think.'

'What?'

'Playing with Danny in the sandpit. Why?'

'You never told me he was here.'

'You never asked. You've been looking for him, have you?'

'Along with several others. Has he been here long?'

'A few days,' Sky said. 'I thought he seemed oddly disinclined to go out.'

'Let's go and have a chat with him, shall we?'

We stood out on the terrace, looking down the steep garden to where Dugdale sat in a patch of afternoon sun at the edge of the sandpit, butt to some game of the youngest Hendersen which chiefly involved having sand poured in his pockets and being hit occasionally with a spade. This seemed to afford the youngest Hendersen a great deal of innocent pleasure; I was struck by the easygoing trust which Dugdale had inspired. He glanced up.

'George,' he said, hand above his eyes to protect them either from the sun or the sight of me. 'How nice.'

I descended the garden steps slowly.

'I used to have a family once, you know,' Dugdale observed. He reached out gently to prevent Danny Hendersen tripping up, and was rewarded with a spadeful of sand down the back of his neck.

'Yes I do actually. Dugdale listen...'

'I'm quite glad you called, George. I think there are one or two things we need to discuss.'

'There certainly are,' I said. 'Why don't we all step into Sky's studio and have a little chat about Professor Holloway and Dylan Thomas?'

'Oh...'

'And Bryn Dando,' Sky put in, joining us. 'And our living room cupboards.'

'Not to mention the penalties for fraud,' I added.

'So you've...?'

'Read your letter, yes. I've got it here.'

We disposed ourselves about the cramped inside of Sky's studio, which in the sober light of day seemed to have been furnished principally with mildew, paint pots and discarded sheets of paper. I set out the gravity of the problem as I saw it, very much from the point of view of my HMG employed persona, though hampered somewhat in the dignity of my delivery by the fact that Danny kept trying to paint my knee blue. I concluded by saying that the only course of action I could see was to go to Holloway in a body, explain the beginnings of the poem as innocent *pastiche* and apologise for a practical joke which had got out of hand.

'I suppose you're right,' Dugdale said with a glum and disarming air of contrition. 'Oh dear.'

'But how did you expect to get *away* with it?' Sky demanded. 'There'd have been television crews all over the house wanting to film the cupboards.'

'When the time came I'd have told you about it and cut you in,' Dugdale said simply.

'Oh. I see. But I mean all the rest of it...'

'But he *was* robbed in a pub in 1934,' Dugdale said. 'It's a matter of record. At least it's a matter of record that he said he was.'

'That wasn't what I meant,' Sky said. 'Actually I think all that stuff about Bryn Dando is brilliant.'

'He really existed, you know. I've been talking to the old girl next door.'

'But that isn't the point, is it. I mean okay, the set up's superb. So is the poem. So's Mr Mukkarjee's calligraphy. But you see, Dugdale dear, when it comes to money people don't just stop there. They have tests you know. Things like the paper and the ink.'

'And that,' said Dugdale, 'is the reason I scoured the junk shops till I found a part-used ledger with entries for 1937, which ought to be close enough. And the ink is what gave me the idea in the beginning. You see Mr Mukkarjee, who has a great literary future behind him, is a wonderfully sentimental custodian of his old ambitions. That's why he's still got the first bottle of ink he ever bought, in about 1952, from some backstreet shop in Bombay whose stock dated back to the Twenties.' He sat back and smiled at us serenely. 'I'm not daft, you know.'

'I see,' Sky said thoughtfully. 'I see. I didn't know about that.'

'*Look*, you two,' I said. 'For Christ's sake. It is absolutely imperative that we knock this thing on the head *now*.'

'How do you suppose Holloway will take it?' Sky asked.

'Not very well,' I said. 'But that's too bad. Why?'

'Well, correct me if I'm wrong, but a conspiracy charge could be as heavy as an actual fraud charge, couldn't it?'

'Possibly, yes. But who'd bring one?'

'Holloway, quite probably. Don't you think? I mean hell hath no fury like a sucker disillusioned. And Dugdale's letter certainly gives him the evidence.'

'But we've got it.' I tapped my pocket.

'Can I see it?' Dugdale asked.

191

I gave it to him.

'Photocopy,' he said, handing it back.

'Oh.'

'Precisely.'

'Actually,' Sky asked, 'as a point of interest, what sort of sum would we be talking about?'

'Ten thousand as a minimum,' Dugdale said smartly. 'Pounds sterling. Thirty would not surprise me in the least.'

'Christ.'

'Five years as a minimum,' I said, 'in view of your record. Maybe a bender for Sky if he's very lucky. Look, what is the *matter* with the pair of you? We have one last golden opportunity to clear this whole thing up...'

'No,' Sky said. 'You and I have the opportunity to step sideways and let Dugdale fall in the shit. This is the real point, isn't it? He's got no income whatever now. As soon as he shows his head above ground he's going to get run in on some petty charge and maybe get his teeth kicked in on the way. In addition to which I'd give three to one Holloway does go for his throat if we tell him the truth, let alone that bunch of provincial wankers in the Dylan Thomas Memorial Affiliation. So he's got to vanish. He needs money. I mean alright, George, we know the Home Office pays your salary and we don't hold it against you, but there's no need for you to be so fucking pompous is there? What is all this – voluntary overtime?'

'Look...'

'What precisely,' he asked, picking Danny up, 'are your moral objections to letting the whole thing go ahead?'

'My moral objections are none.'

'Really?'

'Really. The problem is entirely practical. The risk...'

'Would be ours entirely. I mean wouldn't it? You're not implicated in the least. All you've done is carry a message.'

'No, I did write part of the poem. Not much, I know. But I feel responsible.'

'Oh, to hell with your sense of fucking middle class responsibility,' Sky said. 'D'you seriously think it matters if a few academic vultures get ripped off for ten or twenty grand?'

'Well no, but...'

'And I'll tell you one person who'd be right behind us,' he went on, 'and that's Dylan Thomas. You know he was plagued by debts for his entire life? Positively hagridden. Okay, he used to chuck money away like there was no tomorrow, we know that. But within two years of his death he was making fifteen grand a year. In the Fifties. It would have wiped the slate clean at one stroke and given him more than he could possibly spend even if he'd nailed himself to the bar. He'd laugh like a fucking drain to think of Holloway getting screwed. And d'you know what Van Gogh made in his life-time? Nothing. Nix. Not a *groat*. Why d'you think he went off his trolley? Hmm? Why d'you think he shot himself?'

'But I really can't see . . .'

'It's got *everything* to do with it,' he said vehemently. 'Everything. *Christ*. All those years just living off his brother. Every cheque slowly eroding his self esteem until he snapped. Meanwhile paint paint paint no matter what. They were just waiting for him to die. People like Holloway. People like your wife, like the Arts Council . . .'

'The *Arts* Council?'

'The number of times I've tried getting money out of those bastards,' he said. 'You've no idea. Just a few quid. They want you to grovel. I couldn't do it again, I just *couldn't*. I tell you candidly, George, I could more easily go in there with a machinegun and massacre the lot of them. Artists shouldn't have families, I suppose,' he said, subsiding into a chair. Danny clambered out of his arms and ran into the garden. 'I should have realised. I feel like I'm robbing them all the time. Every day that goes by, you worry about the price of children's shoes, you worry about the gas bill, something for dinner. Never mind the price of a drink or the fact that the roof's leaking in six places. And things like this studio – I still owe Charlotte's mother for the materials. Alright, she's a dear woman and she has a few quid. Not very much though. She still works in some bloody office in London. I wonder if I'm ever going to pay her back in her lifetime. What I see, George,' he concluded, 'is a golden opportunity to get in front for the first time in my life. And you want to piss on it because it isn't kosher.'

'Look you can't . . .'

'And nobody is asking you to join the club. This is the bit that gets me. You don't have to know a *thing* about the poem's origins. You just have to arrange a meeting with Holloway sometime when it's nice and dark and Dugdale can step out of the house without getting his collar felt. Then we flog him the poem, Dugdale buggers off over the horizon and everybody's happy.'

'But look . . .'

'And I can see Holloway if you like. Your involvement can stop right now.'

'No. No I'll *see* him,' I said wearily. 'I mean okay, I'll *do* it. But you're both insane.'

'Thankyou, George,' Dugdale said.

'Don't *thank* me. If you ask me I'm insane too. I ought to be on the blower to the Old Bill right now to tell them you're here, that's what I ought to be doing. But don't worry, I won't.' I drew up a stool and sat down, leaning on my knees. 'God, this bloody job gets me down sometimes, I don't mind telling you.'

'You do rate a share, you know,' Dugdale said. 'If you want one.'

'Dugdale *no*. I'll tell you what, though,' I said. 'If Mr Mukkarjee doesn't get an anonymous gift of twenty per cent of the spoils I shall run you in cheerfully.'

'But of course,' Dugdale said equably. 'What a very good idea. When actually do you intend seeing Holloway?'

'Tonight. I want to get the whole thing over with.'

'I wonder if you might give him this?' he asked, handing me some paper. 'I think it's about time he saw a photostat of the entire poem. That wouldn't compromise you, would it? You need have no opinion as to its origins?'

'What's the difference?' I said, pocketing the thing. 'Alright. Well, I'd really better go and do something normal now, like serve a few summonses.'

We all went up to the house, where Charlotte sat drinking tea, a shopping bag on the floor at her feet. She gave me a lovely smile which pierced me to the quick. How they intended to square the whole thing with her I couldn't begin to imagine. I'm so *sorry*, madam, I thought. One would have thought that a penniless mad husband and twenty-five

194

assorted cats and children were enough for you to contend with already. However, I am afraid that Dugdale and your husband are currently plotting to increase your burden by perpetrating the biggest literary fraud of the century as casually as though they were fiddling the railways. And I am acting as an indemnified accessory. I'm afraid I was subjected to a harangue of wild and bloodthirsty bohemian rhetoric until I just couldn't stand any more of it and I caved in. At bottom I just want a quiet life, which could be the reason I never get one. I will certainly own that with my temperament I am in the wrong job, possibly the wrong century or the wrong incarnation. I should like innumerable similar lapses to be taken into consideration before you pass judgement.

'Just a casual call,' I said, smiling at her inanely and picking up my briefcase. 'So long, you two. I'll be in touch.'

# 35

Holloway was sitting in the Cheerioh Bar with his wife, no trace of the previous evening's debauchery in evidence about his person. It was as if he'd stepped fully clothed into a dry cleaning machine. At the sight of me he sprang to attention and bought me a drink.

'Well?' he asked.

I sat down and looked at each of them in turn. 'Well, I found him,' I said.

'That's marvellous. And?'

'And he wants to meet you. He also asked me to give you this. I've no idea what it is,' I added, having taken the perhaps ignoble precaution of placing the poem in an unmarked sealed envelope.

Mrs Holloway took it, Holloway gazing avidly while she ripped it open. She bit her lip and scanned both sheets voraciously, her frown one of approbation rather than doubt.

'But my God,' she exclaimed on a rising note. 'Somebody's been scribbling on the bottom.'

'This is only a copy, honey,' Holloway said placatingly.

'Oh yes. I guess it is. But all the same . . .'

'I think,' I said, drawn in spite of myself, 'that must be Dugdale's construction of the last two and a half lines. I do seem to remember his mentioning that.'

'Oh yes,' Mrs Holloway said, squinting. '"is flat like cardboard and as sharp as . . ." What's that word?'

'I dunno, honey. Look can we read the poem from the beginning and give it a little dignity?'

'Okay, Clarabelle. Let's read.'

They read. Holloway's lips were moving and he beat time surreptitiously with one finger. Once or twice he wiped his eyes. They concentrated silently for a long time, at the end of which they exchanged a smile, tremulous with unendurable satisfaction. I wanted to throw up. Disgust had nothing to do with it. I felt guilty and scared.

'That's just amazing,' Holloway said. He found speech difficult. 'Amazing.'

'It certainly is,' Mrs Holloway said. 'I sure hope he didn't scribble on the original.'

'I rather doubt it,' I said.

'Yeah, let's look at these last two and a half lines now, shall we honey?' Holloway said, taking the poem. 'I *think* that's "Flat like cardboard and as sharp as fear".'

'Mmm. Yes it is. And where is that in the margins?'

'Right down the bottom here.'

'Oh yes,' she said. 'And how does it go on? "The cat flops, spent as . . ." What's that? His handwriting's terrible.'

'Sure is.' Holloway chuckled. 'It's even worse than Dylan's. I think that reads "spent as money".'

'Oh that's lovely. Have we got it anywhere though?'

'Yup. Top left hand corner. See? Then we conclude "at the lockjaw fender's rim/His own dead, bright banana in his hangdog mouth."'

'And does Dylan have all that around the margins?'

'Looks like it,' Holloway said, searching the margins with his fingers. Yeah.'

'But look,' she objected. '"Lockjaw" is crossed out there. I

196

mean Dylan crossed it out. He's tried "hangdog" instead. See? "Hangdog fender".'

'Yes, but then we have the whole thing reversed again up the left hand margin here. He was obviously switching the two adjectives around. Dylan did that quite a lot during composition. We've got it again here, too. Look. He's been reversing "dead" and "bright".'

'So he has,' she said. 'You know, personally I think "Bright, dead banana" might have been better.'

'I'm not *sure*,' Holloway said. 'My opinion is that when in doubt, Dylan would always go for direct alliteration. I guess Dugdale feels the same way.'

'Okay, okay,' she said in a singsong tone, ironically holding up her hands as if at gunpoint. 'You're the professor of English and I'm the dizzy housewife.'

'Now, honey. You *know* I didn't...'

'Ah, I was kidding.' She punched his shoulder. 'Bright, dead banana. Dead, bright banana. Red, white, black and blue banana. Who cares? It's all very academic.'

'In the literal meaning of the term,' Holloway said. 'Well...' They looked at each other again.

'Tell Dugdale,' Mrs Holloway said, laying a hand on my sleeve, 'that of course we can't absolutely commit ourselves on this, this copy, but...'

'Actually,' I said, 'I'd rather you told him.'

'Okay George. But I don't mind admitting to you that we're pretty excited. Are we going to run up a phone bill tonight or are we going to run up a phone bill?'

'We're gonna run up a phone bill,' Holloway agreed happily.'

'I do think,' I said, 'that you should be, well, as discreet as possible at this stage.'

'Oh, believe me, George,' Holloway said, quite misinterpreting my admittedly obscure meaning, 'we intend to be very low-profile and caring and whatever. We've discussed this.'

'We have,' Mrs Holloway said. 'We don't want to do this – here comes America. Grab. Y'know?'

'We're going to make damn sure we do some good for Swansea along the way,' Holloway said. 'And the Affiliation.

197

And of course the most important thing of all, is to enhance Dylan's reputation.'

'Sure,' she said. 'Mind you,' she confided to me, winking, 'the professor here won't exactly have his reputation suffer when the story breaks.'

'Aw . . .'

'It'll be about time too,' she said, grinning. 'During his illustrious career he must have missed every boat that left. He wasn't liberal, radical chic, new wave philosophical and he's not radical right,' she said, ticking off these glittering choices on her fingers. 'The students don't love him and they don't hate him. They don't know he exists. Know what I mean? Not so much a has been, more a never was.'

Holloway was chuckling with helpless embarrassment; clearly this gag was an old part of their act.

'But what the hell,' she concluded. 'He's mine. He pays the bills. And he's not bad in the sack either, if you get him in the right mood.'

'I see,' I said, probably sounding very British and stuffy. 'How nice. Well look, I . . .'

'So we've gotta see Dugdale,' Holloway cut in.

'Of course. What should I . . .?'

'Hell we're right here. Have him phone us.'

'What a good idea.'

'And soon.'

'Yes.' I stood up.

'You're not going?'

'I've an appointment,' I said, my feet beginning to run of their own accord.

'Thanks for everything, George.'

'Don't thank me,' I pleaded over my shoulder. 'Don't *thank* me.' I took the stairs three at a time down to the lobby.

Beau was there. He was leaning on the reception desk chewing his wrist and staring intently about the room without really taking anything in.

'Hi,' he said sepulchrally. 'Just waiting to see the manager,' he volunteered. 'See if I can rescue the Fringe Club at the last minute. I mean the cops gave us a licence on the understanding that there'd be two directors on the door every night. So I drew up a roster – *weeks* ago this is – and sent it out to all of them and not one of them objected. Now all of a sudden half of them can't do it. I mean what's the *point*, George? What is the fucking point? Everything I set up falls to pieces as soon as I turn my back. The whole *thing* starts the day after tomorrow. I dunno...'

He thrust his hands in his jacket pockets and pulled them out again.

'Oh,' he said. 'I nearly forgot this.' He was holding an envelope with my name on it. 'Some Indian guy brought it round this afternoon.'

'Thanks.' I took the envelope and set off for Sky's house, to deliver Holloway's message and end my involvement with the whole lunatic and felonious scheme as fast as possible. I felt terrible about what I had set in train, at the same time as being sharply aware that I had no right to the feeling at all. My sentiments were those of a puritanical acting unpaid ponce trying to stop an orgy in a brothel when every single other person in the place was extremely keen on the idea. Well, it was after all an American trait to describe doing business as getting into bed together. I stopped at the corner and moodily ripped open Mr Mukkarjee's envelope, expecting a tearful note of apology and despair.

Instead, there was sixty five quid wrapped in plain paper. It was the first hopeful thing to have happened all day.

# 36

'I wish you'd go to bloody sleep, George. What's the matter?'

'Oh sorry. Was I fidgeting?'

'Just a bit.'

'Oh. I suppose it's this private view of ours,' I said. 'It's the day after tomorrow. Sky seems to take it all in his stride but I'm positively dying of nerves. D'you realise there's going to be all sorts of people standing around looking at my sculpture and sneering at it? It's intolerable.'

'I shouldn't worry,' she said. 'At a private view they'll be more interested in the drink.'

'That's deeply reassuring. Thanks.'

She laughed. 'Who've you invited?' she asked.

'*Le tout* Swansea,' I said. 'Plus a few bums that Sky knows. Why?'

'I just wondered. *Le tout* Swansea's nothing to worry about provided you're brazen enough.'

I sighed. 'I suppose not. Actually there is something else I'm worried about.'

'What?'

I told her, all about the Wellspring Banana Cat and its Byzantine ramifications. 'Maybe it's stupid,' I concluded, 'but I do have such a feeling of dread about it.'

'I should fucking well hope so,' she said, sitting up and lighting a cigarette. '*God*. This is pretty extreme even for my father. Why the hell didn't you stop them?'

'I tried,' I protested. 'But they persuaded me I was just being stuffy and old maidish.'

'They're dreadfully naive,' she said. 'The pair of them. Dreadfully. So are you.'

'Why, especially?'

'All that paper and ink bit, thinking they're so bloody *clever*. I mean there's *all sorts* of tests.'

'Like what?'

'Like, oh – you don't read thrillers do you?'

'No.'

'Well if you did,' she said, 'you'd just *know*. Oh I *wish* you'd told me about this before. It's not at all difficult to tell how old the creases in a piece of paper are, for example. How long the ink's been dry, and Whatsisname's facsimile Dylan Thomas handwriting might look wonderful to the naked eye, but handwriting tends to have all sorts of characteristic pressure points and things which are fairly constant and can be measured. What's going to happen is the whole thing will look great at first glance, and those Americans will go all dewy eyed and find of the century, then somebody will take a proper look at the poem and once they've stopped laughing they'll phone up the Fraud Squad. You've *got* to stop them.'

'Oh.'

'What's the matter.'

'I think the dewy eyed find of the century bit will already have happened,' I said. 'We are now in that period of deceptive calm before the outbreak of hilarity and phoning the Fraud Squad.'

'Oh *shit*. God, George you're such a *fool*.'

'I expect you're right.'

'I'm bloody sure I am.'

'Part of me must have been wanting them to succeed,' I said. 'That's the only way I can explain it.'

'They've got one thing to do,' Sophie said, ignoring this. 'That's take their deposit and piss off.'

'Deposit?'

'Yes. Goodwill payments of ten percent are normal in most things,' she said. 'And I can't see my father being backward about asking for it. Can you? They'll just have to split with the down payment like the best con men always do.'

'But Sky can't,' I said. 'He's got a family. A house.'

'It's that or jail,' she said simply.

'His wife doesn't even know about it.'

'I should hope not,' Sophie said. 'I've met Charlotte. She's a sensible woman. She'd have put the block on it right away. But they've *got* to blow, you know. To Ireland at least. Sky will either have to pretend to desert his family, or take them with him and leave the house with an agent. The only other thing to do is steal the poem and destroy it.'

'Gosh.'

'Things are rather gosh already,' she said. 'So there's nothing to lose. Now look, it so happens that if the weather's calm tomorrow we're due to take the Americans to Laugharne in the *Polly Garter*. And if it's rough we're going in a minibus. This is our chance to sound them out about where the poem is.'

'I'm not sure I could face the *Polly Garter* a second time.'

'I wasn't *asking* you, sweetheart,' she said. 'You're coming to Laugharne.'

# 37

The weather was calm, with a decently warm sun even first thing and a nice flat glistening grey sea. Sophie and I got to the quay at about half past seven to find Alice and Delderfield there already with the Holloways, drinking coffee from a thermos. Haydock Williams was aboard the *Polly Garter* doing something fussy and last minute with a can of paint.

It was a different boat altogether. Bright red, green and white, with an awning behind the cockpit, and all sorts of little luxuries like lifebelts and a boathook, eloquent of considerable concentrated effort, probably under Sophie's instruction. There was also a two-way radio and even, for some reason, a PA system. I wondered if he intended addressing people on the Gower beaches next time local elections came round. Sophie went aboard to make sure he had proper charts, and a compass and the tide table and latest weather reports, while I said good morning to the Holloways, trying to gauge their state of mind and thereby take a guess at the location of the poem; a pretty tenuous exercise of course. I was going to have to ease the subject into conversation some time. Their eyes seemed very bright, which could have meant anything.

'How nice to have you along, George,' Alice said. I didn't like the way she smiled at me.

'It sure is,' Holloway agreed. 'I think it's going to be a grand day, don't you?'

Sophie hopped up onto the quay. 'The tide will be full at Laugharne at just the right time of day to allow us to visit the Boat House and have a drink,' she announced. 'However we'd better start now.'

'After you,' Alice said to the Holloways. 'Our little coxswain seems to have everything well in hand, doesn't she?'

'She sure does,' said Mrs Holloway, quite unaware of the bitchery intended, beaming at Sophie as she let her help her about four foot down a rotting wooden ladder to the boat. Surely there was something contemptible and corrupt in that kind of innocence; it was plain ignorance really, perceptual sloth.

'Best help Alice down, Sophie,' I called. 'She seems to be wearing her Forties pencil skirt, which isn't very nautical, and she's always been rather clumsy on her feet at the best of times.'

I could hear Alice growling under her breath, but she was too compulsive a tactician to respond openly. Holloway looked at me with mild surprise. Delderfield was not aware of us; he was rubbing his balls thoughtfully as he put away the Thermos and perused the contents of the large hamper.

'Extra mouth, since you're here, George,' he said to me. 'Just wonder how it'll all . . . Still, you're not a great sandwich and cold meat man, are you?'

'No,' I said, thinking how much I loathed people who described one as such and such a man a propos of some trivial trait or preference. I should have liked to clout him in the nuts with the champagne bottle and push him in the dock; perhaps this was a sign of strain. Together we swung down the hamper and got ourselves aboard, Delderfield stumbling rather so that you could see his underpants over the top of his trousers. I remembered Sophie describing this to me as one of the great turnoffs and started laughing to myself.

Sophie and I cast off and she started the engine and took us on a nice clean course towards the sea. It seemed there was to be no question of Haydock Williams attempting to skipper the boat other than nominally, which was a relief.

'Not many longshoremen around,' Holloway observed, sitting beside me in the stern and waving at the docks as we passed them.

'It's Sunday,' I said. 'Mind you, you never see a lot of activity. Ships come and go all the time, but they must be operating at about one tenth capacity.'

'Mmmn,' he said. 'It looks a little run down.'

'That's just the beginning,' I told him. 'All the docks in the country have just been flogged off to some business consortium. Anywhere which produces under three hundred per cent profit will be let slide back into the sea.'

'Really?'

'If they're allowed. But I think we might get them back soon.'

'We?'

'The government. Not this government. Another one.'

'Oh.' He wiped his brow with his fingers. 'There's going to be legislation anyway George, that's what you're saying?'

'There could be. Or I dunno,' I said. 'Maybe we'll just cut their throats and fling the bastards in the sea.'

'Cut whose throats?' he asked, feeling his own.

'The government's, for a start.'

'But you said . . .'

'I mean this government's. And the dock owners' while we're about it. I mean why waste a good knife?' Stop it, I said to myself. Playing the Dangerous Red is not the way to gain his confidence. But it was too late.

He said: 'Well George, it's certainly been interesting. Think I'll go up front now and see how Gina's getting along in the cabin. She gets a little *queasy* sometimes,' he confided.

Mrs Holloway was in the cabin with Alice. I registered this as a fact of probable significance without knowing quite why. Haydock Williams was poncing about the place in a peaked hat and white trousers pointing out the boat's new features to Delderfield, who was bored stiff by the whole performance: he was leaning against the side eating a small pork pie with an expression of distant rumination. Or perhaps it was just wind. The function of the PA system became apparent once we breasted the sea. Haydock Williams switched it on and blew into the mike, frowning and simpering, and said: 'Testing one two. Now ladies and GENtlemen welcome abOARD THE *Polly Garter*. We SHOULD BE arriving . . . I'll start again.' Having been twiddling the volume knob as he spoke, he now set it carefully with the mike switched off. The others had come out of the cabin and sat watching him, the Holloways with bland expectancy, hands folded in their laps like prayerbooks.

'Ladies and gentlemen.' Haydock Williams assumed a position standing on the seat which ran right around the sides and the stern, the better to point out places of interest and be the focus of attention, grasping the edge of the canopy for support. 'Distinguished guests, fellow members of the Dylan Thomas Memorial Affiliation. Welcome aboard what I hope will be the first of many pilgrim voyages of the good ship

*Polly Garter.* The aim of the Affiliation is to foster a proper appreciation of the stature of Dylan Thomas, not just in literary terms but as an honoured citizen of Swansea. We are of course extremely fortunate to have forged such links with our friends from the New World so soon after our inauguration, and our thanks are certainly due to them – oh no, there's no need to be modest – our thanks are due to them for the attention they have shown us. For our part, let's hope we can show them Dylan's haunts in their true native light. Now the object of these little voyages will of course be to enjoy ourselves. I'm quite sure Dylan would have wanted nothing less. But at the same time, it is of course to continue our pursuit of the man in a proper spirit of dedication...'

'Hear hear,' Holloway murmured. He rapped his knuckles on his thigh to suggest applause.

'Now today,' Haydock Williams said, 'we should be arriving at Laugharne at approximately eleven thirty. Unfortunately we do not know for certain if the castle will be open, but we shall be able to go for a drink in Brown's Hotel, visit the Boat House where there are rooms laid out just as they were when Dylan lived there with his family, and have some tea downstairs in the kitchen. In addition, Tom Delderfield has kindly provided some refreshments and we can have a picnic beside the estuary when we arrive. But before we get to Laugharne, there are in fact many places of interest which may be worth looking at. Over to the right now, to starboard I should say, we are just passing or have just passed the sand dunes which are mentioned in "Just Like Little Dogs". Of course the railway arches where the two men stand will have been behind them, but have since been demolished. The foreshore was thick with railways at that time, indeed the Mumbles Tram Railway ran right along the front until the early nineteen sixties, with stations along the promenade every quarter of a mile or so, right out to the pier, and tram lines all over the city in addition, and we know Dylan was a frequent passenger, trekking out to the Mumbles for a drink at the Mermaid, where he broke his tooth. He had as we know a great fondness for amateur theatricals, and bit a lampost during a dog imitation.

'Up there, about halfway up the hill, you will see the new

technical college, built on the site of the school where Dylan had the fight with Daniel Jones which led to their lifelong friendship. Now just behind the sea wall there to the right of the Guildhall tower, is Victoria Gardens, where it is thought stands the urinal outside which he meets the fascinating girl in the green dress, reading a novel, in "One Fine Saturday". The beach of course in those days will have been packed with families on public holidays, as Dylan describes it. Since then people have got the habit of going to Torremolinos and Benidorm, or indeed of running out to the Gower, which has some of the finest beaches in the world. But as you will see, Swansea itself has a particularly fine, extensive beach, and now actually with unemployment, we are again seeing more people in the summer just strolling through the town with bucket and spade to take advantage of this splendid amenity on their doorsteps. Unfortunately, although just around the corner along the Gower peninsula the sea is particularly clear, in Swansea we have the dubious distinction, as well as having a football team which popped into the First Division and popped out again, of having one of the most polluted patches of sea in Europe, second only to Naples I think. As a result of this, swimming is not advisable, although some do risk it and some of us on the Council are doing what we can to push through proposals about improved sewage disposal and so on.

'Now right back behind the town there, below the council houses on the hilltop, you will see the trees of Cwmdonkin Park which was so important to Dylan in his childhood, and nearby that of course there is Cwmdonkin Drive where he lived, unfortunately not easy to pick out at this distance. The old town centre was of course bombed flat during the war, and Dylan would have a hard time finding his way around there now, except for one or two places which miraculously survived. We know he was reduced to tears by the sight of it. The bomb damage I mean, not the new buildings. Well ladies and gentlemen, that concludes the ship to shore Dylan trail for the time being. We will resume it later on when we get out by Rhossili, and of course in Laugharne itself. I think it will shortly be time for some midmorning coffee and a sandwich, and I shall of course be pleased to answer any questions informally which you might like to put to me.'

He stepped down and we all applauded, the Holloways because they wanted to and the rest of us to please them, though really I had to admit to having found the speech rather poignantly endearing. As Haydock Williams sat down the Holloways were all over him.

Delderfield slouched over and sat by me in the stern, an action which perceptibly altered our stability. 'Promising,' he said.

'What is?'

'This. Nobody else goes to Laugharne in a boat, do they?'

'I suppose not.'

'No. And this boat could take what – perhaps another three people? Four? Not many. So there'll be a sense of privilege in coming along. One should always make things a little difficult,' he said. 'Have a sandwich.'

'Yes alright. I wonder if I might have some of that brandy?'

'I don't see why not,' he said, glancing up furtively as he reached into the hamper for it. 'Just a drop for now. Let's drink it surreptitiously shall we? There isn't much.'

There was in fact a half bottle. Once we had both swigged from it he slipped it into his pocket. Then we all officially had elevenses, after which Delderfield set the alarm on his watch for lunchtime and fell asleep. Out past the end of the Gower, with the sea like a blue mirror and positively no craft nearer than a half mile away, once he had finished his spiel about Rhossili and 'Who Do You Wish Was With Us', Haydock Williams was permitted by Sophie to take the helm for a while. She came and sat with me.

By this time I was feeling stunned with sunlit pleasure, rapt by a warm, vaulted blue misty world which went on forever and where sea and sky mingled not just at the horizon but all around us. The bits of land which were visible seemed dreamlike and insubstantial; it was as if my slow, sea cradled wellbeing were the only real thing left. Sophie leaned on me with lovely animal self confidence and I noticed Alice, browning her knees on the cabin roof, glance up and frown at us. Sophie turned round and trailed a hand in the water, gazing at the wash.

'They've got it with them,' she murmured.

'Got what?'

'Quiet,' she said. 'The poem. I heard them talking to Alice in the cabin.'

'Oh Jesus no,' I said. 'So she knows about it.'

''Fraid so. I heard her say something about the way back. This could mean an announcement. We'd better be ready.'

'But what can we *do*?'

'I don't know.'

# 38

As we came up the estuary towards Laugharne I had an opportunity to slip into the cabin for a look round. No one else was in there and I muttered something about getting out of the sun and went in and searched the cupboards, operating on the admittedly remote possibility that the poem might be there, which it wasn't. There was some evidence that Haydock Williams had adopted the boat as a den, personal territory outside the province of his wife and perhaps the auditors. There was a book of what seemed to be accounts of some unregistered building company, a few old school photographs, back numbers of *Hotspur* and *The Eagle*, and some quite staggeringly lurid magazines with plainish covers and rather monosyllabic titles, many of them not English. I put everything back quickly and went out again.

We were now mooring some way out into the estuary by dropping anchor, and Sophie was patiently explaining the necessity of this to Alice, who was being snooty about having to go ashore in the self-inflating dinghy which had been produced from under the seat.

'If we get any further in,' Sophie said, 'we're going to run aground, in which case we'll have to wait for the tide to refloat us and be here for hours. I'm afraid the only way to avoid using the dinghy is to go back to Swansea and get a bus, assuming there is one.'

'Oh indeed no,' Mrs Holloway muttered, embarrassed by all this. 'We love it, I can assure you. Real pioneer stuff.'

Sophie leaned over the side to hold the dinghy in close, at which Alice entered it with a certain flounce and got her bum wet. It was about a hundred yards to the beach. Sophie did all the ferrying. She took Alice and Haydock Williams first, then the Holloways, then Delderfield by himself, then came back for me and the hamper.

'It isn't in the cabin,' I said.

'I didn't think it would be.'

On the beach we all sat around for a while admiring the outside of the castle, which seemed to be closed, and looking at what could be seen of the town, much of which seemed to be closed also. It was Sunday and not yet opening time and there followed an indecisive discussion with Haydock Williams leading the indecision, about whether pubs in Carmarthenshire were open on Sundays, and whether or not this would have been altered by the fact that Carmarthenshire was now part of Dyfed. There seemed after the most exhaustive rumination to be no reliably constitutional answer to that one, and in any case he couldn't quite remember if Carmarthen had been one of the dry counties in the old days or not. During the week mind, it was a particularly *wet* one. And no doubt if one actually lived locally and was on friendly terms with the landlord then something could be arranged. The Holloways found all this highly folkloric and captivating and I lay back with my eyes closed, thinking how many things in Wales were officially impossible though the same old things just kept on happening in any case. It was at length decided that we didn't want to risk the disappointment of going to the pub to find it closed. Holloway himself had a great yen for Brown's Hotel but his wife beat him down; it seemed to symbolise some fundamental point of contention between them. Why didn't we just enjoy the shore here and have our lunch and go for a walk up to the Boat House? So in the end that was what we did. I went off to find Alice who had gone to try and dry her skirt behind some rocks, and Delderfield, who had vanished, and tell them that we had arrived at a democratic decision about what was to happen next. I came across both of them together. Alice was dressed from the waist up and had her other clothes lying in the sun. She was leaning forward over a rock with her hand in Delderfield's trousers while he whacked her bum rather unenthusiastically with a limp bunch of seaweed. They didn't see me and I slipped off.

'They'll be along in a minute,' I told everyone. 'Let's unpack the hamper.'

After lunch we all went to the Boat House. Generally it just reeked of museum but there was one room with some books and a record player in it which *did* look as it might have done when in use, and I felt shifty and out of place, as though the family were out for the day and I had broken in to gawp. I hung about unhappily upstairs trying to think of something rude to write in the visitors book, and then went down to join the others for tea, served to us in an offhand amiable way by two women, the quite probable descendants of Captain Cat, Mary Ann Sailors, Mr and Mrs Dai Bread etc, who were simply doing what they had always done – making a bob or two while they waited for the previous generation to move over and the next one to come along. But for all their quiescent rustic tenacity you could tell by their eyes that they knew their lives had been deeply redefined by the Universal New Map. This had once been a small town but was now a Place of Interest.

I sat gloomily staring at my cup thinking that cities, towns and villages had effectively ceased to exist. Now, there were Dormitory Districts, or Dead End Districts, or Shopping Districts, or Working Districts or Desirable Districts or Somewhat Less Desirable Districts, or Places of Interest. People talked a lot of sentimental cock about the destruction of the countryside – organically and culturally so much vegetable matter – and blamed the city for it. The fact was that both the city and the country had been consumed by the Universal Suburb, and the city was a far greater and less replaceable loss. I was feeling pretty misanthropic by the time we set off back towards the dinghy.

By contrast Haydock Williams and the Holloways were high by now, tripping along the path in a perfect lather of mutual congratulation. We stopped to look into the shed where Thomas used to sit writing or gazing out of the window, and this again looked – or I felt it did – just as it would have done when he was using it. I think it gave all of us a pang, even Alice, so that for the first time that day we started feeling like members of the same party. We sat on the beach and drank the last of the champagne while Sophie assured Alice, with the very minimum of acrimony, that the slight deflation which had occurred to the dinghy in our absence wasn't serious. I was thinking that my feeling on seeing the inside of the shed had been curiously like glimpsing my own past. Sometimes a sound or smell, an object or place will bring a younger version of yourself bang up in front of you, which is exquisitely painful because you remember vividly how mysterious and promising the future seemed, whereas here you are with the future all around you and it's dull as porridge.

I didn't know why Thomas's chair and table, and books and photographs and bits of paper should have affected me the same way, but there it was. Perhaps it was because with his postcard cubist reproductions, and tacked up pictures of Isherwood and Auden, I had sensed his pride in being a singular part of a modern movement, whereas now it seemed there was no modern movement, no art really, just museums and television and sociologists and boredom.

Sophie got the first passengers aboard the dinghy and took them out to the *Polly Garter*. It was time to go.

# 39

The announcement came about halfway back, and was made by Alice. Things had by this time got to the community singing stage, with Haydock Williams teaching the Holloways 'Sospan Bach', conducting wildly with both hands and oozing encouragement. Having pulled the brandy from his pocket, drunk the rest off quickly and dropped the bottle in the sea, Delderfield was asleep again. The weather had deteriorated slightly and every now and then some spray would be flipped in his face, at which he stirred fitfully without gaining consciousness. Alice took the mike and switched on the PA. She said:

'Boys and girls. Wake up, Tom. Everybody. Listen. Now some of you already know what I'm going to say. I would like the rest of you to try and imagine the most exciting thing that could possibly happen, and then see if it even begins to match up with what I have to tell you.'

Haydock Williams was probably the only one of us who didn't know what she was going to say, though of course Delderfield, Sophie and I in our different ways were not supposed to. It was Haydock Williams she played to; he was the little kid opening his present and we were all the uncles and aunties. The Holloways loved it.

'Bill,' Alice said. She hopped up into the position he had adopted to speak from earlier, standing on the bench seat and holding rather precariously to the canopy. The breeze ruffled her hair. 'I wonder if you can tell me what this reminds you of.' She drew the poem from inside her blouse. It was in a clear plastic folder.

Haydock Williams took it out of the folder and gasped. You could have printed the entire take straight off. He said: 'But this looks like . . .'

'It doesn't *look* like it, Bill,' she said, leering at the gallery. 'It *is*.'

'But, I mean how . . .' He scanned it again. 'But Alice,' he said. 'I don't recognise the verses.' He was a natural – word-perfect with no script.

'*That*,' Alice said, 'is because you're one of the first people to *see* them, other than the author.'

'You don't mean . . .' He collapsed onto the seat.

'Yes I do, Bill,' she said. 'Of all the people who've been hunting for a Thomas original for years, we've had the fortune, the *extraordinary* good fortune to find one.'

Haydock Williams was in tears. She reached down gently to take back the poem from him. 'Before I go into *how* we found it,' she said, 'I can hardly think of a better way to end this lovely day than to read it to you all. Are you alright, Bill?'

'*Yes*,' he sobbed. 'Go on Alice. Please.'

She coughed and assumed a voice of deep schoolgirl solemnity. 'How should my wellspring cat,' she intoned, sweeping us with her gaze to be sure we were all paying attention.

'Electric lard, within a mottled tomb of cancer

'And the shouts of – *ooaagh* . . .'

I don't know what it was. Perhaps we passed over rocks, or some wayward submarine confluence of currents, twining about each other like toffee and throwing bubbles of force up to the surface. At any rate we seemed to hit one of those bits of inexplicable turbulence which come and go about the sea, which was noticeably rougher now in any case. Alice was flung clean overboard, and in a jiffy Sophie was circling around to pick her up.

Alice was shouting something, red either with fury or the effort of treading water in a tight skirt. I threw her a lifebelt and called: 'What?'

'I said you *stupid* girl,' she said savagely, catching it. 'What did you have to turn the *wheel* for?'

'I *didn't* turn the bloody wheel,' Sophie said. 'Why were you clambering around like that when you could see the weather was rough?' She employed the boathook to pull Alice in close, none too gently, and then dragged her aboard.

'Well if you're such a brilliant mariner,' Alice spluttered, 'why couldn't you have warned me about the state of the weather? Just look at this *manuscript*, you stupid child. It's *ruined*.'

'*Look here*,' said Sophie. She went and switched off the engine: now, we were making no way at all and it was clear how strong the sea had got; we were bouncing like a cork. 'Everybody listen. If *anybody* thinks I was in *any* way responsible for Mrs Waddington going overboard would they kindly say so *now*. I should hate to prejudice your opinion, but I must tell you that if I hear the *slightest murmur* of assent from *anyone*, including Mrs Waddington, I am going to take that fucking dinghy out and row myself ashore. The rest of you can then pool your intelligence to try and pilot this pile of scrap back to Swansea. I'd give you about one chance in ten of getting back alive.'

213

Not unnaturally no one said anything to this, and after glowering at us all she went and started the boat again. Everybody was sitting around Alice, wrapping her in every available warm garment, digging in the hamper for soup or coffee – Delderfield pretending he couldn't find the brandy – and keening over the state of the poem, which was of course obliterated. A few phrases could still be made out among the blur, and there was gloomy speculation as to whether it was any use at all, coupled with some tentative expressions of relief that at least the text had been copied down so the words weren't lost. Haydock Williams and the Holloways were weeping openly, and shortly after that everyone got sick except Alice, who sat staring straight ahead dripping with as much dignity as she could manage, a bit like Britannia being deported from her native shore and seeking to pretend that no one had flung a bucket of water at her.

And of course Sophie wasn't sick either. Poised with a perfect and careless grace against the bucking of the sea – now real howling grey October stuff flying savagely on the heels of Indian Summer – she brought us all back safely, dripping and shivering to the mooring. It took about three hours. My legs felt fuzzy and weak when I stood up; I had been deeply scared several times. Nobody said a word. Sophie tied up the boat and walked straight over to my car, waiting with smouldering impatience for me to come and let her in.

'I'm sorry,' I said.

She got in and sat gazing blankly at the dashboard, so bored with feeling so angry for so long that she was practically in tears. 'Why are you sorry, for Christ's sake?' she asked.

'I'm sorry Alice was such a cow. But you seemed to handle her quite well, so . . .'

'Oh shut up, George. Sometimes I think your mania for apology is obliquely egocentric.'

'All I'm saying,' I said, starting the engine, 'is that you did wonderfully.'

'Eh?'

'I mean it was too late to destroy the poem, wasn't it?' I eased the car off the rough ground onto the dock road. 'So drowning it was a real piece of lateral thinking.'

'George.' She picked up the monkey wrench from beside the passenger seat. 'Would you like me to tighten this thing on your nuts and give it a good twist?'

'No, not particularly,' I said. 'What on earth's the *matter*?'

'*I didn't flip the fucking wheel*,' she said, pummelling my shoulder with her fists and nearly sending us into an oncoming timber lorry. 'I happened to be watching your dear wife at that point. And I could positively swear that she chucked herself overboard on purpose.'

# 40

'Three hundred quid,' Sky said. He sucked the last breath of life from a cigarette clamped tight between his fingers, and ground it into the gallery floor. 'It was all Holloway had about him at the time.'

'What did he actually settle for?' I asked.

'Fifteen grand. Dugdale reckons he still owes us the rest.'

'That's pushing it.'

'I know. But he does, doesn't he? Give us a hand with this light.'

I leaned carefully on the mobile scaffold tower till Sky had it where he wanted it, then steadied the thing while he clambered up to make an adjustment to the overhead spotlights. Our private view opened in less than an hour and I felt like Piglet on his way to meet the Heffalump; perhaps my nerve wasn't adequate to putting sculpture on public view after all.

'I suppose three hundred's better than nothing,' I said.

'Oh sure,' said Sky. 'And it beats being done for fraud by a long way. Mind you, we've blown two hundred already.'

'Oh?'

'Mmn. Packing Charlotte and the kids off to her sister in the Hebrides. Wanted to get them out of the way when the big story broke, you know.'

'How did you explain the money?'

'Oh, that was the best part of all.' The scaffold wobbled as he began laughing, balanced precariously at the top. 'Dugdale pretended to have won it on the dogs.'

This of course reduced me to instant jelly and we were quite lucky to get Sky down in one piece. I suppose a lot of it was pre-exhibition nerves. We now decided that the layout and lighting were as good as they ever could be and it was time to tidy away the scaffolding and open the wine, so we did.

It was a pleasant gallery, converted from a seaman's chapel down near the South Dock, clean and well lit and giving a sense of deep seclusion, without being *too* clean or costing too much; we were very happy with it.

Beau had given me a tranquilliser, a fat and lethal looking capsule devised by a team of gnomes in Basel, packed with round and many coloured grains like rainbow caviar which were designed to explode into the blood at precisely computed intervals to keep one on an even keel. I took it with a glass of white wine which I sipped cautiously, since Beau had delivered a long talk about the strange effects which might result if one drank with it at all. I decided that he was as usual being insanely overcautious in this but as it happens I was wrong. I was rather keen to induce a sense of dissociation from the half dozen lumps of wood which stood with such lewd obtrusiveness about the gallery, beplinthed and spotlit and flagrant to the public gaze; the only way I could face this was by coming to feel like they'd been done by somebody else. It seemed to work after a fashion: by the time the first guests began to arrive I was too detached to notice the transition, so that before I knew it the room was absolutely heaving with people.

'Rather nice, George,' Delderfield was saying to me at one point, beside a piece which had part of a female form emerging from the rough hewn wood, based largely on Sophie's bum done from my well schooled memory. It was one of the pieces Sky had made me leave alone. I could see Delderfield's hand reaching out to caress it but something in my look must have stopped him. My next memory is of my sheer amazement at finding Mr Mukkarjee in front of me in a beautiful pale green suit, thrusting another envelope in my hand which later proved to contain upwards of two hundred quid. He was beaming widely and smoking a cigar.

'Look,' I said, 'you really must stop giving me money.'

'But this is a fifty fifty operation,' he said defensively, as though I were threatening his honour as a sportsman.

'Just at the beginning,' I said. 'You can't stay in my debt for ever, can you? Excuse me, I'm going to the lavatory.'

When I got back he was gone, or at least I couldn't see him. Alice stood plumb in the middle of the room, like a statue, hands on her hips and scanning everything with eyes which seemed preternaturally bright even for her.

'Ah, there you are,' she said, as though she'd been here all the time and I was late. 'Some of this isn't bad at all.'

'I'm so glad you think so.'

'I should think you are,' she said. 'Now listen...'

'Back in a sec,' I said, taking off towards some entirely fictitious social contact just to get away from her. At the far end of the gallery I encountered Dugdale. He was slumped in a chair by the drinks table looking tired and emotional.

'Cheer up,' I said, pouring myself a drink.

'Piss off, you social working creep,' he said, which I felt to be less than fair.

'It isn't the end of the world,' I retorted, 'and you don't have to be so damnably rude.'

'Yes I do and it is,' he said. 'What do you know? This was going to be the big one – I don't think there's an ounce of deception left in me.'

'You're beginning to talk like a criminal.'

'About time,' he said. 'That's what I am, isn't it? I should have realised it years ago and I might have made out. D'you know, I used to have a family and all sorts of serious literary ambitions? That was my undoing of course. I wanted to be happy. Hah! People think happiness is a soft option, don't they? Let me tell you, George, it's the ultimate Faustian con trick. It costs everything...'

He broke off suddenly. His eyes had gone wide. And then to my astonishment he followed this up by sliding right under the table like a ham actor miming inebriation.

'Contract is a bloody *contract*,' Bassett's voice cut like a rusty saw through the seething hubbub of the gallery. 'An' I wants my *end* of it, my girl.'

'This contract,' Alice said, waving it aloft (they were over by the door evincing a positively physical malevolence) 'isn't worth the paper it's written on. It was given you by someone who had no right to make it and any court of law would throw it out. Nevertheless I am prepared to give you your forty pounds back provided you never bother me again.' She ripped the contract into four pieces which she tossed over her shoulder, thrust some money in his hand and then actually took him by the sleeve and marched him out.

The noise of voices came up again at once, shriller and more broken than it had been. I saw the Holloways picking up the pieces of contract and frowning over them in puzzlement. Sophie arrived at my elbow looking breathless and gave me a kiss.

'Sorry I'm late, darling,' she said. 'Have you heard the news?'

'News?'

'There's reporters everywhere,' she said. She sat on a chair. 'How she did it I simply can't imagine.'

'Did what?' I demanded. 'Who?'

'Alice,' she explained. 'I've been talking to Haydock Williams. The trouble with him is his grasp of reality is never terribly good – I mean he does tend to be hysterically optimistic, doesn't he? He's over the moon, you see. It seems they've had some stuffed shirt down from the National Book League or somewhere to look at the remains of the manuscript. And after a lot of deliberation and hoo ha, it's been given the Papal blessing.'

'*What*?'

'Right,' she said. 'I told you she fell in on purpose, didn't I? Everybody's here,' she said. 'The *Guardian*, the *Mirror* . . . even somebody from *Vogue*, for Christ's sake. They must have chartered a helicopter. She's called a press conference, you see. In the Dogfish. It starts in about ten minutes.'

I gazed about the gallery trying to gauge my own reactions to all this; my feelings were swimming elusively about my head like large fish. The room swayed and righted itself. I noticed that Alice and the Holloways had gone.

'Right,' I said, striding for the door.

'Where are you going?' ·

'To murder my wife,' I called over my shoulder. 'I've been putting it off for years.'

# 41

At the Dogfish, the Press conference was in the process of moving itself from a suite of rooms into the ballroom. This was because of the crush. I was astonished to see well over a hundred people standing about the ballroom while staff ran in and out of the place with trays of drinks and chairs, microphones and tablecloths and all the rest of the paraphernalia which had been set up in the other rooms until so many people arrived that they started to suffocate.

There was not only *le tout* Swansea but a mass of what looked like passers by, as though word had gone around the streets like the rumour of plague in a mediaeval city. Perhaps some of them thought they were at a free booze up to inaugurate the Fringe: I noticed Beau sitting slumped in a corner methodically tearing his hair and muttering, but it transpired later that he had come in order to discuss yet another problem about the Fringe Club with the manager and had then stayed because this seemed a good place to hide from all the people who might be looking for him.

The Press were hanging about the drinks table which had been placed near the stage, pointing cameras experimentally at the long table, now draped with a red cloth and set with microphones, from which Alice was due to make her voluntary contribution to English literature once everything was ready. She was nowhere to be seen at the moment. I edged over to get myself a drink.

'Inside a book,' a reporter was saying. He looked tall and

219

cheerfully misanthropic, dressed in a well tailored, loudly chalk-striped brown suit like the Platonic original of a cheap one, largely concealed by a grimy off white flasher's mackintosh.

'Oh yeah?,' said his mate. By contrast he was short and fat, with a red shirt the same colour as his face and a dark blue tie with red polka dots. 'She opened it and it fell into her lap?'

'Just like that,' Flasher's Mac said, nodding. 'You got it in one.'

'And after that she took it for a boat ride and accidentally fell in the sea with it.'

'I invent stranger things every day. You don't mean to tell me you're taking a sceptical line?'

'Of course not. 'Less somebody trips her up of course. I mean fraud is commonplace, right? But a new Dylan poem is history.'

'Right,' Flasher's Mac said. He replenished his glass from a hip flask of whisky. 'You ever read any?'

'Do me a favour, I don't even read my own paper. Have you?'

'One or two. Couldn't understand a fucking word. If you ask me, he was permanently paralytic. He used to be a reporter once, did you know?'

'Yeah, someone on the local rag was telling me. I'm using it as background. He was a real shower of shit apparently. Used to make things up all the time.'

'No ethics.' Flasher's Mac shook his head. 'That's artists all over for you.'

I went and sat in a row of chairs near the back. I didn't know what course of action I intented to take yet, if any. I was mesmerised of course. After all the labour of composition and calligraphy and mendacity had been done by other people, brought to the point of fruition and abandoned, Alice had picked the whole thing up and seemed on the point of turning it into money and prestige for herself; this just had to be the quintessence of the capitalist genius and I couldn't tell for certain whether I wanted her to fail or not. My heart was thumping erratically and as Alice emerged from a side door to take her place at the table on the stage a revolver fantasy flitted through my mind: I mentally pulled out a revolver and fired but the bullets flopped harmlessly onto the stage before

220

they reached her. The implications of this waking dream frightened me rather and I pinched myself and tried to pay attention.

The table was now filling up to either side of her. There was Delderfield and Haydock Williams and the Holloways and several men I didn't know. They all looked subdued and pasty while Alice's expression was beacon bright as though she were about to eat raw human flesh secure in the knowledge that nobody could stop her. Memories of Thatcher being interviewed on television came back to me and I shuddered.

The first speaker was called Harcourt Foglamp or something similar; since Delderfield introduced him it was difficult to be sure. It seemed that Harcourt Foglamp was an archivist and a fellow of several universities and the man Christie's and Sotheby's called on when they were a little bit doubtful about first editions. In short, when it came to literary verisimilitude he was the nearest thing to a burning bush in the visible landscape. It transpired that Alice had first phoned him the day *before* we all went to Laugharne and I couldn't help admiring her presence of mind.

I had anyway harboured only the mildest intention to spring up and denounce everything, and the futility of doing so became rapidly apparent: once Harcourt Foglamp had finished muttering through his beard about there being no doubt in his mind about the poem's authenticity I felt like Galileo at a gathering of the Flat Earth Society; there was simply no premise from which I could have begun. It remained to be seen whether Alice might incriminate herself but she didn't.

After a neat build up about Dylan Thomas and Swansea and the value of the Memorial Affiliation and the transatlantic interest shown in it she moved into the big story; by this time the audience was expecting nothing less than Wonderful Coincidence and that's what she gave them. She said she had found the poem in a secondhand encyclopaedia, and held the book up for inspection and photographs, as well as the manuscript which was now in a gilt frame in the charge of a uniformed security guard who had been waiting in the wings.

She said she had bought the book several weeks ago, and

had the dealer there to corroborate this. I had thought he looked a bit familiar and now dredged my memory to come up with his name, which was something like Gramphold. More to the point, the last time I had seen him had been several years ago in my office when I first came to work in Swansea and he was just finishing a period of probation for nicking cans of beans. It appeared he now had some sort of junk shop out Brynmill way and would you believe it, he just *couldn't* think where the book had come from. Yes, it was part of an incomplete set dating back to the thirties, but what with him being in the house clearing game and all the stuff that passed through his hands there was just no way of knowing where things had originated. He said with a bleak and shifty smile that it wasn't the sort of thing he kept records about.

I decided that Alice must have flashed over to Hay on Wye to get the book herself and that Gramphold would have cost her about twenty five quid, once she'd learned enough about him to put the screws on if he started getting difficult. By the time she had finished answering questions about the probable value of the poem and whether or not the Americans might buy it – both she and they were very coy about this – and the whole gang of them had been aligned in twenty seven different ways for photo calls, it was clear that everything was over bar the hyperbole of tomorrow morning's papers and I got up to leave. At that point several things happened at once; it could be that all the flashbulbs had broken some sort of spell.

First of all Dugdale sprang to his feet and shouted: 'This whole thing is a sham and a farce and I . . .', just as Bassett rose at the other side of the room to say: '*That* bloody poem is 'alf *mine.*'

They looked at each other. The whole room was silent.

'And *that* bugger is responsible,' Bassett shouted. 'Apparently 'e've nicked the bloody poem off that woman in the first place.'

Dugdale's eyes switched from one side to the other; you could see him wondering whether to counter this blatant lie with an even better one but nobody was interested. He had come in at the wrong time in the wrong play; the drama was over now and he was a bit of light relief like a clown in Shakespeare. Having seen this he swung out his arms like Tom and Jerry and took flight as Bassett grabbed up a bottle and ran after him. The room relaxed and buzzed with talk and laughter and nobody bothered to follow him except me, and Sophie who had been there for about ten minutes searching for me.

I saw the tails of Dugdale's coat vanish as he hurled himself down the stairway, just as Mr Mukkarjee emerged from the Gents to reach the stairwell fractionally in front of Bassett. With a truly wonderful deadpan insouciance he held out an elegant foot to catch Bassett's ankle and send him crashing down head over heels.

There was a rather sickening crunch. I ran up. Bassett was lying on the first half landing like a sack of manure, making no attempt to move.

'Concussion, I expect,' Mr Mukkarjee said, adjusting his tie. 'Hit his head on the wall.'

Sophie had now caught me up and held with both hands onto my arm as though I might try to escape. She surveyed Bassett, looked up and down the corridor and said: 'Nobody seems to have seen that. Why don't we move?'

'Good idea,' I said. We went down in the lift.

'What a fascinating crook,' Mr Mukkarjee observed.

'Who?'

'That woman.'

'Actually she's my wife.'

'Really? She's like something out of the Borgia family.'

'She is rather,' I said. 'Weren't you annoyed?'

'Oh no.' He shook his head. 'I was far too interested. What a character.'

We emerged into the foyer.

'I think I'd better scarper,' Mr Mukkarjee said, doing so with commendable lack of haste.

Suddenly my knees were not able to support me and I sat on a leather couch.

'What is it?' Sophie was asking, feeling my brow. There seemed to be a lot more people around now and it occurred to me that I might have passed out for a minute or two.

'It's either that pill Beau gave me,' I said, 'or it's Alice.'

223

'Alice?'

'I just can't stand to see her *winning* like this.'

'Oh come on, George, you're letting...'

'You don't *know*,' I said. 'You just don't know what it's *like*. If Alice is going to get away with this, then everything I try and do is worthless. Everything I stand for is meaningless. Can't you *see*?'

'No.'

'In that case I doubt if I can explain it.'

'So do I.' There was an edge of contemptuous disappointment in her voice. 'Alice has nothing more to *do* with you now,' she said. 'Just let her go her own way. Forget her.'

'If only I could,' I said. I seemed to be in a semi trance. Sight and sound were clear but at one remove, echoing and shimmering. Speech and movement were difficult so I gave them up.

'Not such a big deal when you think about it,' I heard Flasher's Mac say. He was standing beside the couch.

'Maybe not,' said his mate.

The foyer was full of people; Alice and her gang seemed to have gone but it was otherwise as if the Press conference had been teleported down a floor. Perhaps people were reluctant to leave the party, and the interest generated by Bassett's accident gave them excuse enough to hang around. Two ambulance men now threaded their way through the crush to wheel him off on a stretcher.

'Bit of colour,' Flasher's Mac remarked, observing this.

'Yeah, we need it.' Red Face picked his nose and scraped his finger on a rubber plant. 'I mean you did have a point there. The bloody poem might be history but is it Front Page?'

'Right. But if it causes a *punch up* ...'

'Exactly. Pity there's no sex angle.'

'Right,' Flasher's Mac said again. 'There is this play though.'

'Play?'

'Nude version of *Under Milk Wood*. Or something. That woman's in it – I heard her telling the Telegraph man.'

'Now that might be interesting. Can we take pictures?'

'Oh, I wouldn't wonder. You know what these provincial actors are like. They'll do anything.'

224

'Mmnn . . . So you think it could be worth a look?'

'Yeah. Anyway I've got to do something this evening besides drink. I'm booked in this bloody dosshouse on expenses.'

'Me as well. I'll get my photographer then. It'll save printing the fucking poem, won't it?'

'Oh, we wouldn't do that anyway. Leave it to the *Guardian*,' Flasher's Mac said. 'They can get all the lines reversed and see if anybody notices.'

'George.' Sophie's voice echoed in my ear. 'You really don't seem to be very well.'

'You could be right.'

'I think I'll go and get a cab.' She patted my arm twice. 'And bring it round here. You ought to go home.'

'Eurgh,' I assented. She left.

Actually I was beginning to come round. A plan was forming in my brain so fiendish that I didn't even know what it was. No doubt this all had to do with the workings of the unconscious mind, or not inconceivably with Beau's funny tranquilliser. At any rate I waited till Sophie was out of sight and then slipped off like an escaping lunatic towards the South Dock.

# 42

There was no one left at the gallery except a woman with a small dog, and Sky who was upending the last bottle into his glass and staring at the wall. Everyone else had moved over the road to the White House Theatre, where I went myself. I was hunting for Alice again of course; this was becoming clear now.

The entire town seemed to be milling around in the foyer, which was fortunately a large one. *Le tout* Swansea, people from our private view, people from the Press conference and yet more passers by including a couple of dossers from

Dugdale's old residence down the street, who had come in under protective cover of the crowds in search of warmth, free drink and a share in the excitement. Everyone had been caught by the throat by an air of expectancy; clearly there was a great big event taking place somewhere and they were seething around in swarms afraid of missing it. The Press had picked this feeling up at once; they were standing at the bar slopping whisky around tall glasses, trying to give it coherent form.

'You got this festival, right?'

'Fringe festival.'

'Okay, Fringe festival. This is it though – the spirit of Dylan Thomas. Raffish, way out, and then the *same day* it all opens...'

'Oh, do me a favour,' someone cut in. 'We don't want raffish way out. We want big national discovery. We want Nelson at Waterloo. We want Shakespeare.'

'Shakespeare? What the bloody hell has Dylan Thomas got to do with Shakespeare?'

'They're both dead?' someone suggested.

'It's the national hero bit,' the Nelson at Waterloo man asserted. He worked for the *Sun*. 'Alright you got this drama festival thing as background, but leave raffish out of it. The point is this is a bit of British theatre, there's foreigners coming from all over the place to see it and it's knocking 'em dead. Get it? It's the Falklands all over again.'

'The *what*?'

'Of course it is,' Waterloo Nelson said without the least trace of a smile. 'Eyare – try this: "Shoot 'em dead in Stanley, knock 'em dead in Swansea." Well?'

'It does scan nicely,' someone said. 'That I will allow.'

'No,' Flasher's Mac said drily. 'I think I'll leave the Falklands out. It's Thomas I want. Dylan Thomas poem, Dylan Thomas play, Dylan Thomas festival...'

'I thought it was called a fringe.'

'Dylan Thomas Fringe then. Hallo – isn't that the big gaffer?'

'Who?'

'Whatsisname – over there. Willoughby. He wrote it or directed it or something.'

'Did he? Let's grab him then.'

Beau was too late. He had been sliding along the wall with his collar up, possibly trying to avoid someone quite different, and as the Press flapped across like dirty seagulls to surround him he realised he had nowhere to manoeuvre. He flattened against the wall and searched their faces rapidly, as if wondering which one to smash as he made a break for it.

The first questioner nearly put himself in the frame. He asked Beau where he had found the poem; it transpired that this was the *Express* man who had spent the Press conference asleep in the wrong room after a gruelling lunch. Everybody shushed him. A barrage of flashes and questions followed and Beau responded by raising his hands in the air like claws and demanding silence.

'I'll make *one* statement,' he announced. 'Get your pencils out because this is all I'm going to do. Now point one: this is called the *Swansea* fringe. Not the Dylan Thomas Festival or the poetry Fringe – this play tonight is just one among many events over the next fortnight. Swansea, okay? I'll spell it if you like. Now point two...'

'But you did direct the play?' someone cut in.

'No I didn't direct the play!' Beau was hopping up and down with no apparent movement of the legs, as if the sheer psychic force of his exasperation had produced a pogo like and spasmic levitation. 'I didn't write it, I haven't *read* it, I've got nothing to do with it at *all*. It's an adaptation of *Under Milk Wood* done by a group called Theatre of Conflict. You can talk to them about it. Now point two...'

'How do you feel about the success of the Fringe though?'

'What success?' Beau was quite unable to believe his ears. 'The fucking thing hasn't even *started* yet. /This is the *first event*. How can I...?'

'But what about the interest it's generated?'

'You tell me,' Beau said. 'It's you that's interested.'

'So you don't want publicity?'

'This is the *wrong kind*.'

'What's the right kind?'

'Oh *Jesus*.'

'Alright, what advice would you give a young theatre director?'

'I am *not* a *theatre* director.'

'Fringe director then.'

Beau sighed. 'Suicide,' he said.

'Oh come on. The job must have its good times.'

'Yeah, that's right,' Beau said. 'It's nice when you stop. You know why I came here this evening?' he asked rhetorically. 'I've got to talk to the sound man. But I don't control this theatre, you understand. Neither does anybody else. It's run by a bunch of slavering provincial amateurs who close ranks at the least hint of criticism and think they're doing me a big fat favour by letting me pump more money through the place in a fortnight than it takes for the rest of the year put together. Not that this is a bad venue, comparatively speaking. In fact it's about the best one available. They overcharge performers, they lose their contracts, they're not here when they turn up for rehearsals, they don't send them lighting plans, they don't put up their posters or clean the stage and they lose their props under piles of scenery. I have to take responsibility for all that in spite of the fact that there's nothing I can do about it. It's a real barrel of laughs. I have to talk to the sound man this evening to make sure he's memorised all his cues in triplicate and doesn't plug in the electric kettle by mistake when he's supposed to be doing special effects. It costs groups ten quid extra to have him there, he's a geriatric goon who needs a map to find his own arsehole and they won't let us use anybody else. Meanwhile this place is full of a load of drunken idiots who seem to think Dylan Thomas is about to be raised from the dead. And how many have bought tickets? About three I should think. Then there's you lot who'll be going in for free, and all the middle class idiots who run this place going in for free as well; either that or hanging around the bar in dinner jackets talking loudly all through the performance so the actors can't hear themselves fart. That's about all they're good for. And you talk about success. Well if this is success you can stuff it. You can print that if you like. Now excuse me, I'm a bit busy.' He thrust his way clear and made off, to strangle either the White House Theatre sound man or the first person to ask him another question, whichever he encountered soonest.

'Can we use any of that?' someone wondered in the rather

228

stunned pause which followed.

'*Course* we can...' Flasher's Mac asserted, scribbling happily. '"This is the first event of the Dylan Thomas Fringe,"' he read, '"but already the crowds are pouring in. The publicity generated by this poem has been amazing," said Mr Willoughby. '"In a strange way I feel the spirit of Dylan Thomas here in the theatre, giving us his blessing. A young theatre director like me has a lot of hassles to deal with but at the end of the day, when you stop and look back, you realise it's all been worth it. A provincial amateur theatre has a sense of solidarity, this is the thing. They're troupers. Then when it's time for the show they'll don evening dress and come and swell the crowds. Magic. I'm a busy man alright but when I look at the way everyone's pulled together and the success it's brought – well, all I can say is this is what it's all about. This is show business. You can quote me on that. The Thespian spirit is alive and well and living in Swansea. Excuse me a sec."' And with a cheery wave, Mr Willoughby dashed off to sort out a few last minute hassles before curtain up.

'Not bad,' Waterloo Nelson commented, nodding. 'Not quite my line but there's one or two phrases I wouldn't mind there.'

'Fuck off,' Flasher's Mac said, stowing his pad. 'Write your own bleeding copy. Your punters can't read anyway.' He lunged for the bar.

Mark and Alex had now made an appearance among the crowd, doing their audience participation warm up number. They were dressed in white coats and went around the place feeling people's pulses and telling them that group therapy would begin shortly. Slugge followed two paces behind wearing a sandwich board which read: 'UNDER MILK WOOD/THE TOWN THAT WAS MAD' and making notes on a clipboard. Everybody seemed to think this was such marvellous fun and I wanted to throw up. The Press photographed them a lot and when they got to the Holloways Mrs Holloway simpered and made a wisecrack and they stuck a sticker to her forehead which read: 'TERMINAL SCHIZOPHRENIA' without smiling.

I was beginning to think Flasher's Mac must have got it wrong about Alice being involved with the production, but

229

then I saw her blow in the place from the street and go straight backstage. I made to follow her but Mark and Alex stopped me on the basis that patients weren't allowed into group therapy yet. Then I spotted Sophie who seemed to be looking for me so I hid in the crowds and bought a ticket for the performance. In the process I picked up an empty Liebfraumilch bottle from the table and stowed it under my jacket. It was reassuring to feel it there as I took my seat: for someone who intended smashing Alice's skull in it seemed like a perfect piece of ergonomic design.

Once we were all in the auditorium the cast followed us, announced that the doors were locked and launched straight into the production with the house lights up. The first part of it consisted of yanking people out of their seats, breaking up groups and couples and rearranging them according to age, sex and category. I finished up between female depressives and male paranoids although they hadn't actually moved me at all. I still couldn't see Alice.

The cast didn't perform the play themselves. They got people out of the audience, stuck them on chairs on the stage, put scripts in their hands and told them what parts to read. Holloway was the first First Voice. Mark let him get as far as 'sloeblack, slow, black, crowblack, fishingboatbobbing sea' and shouted: 'Speak up. This is meant to develop your social confidence. You're enjoying this, aren't you?' he asked the audience. The three of them were ranged at the back of the stage with their arms folded.

They let Holloway get a bit further on, then pulled him off into the wings for deep therapy and replaced him with somebody else. That's how the whole thing went on. Maybe half a dozen people at one time would be backstage for deep therapy, from which they would emerge giggling in ones and twos a few minutes later while the show went haltingly on. There was no shortage of willing readers and I thought how impossible it would have been to do this if the thing had been free, but since everyone had paid they were determined to enjoy themselves. There was a good crowd too but then *Under Milk Wood* could draw capacity audiences in Alaska, not that this production was quite what it purported to be. Everyone was so disgustingly compliant that I began to see what an easy job Hitler had had of it. After the most exhaustive search I had still failed to locate Alice among all the faces. I stood up and was in the process of leaving when Mark interrupted the girl reading Gossamer Beynon to shout: 'Stop that man! He's a dangerous patient and he needs help.'

To my fury and amazement several people had grabbed me before Mark and Alex could even get over to give them a hand. I lashed out wildly but my arms were pinned. Delderfield said: 'Come on, George. Don't spoil the party' and someone punched me in the kidneys. I went limp and found myself frogmarched onto the stage. When I started struggling they got me into a straitjacket and dragged me backstage.

Alice was there in a white coat, with a circle of people sitting on hardback chairs having their temperature taken. 'Ah,' she said, eyes lighting up. 'An interesting case.' She retrieved all her thermometers. 'You may all go back to the other ward,' she said. 'I'll have no more deep therapy patients for fifteen minutes.'

'Very good, Matron,' Mark said. We were left alone.

'Alice. Get me out of this fucking straitjacket.'

'No,' she said happily. 'It suits you.'

'You're so pleased with yourself, aren't you?'

'Yes I am rather.'

'How did you know the poem was fake?'

'It was perfectly obvious,' she said. 'Dugdale was handling it.'

'So you couldn't resist stealing it for yourself.'

'Not stealing,' she said. 'Please. And Dugdale would never have got away with it; I did the only sensible thing. Now it'll do a bit of good.'

'You mean it'll do you and your mates a bit of good.'

'Quite.' She beamed at me.

'I don't know,' I said, suddenly weary. I leaned back against a table; the room was chock a bloc with furniture of different kinds, costumes and lights and bits of scenery. 'I came into that auditorium tonight with the full intention of killing you, d'you realise?'

'George how *thrilling*,' she said, coming over to caress the back of my neck. I shook my head free. Alice giggled. 'Poor darling,' she said. 'Your hands are a bit tied, aren't they?'

'Yes,' I said glumly. 'And I've lost my bottle.'

'Your figurative bottle or the literal kind?'

'Both. *God*, you're loathsome.'

'*Oooh*, yes,' she said, twining about my legs. 'I am, aren't I?'

'Alice stop it.'

'And who's going to make me?' she murmured as she made the necessary adjustments to our clothing. 'Certainly not you.'

It was the last thing in the world I wanted, but I'd never been able to want Alice unless I particularly didn't, whereas the more I didn't want her the more I did, and this is what made her excited too. I had been hoping I might be too drunk to be raped but the fact is I was too drunk to realise how much drunker I needed to be before I was impotent. We were in a flagrant position on the table when there was a terrific banging noise, and Sophie emerged from a rococo wardrobe.

She shook some bits of cord off her wrists and pulled a gag off. The look she gave me lasted less than half a second but I'll never forget it. She passed out of view, a door banged and she was gone. Alice collapsed in a violent frenzy and fell loose onto me.

'Get off,' I said. 'And get this bloody thing off me.'

She complied rather dreamily. I was at liberty to strangle her now but what was the point? I'd lost everything, but it was she who had robbed me so I was powerless.

'You knew she was there didn't you?' I said, doing my trousers up.

'Of course,' she said, slumped in a chair looking up at me. 'We put her there. She was sneaking around the place.'

'She was looking for me. She wanted to stop me attacking you.'

She shrugged, with a dazed and sated half smile.

I left. The doors out to the foyer were of course not locked, which would have breached the fire regulations. Sophie wasn't there, nor in the street outside.

I noticed the Sanity Patrol van, parked at the edge of the South Dock. On impulse I went over to see if it was locked. To my great joy it wasn't. I reached in and took off the handbrake, then leaned my weight on the back of the van till it started moving.

It rolled forwards very very slowly, then the front wheels dropped over, the chassis caught on the edge of the dock and I was afraid it might be stuck. But it was balanced right on its fulcrum and I was able to rock the van from the back like a seesaw till it tipped forward and slumped into the water like a drunken sea lion. The top few inches hung above the surface for a few seconds while the air was displaced, then it was gone in a swirl of rivulets and bubbles.

It didn't make me feel a hell of a lot better, but it was something.

# 43

'Do you actually choose women?' Sky asked me. 'Or have they always chosen you?'

'Now you mention it, I suppose they have. I'd never thought about it. Why?'

He shrugged. 'That was the impression I had,' he said. 'It puts you at a disadvantage I think.'

'Perhaps it does.'

None of this was particularly relevant but I didn't want to expand about that; I couldn't bring myself to talk about precisely why Sophie had vanished but I couldn't think or talk about anything but the fact that she had. I'd given up the search now and come down to the Dogfish and the late night Fringe Club for company and oblivion. Beau came and sat with us, carrying a pint of lager which he proceeded to drink as though it were lemonade. His eyes were rolling of their own accord and his hands twitched. 'Swansea's a tomb,' he announced.

'Eh?'

'And I've just spent three years proving it. I mean *what* is the *point*? When have the national Press looked at us before? Jeez – I've been six months putting this together. I've booked groups, singers, puppet shows, mime artists, comedians, jugglers, lunatics. Writers who can't write, actors who can't read, musicians who can't play... I've put up posters, put out Press releases, printed tickets, arranged accommodation, found blackout curtains. I've dealt with contracts,' he went on, not without a rather infectious lugubrious relish now he was getting warmed up, 'lighting, insurance, burst tyres, temperament, missed appointments, hangovers. Not to mention doing twelve thousand programmes. And what happens? What's the end result? Do we get audiences? Does anybody in the street know what the Fringe *is* apart from a small circle of bums who never seem to buy tickets anyway? And then all of a sudden we've got reporters crawling all over the place sounding off about how wonderful it is, just because of some fucking poem which if you ask me is a fake anyway.'

I glanced at him shrewdly but this was just pessimism talking.

'Well I think,' said Sky, 'that the whole thing is going splendidly.'

'You would,' Beau said rudely. 'What the hell do you know about it? Christ, I've been running all over town like a drunken jackrabbit this evening. We've got a show on at the Nodge Welfare Hall where a load of kids had broken in stealing props and trying to set the place on fire. We've got another at St Eustacia's Church Hall where the vicar hadn't even told the Girl Guides not to turn up for their regular meeting. They're all up there fighting the bloody cast trying to get on the stage at the same time. Then I nip down the Blue Dragon where the landlord's having a fit because we've got Naked Lunch in the upstairs room...'

'Who's Naked Lunch?' I asked.

'Some group of poets,' Beau said in a harassed tone. 'From Birmingham. They ended up throwing flour at the audience.' He wiped his forehead. 'Then I go down the White House where everything's supposed to be hunky dory ... oh I dunno. I think I'd better go,' he said, going. 'I can't stand the sight of anyone this evening.'

He got nearly as far as the door before the Press got him;

they had been draped semi comatose around a table playing three card brag, and seemed to think his haste an indication that something was about to happen which they might miss. Beau ducked and weaved among them like a rugby player, and then I believe he actually hit one of them, or perhaps he just trod on someone's toe. At any rate there was a cry of pain, Beau made it out through the door and they all shrugged and went back to playing brag with that sour philosophical air with which Press men pace out the greater part of their time.

Sky seemed to have gone somewhere else now, leaving me nothing to do but think about Sophie which I wanted to avoid. I went to the bog and came back to find the Holloways at the bar, clutching drinks as though they were lollipops and looking about them eagerly.

'Hi, George,' Holloway said. 'We're certainly in the thick of things here. What did you think of the show?'

'Wonderful,' I said. I bought a drink.

'I wouldn't exactly say that,' Holloway said.

'Well,' his wife amended. 'It isn't the way we'd stage *Under Milk Wood* maybe, but it was sure fun.'

'Interesting,' Holloway conceded, nodding.

'Everything's interesting or fun to you, isn't it?' I said.

'More or less, George, yes.'

'Yeah, it would be. What's going to happen to that bloody poem now?'

'Now if you're sore about Dugdale,' he said, 'let me tell you he had no right to the poem at *all*. It was good of Alice not to bring any charges, and we wrote off the three hundred to experience. All that stuff about finding it in a cupboard was just a pack of lies.'

'I know. I knew all along,' I said. 'The poem's a fake.'

After a short pause they both laughed. 'That's just sour grapes, George,' Holloway said. 'You're drunk and a bit bitter I guess.'

'I tell you it's a fake,' I said loudly. 'I was there when it was written. I even wrote some of it. Sky and Dugdale did the rest.'

'My advice to you is go home, George,' Holloway said confidingly. 'You're beginning to attract attention. You're just horsing around here,' he said. 'Maybe you've got your problems, I don't know. But you can't tell me and Gina, and all the eminent people who've examined the text of that poem, that it isn't genuine Dylan Thomas. Sure it's a pity about the worksheet,' he said, nodding. 'Sure it is. But at least there's enough there to check the handwriting and make it collectable. We're all really happy about this thing, George. We're having a great time and it isn't very nice of you to try and spoil it.'

I left it. There was absolutely no point in talking to him any more. I went to get another drink, discovered I'd run out of money, remembered Mr Mukkarjee's envelope and opened it. I did a double take at the amount and bought a large one.

Theatre of Conflict were standing beside me in a sealed circle of backs, still wearing their white coats but looking otherwise as subdued as three Arabs with a dead camel. I leaned on the bar thinking that in their own way the Holloways were even more pernicious than Alice. She at least was evil in a small way, but they had the power to reduce the whole of marvellous and terrible creation to interesting fun. Sky appeared at my elbow and said: 'Listen, I've just been thinking. Copyright lasts fifty years after death, right?'

'So?'

'So now the poem's genuine, who does it belong to?'

'... but of *course*,' I said. 'His estate.'

'Right.'

'But surely Alice must have realised that.'

'I don't see why,' he said. 'We never realised it, did we?'

'No.'

'Not unnaturally, of course. Since we wrote it we saw it as our property.'

'But Harcourt Foglamp or somebody will have pointed it out.'

'Why? Harcourt Foglamp will have thought it too elementary to mention, I should think. Shouldn't you?'

'I suppose so. But of course there could be some distinction between copyright and property right. Couldn't there?'

'There could,' Sky conceded. 'That might be a moot point. But can you see it *not* being contested?'

'No.'

'Neither can I. So this means that at the very least Alice is going to have a rough time. Plus she'll have to spend money defending her position. I just thought it might make you feel a bit better.'

'Yes it does a bit,' I said. It did. 'We ought to tell Dugdale as well.'

'Mmn. Mind you that could be a bit difficult,' Sky said. 'He's on his way to Ireland.'

'Oh?'

He nodded. 'He got very pissed and morose and said it was the only thing to do. He took off for the docks over an hour ago.'

'But the Cork Ferry's closed down,' I objected.

'Oh, he isn't going on a ferry,' said Sky. 'He muttered something about stealing a boat.'

'Not the *Polly Garter*?'

'That's it.'

'... Wow.'

'What's the matter?'

'Nothing,' I said. 'Nothing at all. I'll see you.'

I made for the door. I was tremendously elated by the news about Dugdale, and at first I was puzzled by the fact. But then things began falling into place in my mind. Dugdale was taking off because he had the dignified good sense to know he was finished, or finished in Swansea at least. He would now, if he didn't drown in the attempt, turn up in Ireland purged and renewed by the risk he had taken.

But wasn't it the same with me? I'd always been something of a failure as a citizen but that had never bothered me. But then I'd tried to do the other thing, to be an artist, a lover, a real *mensch*, and I seemed to have failed at that too. So what was there left for me to do, I thought, bounding down the stairs, but take off over the briny too, not caring whether we sank or not?

The cab rank was just around the corner and I fell into a taxi to be whisked round to the docks.

# 44

When I first got out of the cab I wondered if I was in the right place. In the deep night of that vast maritime world of warehouses, cranes, decaying hulks and strange pieces of old iron where everything seemed to be half a mile apart, it was easy enough to get lost at the best of times. I went over to the edge of the dock and searched the sheer black water. This did seem to be the right place but there was no boat.

I sat back on an iron bollard with a slump of cold despair in the pit of my stomach; I felt like the lame kid in *The Pied Piper*.

There was a shuffling noise, and Haydock Williams began to appear up the wooden ladder over the edge of the dock. There was a piece of rope in his hand and his legs were wet. I coughed.

He was so startled that he nearly fell clean backwards. 'Who is that?' he demanded.

'Me,' I explained.

'Oh. George, is it? Look at this,' he said, shaking the rope. 'What do you make of that?'

'It's a piece of rope.'

'It is my mooring rope. Cut,' he said.

'You mean, some bastard's cut your boat adrift?'

'I mean some bastard has stolen it. Look.' He put one arm round my shoulder and pointed down the dock at something I couldn't see at first.

Then I made out the boat, in a pool of moon, nearing the end of the South Pier not showing any lights. It seemed to be swaying slightly.

'Any idea who?' I asked.

'Dugdale,' he said grimly. 'This is a police matter, of course.'

'Of course,' I said. 'How did you come to be down here?'

'I had some provisions to put aboard,' he said evasively. 'Ship's provisions. For the boat. They're in the water now,' he said on a rising mournful note. 'The sea has taken them.'

No doubt provisions meant salacious magazines. So several batches of *Groep*, *Rump*, *Export Fukwurst*, *Behave*, *Verboet* and *Thrust* would now be swanning their way towards the bottom to flabbergast passing fish.

'He laughed in my face,' Haydock Williams said. 'Just laughed in my bloody face when I demanded to know what he was doing.' He seemed more distressed by this than the loss of the boat. 'Then he gave me a shove, I lost my footing on the ladder and got my feet wet, and the next thing I knew she was bloody *gone*. Duw.'

So Dugdale had been disturbed; if this bloody clown hadn't showed up there was a good chance I'd have made it. I toyed with the idea of wrapping the rope round Haydock William's legs and shoving him in, but decided against it. I'd shoved enough things into docks for one evening: besides he might float.

'You'd better call on the dock police,' I said.

'Oh I shall.' He walked over to his car.

'Can you drop me in town?'

'Of course, George boy. Of course. Hop in.'

Before getting in himself he paused to gaze at the piece of rope in his hand, either savouring his humiliation or reluctant to drop it in case this action might sever some psychic connection with the boat. He dropped it on the ground and climbed in, fussing like an old matron with his wet trouser bottoms.

'Duw, the wetness of my clothing on this upholstery,' he said. 'We've only just had the car cleaned and serviced.' He drove carefully across the rough ground to the dock road. 'What brings you down here, George?'

'I was looking for someone,' I said, not caring whether I sounded convincing or not.

'Oh.' He pulled up at the police station by the dock entrance. 'Well, I shan't be a minute.'

I watched him walk over to the police station, trip over a step, try one door which didn't open, lean on another and be admitted, stumbling, to the building.

Meanwhile I had started thinking, messing about with the door to the glove compartment in front of me. Ireland was westwards. Somehow I felt sure Dugdale would hug the coast too. This meant there was a good chance of his passing close to the end of the Gower. The glove compartment door flipped open; there was a half bottle of rum inside with the seal intact.

Trivial things often weigh heavy in large decisions, and it was the rum which decided me. I stole it and slipped out and round the corner to the main road. I stopped the first taxi I saw.

'Rhossili,' I said.

'Eh?'

'End of the peninsula, you know? The Worm's Head.'

'But that's *miles*,' the driver said. 'Cost you a packet.'

'I've got a packet.' I waved it at him. 'Okay?'

'Alright, aye,' he said, starting off. 'Missed the last bus, have you?'

'No.'

Half a mile further on he said: 'So your car's broke down?'

'No.'

'Oh. Your car's okay but you're too pissed to drive?' he suggested hopefully.

'No.'

'Oh. You do live at Rhossili though?'

'No I don't,' I said, which effectively put an end to the conversation. I quite soon fell asleep and before I knew it we were there.

'Seventeen pound fifty,' he said as I got out. His breath was misty on the night air. 'After midnight, see, and I've got to drive back. Less you want me to wait.'

'No thanks,' I said, fishing money out. 'Listen – you haven't got a torch, have you?'

'I have, ah,' he said. 'But I needs it.'

'How about selling it to me?'

'Sorry.'

'I'll give you ten quid.'

'No. I mean...'

'Fifteen then. Look – thirty five altogether. What about that?'

'Alright then.' He handed me a torch and took the money. He was convinced I was stark mad and hesitated a minute or two before starting the engine, perhaps wondering whether to offer me his socks or some cigarettes for another fiver. Then he drove away and there was nothing in the entire world but

240

me and the seaborne moon, and a breeze. I was glad it wasn't raining.

The village lay about half a mile away to the north east, dark and silent as a pile of potatoes. I walked down the wide grassy path along the top of the cliffs, to where the land dipped into the water and at low tide became a causeway to the empty, steep bird haunted island of Worm's Head. At the edge of the sea I got out the rum and settled down to wait.

I had to wait a long time, but something stubborn in the pit of me hung on. As a child my way to school used to cross a railway bridge. I would always wait there until I'd seen a train go by before I went on, which sometimes took as much as an hour. Embarrassment, punishment, rows meant nothing in comparison to the compulsive thrill that I craved; I never revealed why I was late either. I now leaned back against a rock, and had nearly fallen asleep when I heard what sounded like a voice.

It would bark and echo and die away again, and come back. It sounded faulty and scrambled, like a station announcer's. Then the deep thrubbing of an engine.

He was dangerously close in to the shore, and as he came round the headland he seemed actually to steer towards what I knew were some dangerous rocks. He still wasn't showing any lights, though there was a faint glow from the cockpit and I fancied I could make out his head.

I began frantically waving the torch, jumping up and down in the surf shouting: 'DUG DALE.'

'*Flah bankling anna* reach of want,' he said over the PA system. I thought at first he was answering me.

'DUG DALE. OVER HERE.'

'To spin, on ashtip summits *okker makke nhor*,'

'A clawtooth minuet of hair raise mawk...'

He had now got the PA working more or less properly and I realised he wasn't talking to me at all. He hadn't heard me, hadn't seen the light, didn't care anyway. The boat began to turn; with an island across his bows even he knew he had to. He'd been hugging the coast too tight with some fuddled intention of knowing where he was, or else he was just dipping and skimming among the rocks for the hell of it.

'DUG *DALE*,' I had run into the surf, which now seemed

241

immensely loud. The water took my knees and I fell over and lost the torch.

I scrambled upright. The boat was still close enough for me to realise I was looking at the stern. Since I was wet anyway I wondered for a second whether to swim after it.

'". . . flat like cardboard and as sharp as fear,"' his voice came back, suddenly bell clear across the dark water.

'"The cat flops, spent as money at the lockjaw fender's rim,

'His own dead, bright banana in . . ."'

He was as suddenly switched out. He had stumbled into a button, fallen into a stupor, simply got bored with it. The engine ploughed on into the black stretches of the sea and it became impossible to know if I was looking at the boat, a distant rock or something dancing in my vision, and the engine faded until it was no longer possible to imagine I was hearing it. I trudged slowly out of the sea and with the mindless resolution of the very drunk walked twelve miles home to Swansea, where I fell asleep in the dawn.

I took an interest in the maritime weather reports over the next few days, that strange and haunting midnight litany of the sea around Fastnet, Lundy, Sole, Malin, Irish Sea, Rockall, Bailey, Shannon, Faroes, Fair Isle . . . but for October it was surprisingly calm and there were no storms. I preferred to believe he'd made it.

First of all I was puzzled because so many of Sophie's things were still there in my room, but then I found her passport was gone so that was that.

I can't claim to have been desperately unhappy about it; I was too used to this mode of life to be shattered by its return. There were just ordinary things to be done now and I felt my old self settle back on me like a winter cough. When I looked out of my window at the sea it seemed a pleasant sort of a view with no magic in it. I wondered how many days' life lay ahead of me.

## Also available in ABACUS paperback:

**FICTION**

| | | |
|---|---|---|
| BANANA CAT | Christopher Hood | £3.99 ☐ |
| GOD HELP THE QUEEN | Geoffrey Cush | £2.99 ☐ |
| LEAN TALES | Alastair Gray, Jim Kelman | |
| | and Agnes Owens | £3.99 ☐ |
| REDHILL ROCOCO | Shena Mackay | £3.50 ☐ |
| HEAVENLY DECEPTION | Maggie Brooks | £3.95 ☐ |
| I WISH THIS WAR WERE OVER | Diana O'Hehir | £3.50 ☐ |
| WELCOME STRANGERS | Mary Hocking | £3.95 ☐ |
| THE CIRCLE OF REASON | Amitav Ghosh | £3.95 ☐ |

**NON-FICTION**

| | | |
|---|---|---|
| SON OF "IT WAS A DARK AND STORMY NIGHT" | Scott Rice | £2.99 ☐ |
| THE WAKING GIANT | Martin Walker | £4.99 ☐ |
| BARS OF AMERICA | Neil Ferguson | £3.50 ☐ |
| IF THIS IS A MAN/ THE TRUCE | Primo Levi | £3.95 ☐ |
| FORESTS IN BRITAIN | Thomas Hinde | £4.95 ☐ |
| HOMAGE TO QWERTYUIOP | Anthony Burgess | £4.95 ☐ |
| MOVE YOUR SHADOW | Joseph Lelyveld | £3.95 ☐ |
| BEYOND POWER: WOMEN, MEN AND MORALS | Marilyn French | £5.95 ☐ |

All Abacus books are available at your local bookshop or newsagent, or can be ordered direct from the publisher. Just tick the titles you want and fill in the form below.

Name _____

Address _____

_____

Write to Abacus Books, Cash Sales Department, P.O. Box 11, Falmouth, Cornwall TR10 9EN

Please enclose a cheque or postal order to the value of the cover price plus:

UK: 60p for the first book, 25p for the second book and 15p for each additional book ordered to a maximum charge of £1.90.

OVERSEAS & EIRE: £1.25 for the first book, 75p for the second book and 28p for each subsequent title ordered.

BFPO: 60p for the first book, 25p for the second book plus 15p per copy for the next 7 books, thereafter 9p per book.

*Abacus Books reserve the right to show new retail prices on covers which may differ from those previously advertised in the text elsewhere, and to increase postal rates in accordance with the P.O.*

# THE WAKING GIANT

## MARTIN WALKER

'This book gives readers a clearer insight into what is happening under Gorbachev than any other I have seen. Brilliantly written by the first resident correspondent the *Guardian* has had in the USSR for fifty years, it is fair, enlightening – and hopeful . . . Martin Walker is reliable, prolific and intensely interesting. His book is a must for all students of Soviet Russia' *TRIBUNE*

'Walker has written the most original and thought-provoking book on contemporary Soviet society and politics to have appeared for a decade. It should be required reading for any politician, diplomat, journalist, businessman or ordinary citizen wishing to understand the nature of the changes currently taking place in the USSR' *LONDON REVIEW OF BOOKS*

'Highly readable, and could well serve as most people's Bedside Guardian Guide to Russia . . . Part of the charm of the book is the sense of hope that it gives for the future . . . Undoubtedly helps to fill a big gap' *DAVID OWEN, GUARDIAN*

'An objective and useful account of Gorbachev's Soviet Union where more change is taking place in political, economic and cultural life than that country has seen since the days of Khrushchev' *NEW SOCIETY*

0 349 13597 5    ABACUS NON-FICTION    £4.99

# IF NOT NOW, WHEN?

## PRIMO LEVI

### Author of THE PERIODIC TABLE

is not often that one feels a better person through reading a book, but this novel somehow has that effect' OBSERVER

his book achieves many things – too many, really, to itemise . . . yet one
left with an enormous sense of optimism and gratitude to the author'
THE LISTENER

'Levi writes of unimaginable hardships: cold above all, pain, terror,
nger and weariness, exclusion from humanity, an almost wolfish sense
exile in marshes and forests, sewers, caves, collapsed buildings. And
of exhilaration, commitment, hope, the longing for a home'
FINANCIAL TIMES

evi is a master whose hand never slips . . . I was convinced by every
detail, and absurdity, shaken to realise at the end that it was indeed
ion, however well grounded in fact. I knew these people, and I wanted
to know more' THE TIMES

0 349 12199 0    ABACUS FICTION    £3.95

Also by Primo Levi in Abacus:
THE PERIODIC TABLE

# The Periodic Table

'One of the most important and gifted writers of
our time . . . an extraordinary and fascinating book'
*Italo Calvino*

'We are always looking for the book it is *necessary* to
read next. After a few pages I immersed myself
gladly and gratefully. There is nothing superfluous
here, everything this book contains is essential. It is
wonderfully pure, and beautifully translated'
*Saul Bellow*

'I was captivated, but also knew that no words of mine
would do this book justice. Nominally it is prose;
in actuality, it is a narrative poem of magical quality'
Frederick Dainton,
*NEW SCIENTIST*

'This is an extraordinary book, eccentric in
construction, protean in genre, grandiose in its
intellectual ambition, and profoundly moving in the
delicacy and depth of its engagement with tragedy'
*SUNDAY TIMES*

'One of the most important Italian writers'
*Umberto Eco*

0 349 12198 2    ABACUS FICTION    £3.95

## Also available from ABACUS paperback:

**ICTION**

| | | |
|---|---|---|
| AWKSMOOR | Peter Ackroyd | £3.95 ☐ |
| OKYO WOES | Bruce Jay Friedman | £3.50 ☐ |
| NDIFFERENT HEROES | Mary Hocking | £3.95 ☐ |
| ASE | Patrick Gale | £3.50 ☐ |
| HE AERODYNAMICS OF PORK | Patrick Gale | £3.95 ☐ |
| IR WAKEFIELD'S CRUSADE | Bernice Rubens | £3.50 ☐ |
| RUSOE'S DAUGHTER | Jane Gardam | £3.95 ☐ |
| VE | Penelope Farmer | £3.95 ☐ |

**ION-FICTION**

| | | |
|---|---|---|
| HE PERIODIC TABLE | Primo Levi | £3.95 ☐ |
| LAME INTO BEING | Anthony Burgess | £3.95 ☐ |
| O BEAR ANY BURDEN | Al Santoli | £3.95 ☐ |
| HIS SPACE TO LET | Ray Lowry | £2.95 ☐ |
| CHUMACHER LECTURES 2 | Satish Kumar (Ed) | £3.95 ☐ |
| HE TRUE ADVENTURES OF THE ROLLING STONES | Stanley Booth | £3.95 ☐ |
| HE FIRST DANCE OF FREEDOM | Martin Meredith | £3.50 ☐ |
| EYOND THE DRAGON'S MOUTH | Shiva Naipaul | £3.95 ☐ |

ll Abacus books are available at your local bookshop or newsagent, r can be ordered direct from the publisher. Just tick the titles you ant and fill in the form below.

ame _____

ddress _____

_____

Vrite to Abacus Books, Cash Sales Department, P.O. Box 11, almouth, Cornwall TR10 9EN.

lease enclose cheque or postal order to the value of the cover price lus:

K: 45p for the first book plus 20p for the second book and 14p for ach additional book ordered to a maximum charge of £1.63.

VERSEAS: 75p for the first book plus 21p per copy for each additional ook.

FPO & EIRE: 45p for the first book, 20p for the second book plus 4p per copy for the next 7 books, thereafter 8p per book.

bacus Books reserve the right to show new retail prices on covers hich may differ from those previously advertised in the text or sewhere, and to increase postal rates in accordance with the PO.